Believers

Charles Baxter

BELIEVERS

A NOVELLA AND STORIES

Pantheon Books
New York

All rights reserved under International and Pan-American Copyright
Conventions. Published in the United States by Pantheon Books,
a division of Random House, Inc., New York, and simultaneously in
Canada by Random House of Canada Limited, Toronto.

Grateful acknowledgment is made to Abkco Music, Inc.
for permission to reprint an excerpt from "Gimme Shelter" by Mick Jagger and
Keith Richards. Copyright © 1969 by Abkco Music, Inc. All rights reserved.

Several of these stories have appeared in earlier form in the following magazines
and anthologies: *American Short Ficiton,* "Saul and Patsy Are in Labor";
The Atlantic, "Flood Show"; *DoubleTake,* "The Cures for Love"; *Glimmer Train,*
"Reincarnation"; *The Sound of Writing,* "The Next Building I Plan to Bomb"; *Story,*
"Kiss Away"; *Triquarterly,* "Time Exposure" (published as "Super Night").

"Kiss Away" appeared in *Prize Stories 1995: The O. Henry Awards,* and "Time
Exposure" (titled "Super Night") appeared in *The Pushcart Prize XX.*

Library of Congress Cataloging-in-Publication Data

Baxter, Charles, 1947–
Believers : a novella and stories / Charles Baxter.
p.   cm.
Contents: Kiss away—Reincarnation—The next building I plan
to bomb—Time exposure—Saul and Patsy are in labor—Flood
show—The cures for love—Believers.
ISBN 0-679-44267-7
I. Title.
PS3552.A8543B45   1997
813´.54—dc20   96-31640
CIP

Random House Web Address: http://www.randomhouse.com/

Book design by Cassandra Pappas

Printed in the United States of America
First Edition
2   4   6   8   9   7   5   3   1

To Loring Staples

and in memory of Loring Staples, Jr.

and for Emily Anne,
Missy, Tom, Greg, and Kate.

Contents

Acknowledgments

This book has had many helpful readers, and for the attention and care they have given to these fictions I am more grateful to them than I can easily say. They include Jonis Agee, Richard Bausch, Nicholas Delbanco, Dan Frank, Russell Fraser, Lawrence Joseph, Margot Livesey, Rosina Lippi-Green, Eileen Pollack, Joan Silber, and Carol Houck Smith. Thank you, thank you.

For help with "Believers" I want to thank Loring Staples, Lewis Baxter, and Stephen Koch. Certain details in the story were suggested by Martha Dodd's *Through Embassy Eyes,* Frederic Prokosch's *The Skies of Europe,* and Ralf Georg Reuth's *Goebbels.*

Thanks also to the Lila Wallace-Reader's Digest Foundation and to the University of Michigan for support in the completion of this book.

Kiss Away

T HE HOUSE had an upstairs sleeping porch, and she first saw the young man from up there, limping through the alley and carrying a torn orange and yellow Chinese kite. He had a dog with him, and both the dog and the man had an air of scruffy unseriousness. From the look of it, no project these two got involved with could last longer than ten minutes. That was the first thing she liked about them.

Mid-morning, midweek, midsummer: even teenagers were working, and in this flat July heat no one with any sense was trying to fly kites. No one but a fool would fly a kite in this weather.

The young man threw the ball of string and the ripped cloth into the alley's trash bin while the dog watched him. Then the dog sat down and with an expression of pained concentration scratched violently behind its ear. It looked around for something else to be interested in, barked at a cat on a window ledge, then gave up the effort and scratched its ear again.

From the upstairs sleeping porch, the young man looked exactly like the fool in the tarot pack—shaggy and loose-limbed, a songster at the edge of cliffs—and the dog was the image of the fool's dog, a frisky yellow mutt. Dogs tended to like fools. They had an affinity. Fools always gave dogs plenty to do. Considering this, the woman near the window felt her heart pound twice. Her heart was precise. It was like a doorbell.

She was unemployed. She had been out of college for a year, hadn't been able to find a job she could tolerate for more than a few days, and with the last of her savings had rented the second floor of this house in Minneapolis, which included an old-fashioned sleeping porch facing east. She slept out here, and then in the mornings she sat in a hard-backed chair reading books from the library, drinking coffee, and listening to classical music on the public radio station. Right now they were playing the *Goyescas* of Enrique Granados. She was running out of money and trying to stay calm about it, and the music helped her. The music seemed to say that she could sit like this all morning, and no one would punish her. It was very Spanish.

She put on her shoes and threw her keys into the pocket of her jeans. She raised the slatted blinds. "Hey!" she yelled down into the alley.

"Hey, yourself," the young man yelled back. He smiled at her and squinted. Apparently he couldn't see her clearly. That was the second thing she liked about him.

"You can't throw that kite in there," she said. "That dumpster's only for people who live in this building." She shaded her eyes against the sun to see him better. The guy's dog was now standing and wagging its tail.

"Okay," he said. "I'll take it out," and when she told him not to and that she'd be down in a second and he should just wait there, she knew he would do what she asked. What she hadn't expected was that he would smile enormously at her and, when she appeared, give her a hug—they were strangers after all—

right out of the blue. She pushed him away but could not manage to get angry at him. Then she felt the dog's tongue slurping on her fingers, as if she'd spilled sauce on them and needed some cleaning.

HE OFFERED to buy her coffee, and he explained himself as they walked. He had once had good prospects, he said, and a future about which he could boast. He had been accepted into the Wayne State University Medical School eighteen months ago but had come down with a combination of mononucleosis and bacterial pneumonia, and after recuperating, he had lost all his interest in great plans. The two illnesses—one virus and one bacteria—had taken the starch out of him, he said. He actually used expressions like that. He had a handsome face when you saw him up close, but as soon as you walked a few feet away something went wrong with his appearance; it degenerated somehow.

His name was Walton Tyner Ross, but he liked to be called Glaze because of his taste for doughnuts and for his habitual faraway expression. She didn't think someone whose nickname was Glaze was ever going to become a successful practitioner of medicine, but in a certain light in the morning he was the finest thing she had seen in some time, especially when viewed from a few inches away, as they walked down Hennepin Avenue for breakfast.

Stopping under a tree that gave them both a moment of shade, he told her that if she wanted him to, he would show up regularly in the morning from now on. He needed motivation. Maybe she did too. They would project themselves into the world, he said. She agreed, and on the next few mornings he appeared in the alley with his dog, Einstein, a few feet behind him. He called up to her, and the dog barked in chorus. She didn't think it was very gallant, his yelling up at her like that, but she had had her phone disconnected, and his passion for her company pleased and moved her.

They would walk down Hennepin Avenue past what he called the Church of the Holy Oil Can—because of its unbecoming disproportionate spire—to one of several greasy smoky restaurants with plate-glass front windows and red and white checkered café curtains and front counters with stools. They always sat at the stools because Walton liked to watch the grill. The first time he bought Jodie a breakfast of scrambled eggs and a biscuit and orange juice. As the breakfast went on, he became more assertive. Outside, Einstein sat near a lamppost and watched the passing pedestrians.

Walton Tyner Ross—looking very much like a fool as he spilled his breakfast on his shirt—was a Roman candle of theories and ideas. Jodie admired his idea that unemployment was like a virus. This virus was spreading and was contagious. The middle class was developing a positive taste for sloth. One person's unemployment could infect anyone else. "Take you," he said. "Take us." He wolfed down his toast slathered with jam. "We shouldn't feel guilty over not working. It's like a flu we've both got. We're infected with indifference. We didn't ask to get it. We inhaled it, or someone sneezed it on us."

"I don't know," she said. In front of her, the fry cook, a skinny African-American kid with half-steamed glasses, was sweating and wiping his brow on his shirtsleeve. The restaurant had the smell of morning ambition and resolution: coffee and cigarette smoke and maple syrup and cheap aftershave and hair spray. "Maybe you're right," she said. "But maybe we're both just kind of lazy. My sister says *I'm* lazy. I think it's more complicated than that. I once had plans, too," Jodie said, indicating with a flick of her wrist the small importance of these plans.

"Like what? What sort of plans?"

She was watching the fry cook and could hardly remember. "Oh," she said. "What I wanted was an office job. Keeping ac-

counts and books. Something modest, a job that would leave
the rest of my life alone and not eat up my resources." She
waited a moment and touched her cheek with her finger. "In
those days—I mean, a few months ago—my big project was
love. I always wanted big love. Like that game, *Careers,* where
you decide what you want out of life? I wanted a small job and
huge love, like a big *event.* An event so big you couldn't say
when it would ever stop."

He nodded. "But so far all the love you've gotten has been
small."

She looked at him and shrugged. "Maybe it's the times.
Maybe I'm not pretty enough."

He leaned back and grinned at her to dispute this.

"No, I mean it," she said. "I can say all this to you because
we don't know each other. Anyway, I was once almost engaged.
The guy was nice, and I guess he meant well, and my parents
liked him. They didn't mind that he was kind of ragged, but almost as soon as he became serious about me, he was taking
everything for granted. It's hard to explain," she said, pushing her scrambled eggs around on the plate and eyeing the ketchup bottle. "It wasn't his fault, exactly. He couldn't do it. He
couldn't play me." She gave up and poured some ketchup on
her eggs. "You don't have to play me all the time, but if you're
going to get married, you should be played *sometimes.* You
should play him, he should play you. With him, there was no
tune coming out of me. Just prose. You know, Walton," she
said suddenly, "you sometimes look like the fool illustration on
the tarot pack. No offense. You just do."

"Sure, I do," he said, and when he turned, she could see that
his ears were pierced, two crease incisions on each lobe. "Okay,
look. Here's what's going to happen. You and me, we're going
to go out together in the morning and look for work. Then in
the afternoon we'll drive around, I don't know, a treasure hunt,
something that doesn't cost anything. Then I don't know what

we're going to do in the evening. You can decide that." He explained that good fortune had put them together but that maybe they should at least try to fight the virus of sloth.

She noticed a fat balding man on Walton's other side, with hideous yellow-green eyes, staring at her. "Okay," she said. "I'll think about it."

THE NEXT MORNING, he was there in the hot dusty alley with his morning paper and his dog and his limp, and she came down to him without his having to call up to her. She wasn't totally presentable—she was wearing the same jeans as the day before, and a hand-me-down shirt from her sister—but she had put on a silver bracelet for him. As they walked to the restaurant he complimented her on her pleasant sexiness. He told her that in the moments that she had descended the back steps, his heart had been stirred. "Your heart. Yeah, right," she said.

Walking with her toward the café, Einstein trotting behind them and snapping at flies, he said that today they would scan the want ads and would calculate their prospects. In the late morning they would go to his apartment—he had a phone— and make a few calls. They would be active and brisk and aggressive. They would pretend that adulthood—getting a job—made sense. Matching his stride, enjoying his optimism, Jodie felt a passing impulse to take Walton's arm: He was gazing straight ahead, not glazed at all, and his shirtsleeves were rolled up, and she briefly admired his arms and the light on his skin.

In the restaurant, at the counter spotted with dried jam and brown gravy, where the waitress said, "Hiya, Glaze," and poured him his coffee without being asked, Jodie felt a pleasant shiver of jealousy. So many people seemed to know and to like this unremarkable but handsome guy; he, or something about him, was infectious. The thought occurred to her that he might change her life. By the time her Belgian waffle arrived, Jodie had circled six want ads for temp secretaries with extensive computer experience. She knew and understood computers backwards and forwards and hated them all, but they were like family members and she could work with them if she had to. She didn't really want the jobs—she wanted to sit on the sleeping porch with her feet up on the windowsill and listen to the piano music of Granados and watch things go by in the alley— but the atmosphere of early morning ambition in the café was beginning to move her to action. She had even brought along a pen.

She felt a nudge in her ribs.

She turned to her left and saw sitting next to her the same fat balding man with horrible yellow-green eyes whom she had seen the day before. His breath smelled of gin and graham crackers. He was smiling at her unpleasantly. He was quite a package. "'Scuse me, Miss," he said. "Hate to bother you. I'm short bus fare. You got seventy-five cents?" His speech wore the clothes of an obscure untraceable Eastern European accent.

"Sure," she said without thinking. She fished out three quarters from her pocket and gave the money to him. "Here." She turned back to the want ads.

"Oboy," he said, scooping it up. "Are you lucky."

"Am I?" she asked.

"You got that right," he said. He rose unsteadily and his yellow-green eyes leered at her, and for a moment Jodie thought that he might topple over, like a collapsed circus tent, covering her underneath his untucked shirt and soiled beltless trousers. "I," he announced to the restaurant, although no one was paying any attention to him, "am the Genie of the Magic Lamp."

No one even looked up.

The fat man bent down toward her. "Come back tomorrow," he said in a ghoulish whisper. Now he smelled of fire-place ash. "You get your prize." After a moment, he staggered out of the restaurant in a series of forward-and-sideways lurch-ing motions, almost knocking over on the way a stainless-steel coat rack. The waitress behind the counter watched him leave with an expression on her face of irritated indifference made more explicit by her hand on her hip and a pink bubble almost the color of blood expanding from her lips. Bubble gum was shockingly effective at expressing contempt, Jodie thought. All the great waitresses chewed gum.

"Who was that?" she asked Walton.

He shook his head like a spring-loaded toy on the back shelf of a car. As usual, he smiled before answering. "I don't know," he said. "Some guy. Tad or Tadeusz or like that. He always asks people for money. Usually people ignore him. Nobody's given him any money in a long time. Come on. We're going to my place to make some phone calls. Then we'll go on a treasure hunt."

When they came out to the sidewalk, Einstein cried and shivered with happiness to see them, barking twice as a greet-ing. Walton loosened her from a bicycle stand to which she had been tethered, while Jodie breathed in the hot summer air and said, "By the way, Walton, where did you get that thing in your walk? Is it, like, arthritis?"

He turned and smiled at her. Her heart started thumping again. She couldn't imagine why men didn't smile more often than they did. It was the most effective action they knew how to take, but they were always amateurs at it. Jodie thought that maybe she hadn't been smiled upon that much in her life. Per-haps that was it.

"Fascists," Walton said, getting up. "My dog and I fought the fascists."

* * *

WALTON'S APARTMENT was upstairs from an ice cream parlor, and it smelled of fudge and heavy cream. Although the apartment had a small study area with bookshelves and a desk, and a bedroom where the bed was neatly made and where even the dog's rubber squeak toys were kept in the corner, the effect of neatness was offset by a quality of gloom characteristic of places where sunlight had never penetrated. It was like Bluebeard's castle. The only unobstructed windows faced north. All the other windows faced brick or stone walls so that, no matter what time of day it was, the lamps had to be kept on.

They went through the circled want ads, made some telephone calls, and arranged for two interviews, one for Jodie as a receptionist at a discount brokerage house and one for Walton as a shipping clerk.

Having finished that task, Jodie dropped herself onto one of the floor pillows and examined a photograph on the wall over the desk showing a young couple, both smiling. Wearing a flowery summer dress, the woman sat on a swing, and the man stood behind her, about to give her a push.

"That's my father," Walton said, standing behind Jodie.

"It's your mother, too."

"I know it. I know it's my mother, too. But it's mostly my father. He always liked to meet my girlfriends."

"I'm not your girlfriend, Walton," she said. "I hardly know you."

He was quiet for a moment. "Want a beer?" he asked. "For lunch?"

HE SAID unemployed people should always seek out castoffs and that was what they would do during the afternoon, but just as they were about to go out to his car, he fell asleep in his chair, his dog at his feet, her front paws crossed.

Jodie sat where she was for a moment, painfully resisting the impulse to go rummaging through Walton's medicine cabinet and desk and dresser drawers. Instead, she brought a chair over next to him, sat down in it, and studied his face. Although it wasn't an unusual face, at this distance certain features about it were certainly noteworthy. The line where the beard began on his cheek—he was cleanshaven—was so straight that it seemed to have been implanted there with a ruler. He had two tiny, almost microscopic, pieces of dandruff in his eyebrows. His lashes were rather long, for a man. His lower lip was also rather full, but his upper lip was so small and flat at the bottom that you might not notice it unless you looked carefully. When he exhaled, his breath came in two puffs: It sounded like *hurr hurr*. He had a thin nose, and his left cheek appeared to have the remnant of an acne scar, a little blossom of reddening just beneath the skin like a truffle. With his head leaning forward, his hair in back fell halfway to his shoulders; these shoulders seemed to her to be about average width for a man of his height and weight. Even in sleep, his forehead was creased as if in thought. His hair had a wavy back and forth directionality, and it reminded Jodie of corrugated tin roofing. She found wavy hair mysterious; her own was quite straight. She reached up to touch his hair, being careful not to touch his scalp. That would wake him. She liked the feeling of his hair in her fingers. It was like managing a small profit after two quarters of losses.

She was sitting again on the floor pillow when he woke up five minutes later. He shook his head and rubbed his face with his hands. He looked over to where Jodie was sitting. "Hi," he said.

"Here's 'hi' comin' back at you," she said. She waved all the fingers of her right hand at him.

*   *   *

THAT EVENING she went to a pay telephone and called her older sister, the married and employed success story. Her older sister told Jodie to take her time, to buy some nice clothes, to be careful not to lend him her credit card, and to watch and wait to see what would happen. Be careful; he might be a psychopath. Sit tight, she said. Jodie thought the advice was ironic because that kind of sitting was the only sort her sister knew how to do. She told Jodie to have her phone reconnected; it wouldn't cost that much, and after all, telephones were a necessity for a working girl in whom a man was taking an interest. She asked if Jodie needed a loan, and Jodie said no.

Her best friend gave Jodie the same advice, except with more happy laughter and enthusiasm. Wait and see, go for it, she said. What's the difference? It'll be fun either way. Come over. Let's talk.

Soon, Jodie said. We'll see each other soon.

HER DREAMS that night were packs of lies, lies piled on lies, an exhibit of lies. Mayhem, penises on parade, angels in seersucker suits, that sort of thing. She woke up on the sleeping porch ashamed of her unconscious life. She hated the vulgarity and silliness of her own dreams, their subtle unstated untruths.

Her job interview was scheduled for eleven o'clock the following morning, and after Walton had called up to her and taken her to the café, she stared down into her third cup of coffee and considered how she might make the best impression on her potential employers. She had worn a rather formal white ruffled blouse with the palm tree pin and a dark blue skirt, and she had a semi-matching blue purse, at the sight of which Walton had announced that Jodie had "starchy ideas of elegance," a phrase he didn't care to explain. He told her that at the interview she should be eager and honest and self-possessed. "It's a brokerage house," he said. "They like possession in places like that, especially self-possession. Be polite. Don't call them motherfuckers. They don't like that. But be honest. If you're straightforward, they'll notice and take to you right away. Just be yourself, you know, whatever that is."

But she wasn't convinced. At the moment, the idea of drifting like a broken twig on the surface of a muddy river was much more appealing. All through college she had worked at a clothing store as a checkout clerk, and the experience had filled her with bitter wisdom about the compromises of tedium and the hard bloody edge of necessity. She had had a gun pointed at her during a holdup her fourth day on the job. On two other occasions, the assistant manager had propositioned her in the stockroom. When she turned him down, she expected to be fired, but for some reason she had been kept on.

"There you are." A voice: her left ear: a phlegm rumble.

Jodie turned on her stool and saw the fat man with yellow-green eyes staring at her. "Yes," she said.

"I hadda get things in order," he said, grinning and snorting. He pulled out a handkerchief speckled with excretions and blew his nose into it. "I hadda get my ducks in a row. So. Here we are again. What's your three wishes?"

"Excuse me?"

"Just ignore the guy," Walton said, pouring some cream into his coffee. "Just ignore the guy."

"If I was you," the fat man said, "I'd ignore *him*. They don't call him Glaze for nothing. So what's your three wishes? I am the Genie of the Magic Lamp, like I said. You did me a favor, I do you a favor." Jodie noticed that the fat man's voice was hollow, as if it had emerged out of an echo chamber. Also, she had the momentary perception that the fat man's limbs were attached to the rest of his body with safety pins.

"I don't have three wishes," Jodie said, studying her coffee cup.

"Everybody's got three wishes," the fat man said. "Don't bullshit the Genie. There's nobody on Earth that doesn't have three wishes. The three wishes," he proclaimed, "are universal."

"Listen, Tad," Walton said, turning himself toward the fat man and spreading himself a bit wider at the shoulders. He was beginning, Jodie noticed, a slow threatening male dancelike sway back and forth, the formal prelude to a fight. "Leave the lady alone."

"All I'm asking her for is three wishes," the fat man said. "That's not much." He ran his dirty fingers through his thinning hair. "You can whisper them if you want," he said. "There's some people that prefer that."

"All right, all right," Jodie said. She leaned toward him and lowered her voice toward the Genie of the Magic Lamp so that only he could hear. She just wanted to be left alone with Walton. She wanted to finish her coffee. Her needs were small. "I want a job," she said softly, "and I'd like that guy sitting next to me to love me, and I'd like a better radio when I listen to music in the morning."

"That's it?" The fat man stood up, a look of storybook outrage on his face. "I give you three wishes and you kiss them away like that? What's the matter with you? Give an American three wishes, and what do they do? Kiss them away! That's the trouble with this country. *No imagination when it comes to wishes!* All right, my pretty, you got it." And he dropped his dirty handkerchief in her lap. When she picked it up to remove it, she felt something travel up her arm—the electricity of disgust. The fat man rose and waddled out of the restaurant. She let go of the handkerchief and it drifted toward the floor.

"What was that?" Jodie asked. "What just happened?" She was shaking.

"That," Walton told her, "was a typical incident at Clara's Country Kitchen Café. The last time Tad gave someone three wishes, it was because the guy'd bought him a cup of coffee, and a tornado hit the guy's garage a couple of weeks later. Fat guys have really funny delusions, have you noticed that?" He waited. "You're shaking," he said, and put his hand on her shoulder. "What'd you ask for, Jodie?"

She turned to look out the front window and saw Walton's dog gazing straight back at her in an eerie manner.

"I asked for a job, and a better radio, and a million dollars."

"Then what was all that stuff about 'kiss away'?"

"Oh, I don't know. Walton, can we go, please? Can we pay our bill and leave?"

"I just remembered," Walton said. "It's that Rolling Stones tune. It's on one of those antique albums. 'Gimme Shelter,' I think." He raised his head to sing.

> Love, sister, is just a kiss away,
> Kiss away, kiss away, kiss away.

"I don't think that's what he meant," Jodie said.

Walton leaned forward and gave her a little harmless peck on the cheek. "Who knows?" he said. "Maybe it was. Anyhow, just think of him as an overweight placebo-person. He doesn't grant you the wish because, after all, he's just a fat psycho, but he *could* put you in the right frame of mind. We've got to think positively here."

"I like how you defended me," Jodie said. "Getting all male and everything."

"No problem," Walton said, holding up his fist for inspection. "I like fights."

SHE THOUGHT that she had interviewed well, but she wasn't offered the job she had applied for that day. They called her a week later—she had finally had a phone installed—and told her that they had given the position to someone else but that they had been impressed by her qualities and might call her again soon if another position opened up.

She and Walton continued their job-and-castoffs hunt, and it was Walton who found a job first, at the loading dock of a retailer in the suburbs, a twenty-four–hour discount store known internationally for shoddy merchandise. The job went from midnight to 8 A.M.

She thought he wasn't quite physically robust enough for such work, but he claimed that he was stronger than he appeared. "It's all down here," he said, pointing to his lower back. "This is where you need it."

She didn't ask him what he was referring to—the muscles or the vertebrae or the cartilage. She had never seen his lower back. However, she was beginning to want to. On the passenger side of his car, she considered the swinging fuzzy dice and the intricately woven twigs of a bird's nest tossed on the top of the dashboard as he drove her to her various job interviews. His conversation was sprinkled with references to local geology and puzzles in medicine and biology. He was interested in most observable phenomena, and the pileup of souvenirs in the car reflected him. She liked this car. She had become accustomed to its ratty disarray and to the happy panting of Einstein, who always sat in the backseat, monitoring other dogs in other cars at intersections.

At one job interview, in a glass building so sterile she thought she should wear surgery room snoods over her shoes, she was asked about her computer skills; at another, about what hobbies she liked to fill her spare time. She didn't think that the personnel director had any business asking her such questions. These days she filled her spare time daydreaming about sex with Walton. She didn't say so and didn't get the job. But at a wholesale supplier of office furniture and stationery, she was offered a position on the spot by a man whose suit was so wrinkled that it was prideful and emblematic. He was a gaudy slob. He owned the business. She was being asked to help them work on a program for inventory control. She would have other tasks. She sighed—those fucking computers were in her future again, they were unavoidable—but she took what they offered her. If she hadn't met Walton, if Walton and Einstein hadn't escorted her to the interview, she wouldn't have.

To celebrate, she and Walton decided to escape the August heat by hiking down Minnehaha Creek to its mouth at the Mississippi River across from Saint Paul. He didn't have to be at work for another four hours. Walton had brought his fishing pole and tackle box, and while he cast his line into the water, his dog sat behind him in the shade of a gnarled cottonwood and Jodie walked downriver, looking, but not looking for anything, exactly, just looking without a goal, for which she felt she had a talent. She found a bowling ball in usable condition and one bruised and broken point-and-shoot camera that she left under a bush.

She walked back along the river to Walton, carrying the bowling ball. On her face she had constructed an expression of delight. She was feeling hot and extremely beautiful.

"See what I've found?" She hoisted the ball.

"Hey, great," he said, casting her a smile. "See what I've caught?" He held up an imaginary line of invisible fish.

"Good for you," she said. His eyes were steady on her. He had been gazing at her for the last few days in a prolonged way; she'd been watching him do it. She could feel his presence now in her stomach and her knees. She heard the double blast of a boat horn. Another boat passed, pulling a water-skier with a strangely unhappy look on her face. The clock stopped; the moment paused: When he said he wanted to make love to her, that he almost couldn't wait, that he had lost his appetite lately just thinking about her and couldn't sleep, she didn't quite hear him saying it, she was so happy. She threw the bowling ball out as far as she could into the river. She didn't notice whether it splashed. She took her time getting into his arms, and when he kissed her, first at the base of her neck and then, lifting her up, all over her exposed skin, she put her hands in his hair. Suddenly she liked kissing in public. She wanted people to see them together. "Walton," she said, "make love to me. Right here."

"Let's go to your place," he said. "Let's go there, okay?"

"Happy days," she said in agreement, putting her fingers down inside his loose beltless jeans.

HE WAS A slow-motion lover. She had made him some iced tea, but instead of drinking from it, he raised the cold glass to her forehead. Einstein had found a corner where she was panting with her eyes closed.

She had taken him by the hand and had led him out to the sleeping porch. You couldn't have known it from the way he looked in his street clothes, but his body was lean and muscular, and he made love shyly at first and didn't really become easy and wild over her until he saw how she was responding to him. She was embarrassed by how quickly and how effortlessly he made her come. She put her arms up above her head and just gave in. Women were supposed to take longer than this. Her swift ecstasy made her feel cheap. Maybe it was his slow fire burning away down on her. When she came the first time, a window shade flew up in her mind, and she could see all of her feelings waiting to be touched and moved, like passengers in a bus station. When she called out, she discovered it was Walton's name she was calling. She kissed all of his scars. She kissed his knuckles.

Maybe fools made the best lovers. They were devotees of passing pleasures, connoisseurs of them, and this, being the best of the passing pleasures, was the one at which they were most adept. His fire didn't burn away. He wasn't ashamed of any impulse he had, so he kept having them. He couldn't stop bringing himself into her. "Look at me," she said, as she was about to come again, and he looked at her with a slow grin on his face, pleased with himself and pleased with her. When she looked back at him, she let him see into her soul, all the way down, where she'd never allowed anyone to own her nakedness before.

" s o . Happy ever after?"

Walton was asleep after a night's work, and Jodie had gone down to Clara's Country Kitchen Café by herself. This morning the fat man with yellow-green eyes was full of mirthless merriment, and he seemed to be spilling over the counter stool on all sides. If anything, he was twice as big as before. He was like a balloon filled with gravy. Jodie had been in the middle of her second cup of coffee and her scrambled eggs with ketchup when he sat down next to her. It was hard to imagine someone who could be more deliberately disgusting than this gentleman. He had a rare talent, Jodie thought, for inspiring revulsion. The possible images of the Family of Humankind did not somehow include him. He sat there shoveling an omelet and sausages into his mouth. Only occasionally did he chew.

"Happy enough," she said.

He nodded and snorted. "'Happy enough,'" he quoted back to her. Sounds of swallowing and digestion erupted from him. "I give you a wish and you ask for a radio. There you have it." His accent was even more obscure and curious this morning.

"Where are you from?" Jodie asked. She had to angle her left leg away from his because his took up so much space under the counter. "You're not from here."

"No," he said. "I'm not really from anywhere. I was imported from Venice. A beautiful city, Venice. You ever been there?"

"Yes," she said, although she had not been. But she did love to read histories. "Lagoons, the Bridge of Sighs, and typhoid. Yeah, I've been there." She put her money down on the counter, and when she stood up, she felt a faint throbbing, almost a soreness but not quite that, Walton's desire, its trace, still inside her. "I have to go."

He resumed eating. "You didn't even thank me," the fat man said. "You smell of love and you didn't even thank me."

"All right. Thank you." She was hurrying out.

When she saw him in the mirror behind the cash register, he tipped an imaginary hat. She had seen something in his eyes: malice, she thought. As soon as she was out on the sidewalk, under the café's faded orange awning, her thoughts returned to Walton. She wanted to see him immediately and touch him. She headed for the crosswalk, all thoughts of the fat man dispersing and vanishing like smoke.

ON THE WAY BACK, she saw a thimble in the gutter. She deposited it in her purse. A fountain pen on the brick ledge of a storefront income tax service gleamed at her in the cottony hazy heat, and she took that, too. Walton had given her the habit of appreciating foundlings. When she walked onto the sleeping porch, she took off her shoes. She still felt ceremonial with him. She showed him the thimble and the fountain pen. Then they were making love, their bodies slippery with sweat, and this time she stopped him for a moment and said, "I saw that fat man again," but he covered her mouth, and she sucked on his fingers. Afterward, she showered and dressed and caught the bus to work. Einstein groaned in her sleep as Jodie passed her in the hallway. The dog, Jodie thought, was probably jealous.

On the bus, Jodie hummed and smiled privately. She hadn't known about all these resources of pleasure in the world. It was a great secret. She looked at the other passengers with politeness but no special interest. Her love was a power that could attract and charm. She was radiantly burning with it. Everyone could see it.

Through the window she spotted a flock of geese in a V-pattern flying east and then veering south.

FROM TIME TO TIME, at work—where she was bringing people rapidly into her orbit thanks to her aura of good fortune—she would think of her happiness and try to hide it. She remembered not to speak of it, good luck having a tendency to turn to its opposite when mentioned.

She called her sister and her mother, both of whom wanted to meet Walton as soon as possible. Jodie tried to be dryly objective about him, but she couldn't keep it up for long; with her sister, she began giggling and weeping with happiness. Her best friend, Marge, came over one stormy afternoon in a visit of planned spontaneity and was so impressed by Walton that she took off her glasses and sang for him, thunder and lightning crashing outside and the electric lights flickering. She'd once been the vocalist in a band called Leaping Salmon, which had failed because of the insipid legato prettiness of their songs; when they changed their name to Toxic Waste and went for a grunge sound, the other band members had ousted her. Singing in Leaping Salmon had been her only life-adventure, and she always mentioned it in conversations to people she had just met and wanted to impress, but while she was singing in her high honeyed soprano, Walton walked over to Jodie, sat down next to her, and put his hand on the inside of her thigh. So that was that.

I have a lover, Jodie thought. Most people have lovers without paying any attention to what they have. They think pleasure is a birthright. They don't even know what luck they have when they have it.

At the end of the day she couldn't wait to see him. Every

time she came into the room, his face seemed alert, relaxed, and sensual. Sometimes, thinking about him, she could feel a tightening, a prickling, all over her body. She was so in love and her skin so sensitive that she had to wear soft fabrics, cottons repeatedly washed. Her bras began to feel confining and priggish; on some days, she wouldn't wear them. The whole enterprise of love was old-fashioned and retrograde, she knew, but so what? Sometimes she thought, *What's happening to me?* She felt a certain evangelical enthusiasm and piety about sex, and pity for those who were unlucky in love.

Her soul became absentminded.

On some nights when Walton didn't have to go to the loading dock, she lay awake, with him draped around her. After lovemaking, his breath smelled of almonds. She would detach herself from him limb by limb and tiptoe into the kitchen. There, naked under the overhead light, she would remove her tarot pack from the coupon drawer and lay out the cards on the table.

Using the Celtic method of divination in the book of instructions, she would set down the cards.

This covers me.

This crosses me.

This crowns me, this is beneath me, this is behind me, this is before me, this is myself.

These are my hopes and fears.

The cards kept turning up in a peculiar manner. Instead of the cards promising blessings and fruitfulness, she found herself staring at the autumn and winter cards, the coins and the swords. This is before me: the nine of swords, whose illustration is that of a woman waking at night with her face in her hands.

She had also been unnerved by the repeated appearance of the Chariot in reverse, a sign described in the guidebooks as "failure in carrying out a project, riot, litigation."

* * *

PROPPED UP in her living room chair, she had been dozing after dinner when the phone rang. She answered it in a stupor. She barely managed a whispered "hello."

She could make out the voice, but it seemed to come from the tomb, it was so faint. It belonged to a woman and it had some business to transact, but Jodie couldn't make out what the business was. "What?" she asked. "What did you say?"

"I said we should talk," the woman told her in a voice barely above a whisper, but still rich in wounded private authority. "We could meet. I know I shouldn't intrude like this, but I feel that I could tell you things. About Glaze. I know that you know him."

"Who are you? Are you seeing him?"

"Oh no no no," the woman said. "It isn't that." Then she said her name was Glynnis or Glenna—something odd and possibly resistant to spelling. "You don't know anything about him, do you?" The woman waited a moment. "His past, I mean."

"I guess I don't know that much," Jodie admitted. "Who are you?"

"I can fill you in. Look," she said, "I hate to do this, I hate sounding like this and I hate being like this, but I just think there are some facts you should know. These are facts I have. I'm just . . . I don't know what I am. Maybe I'm just trying to help."

"All right," Jodie said. She uncrossed her legs and put her feet on the floor and tried to clear her mind. "I get off work at five. The office is near downtown." She named a bar where her friends sometimes went in the late afternoons.

"Oh, there?" the woman asked, her voice rising with disappointment. "Do you really like that place?" When Jodie didn't respond, the woman said, "The *smoke* in there makes me *cough*. I have allergies. Quite a few allergies." She suggested another restaurant, an expensive Italian place with lazily stylish wrought-iron furniture on the terrace and its name above the door in leaded glass. Jodie remembered the decor—she hadn't liked it. However, she didn't want to prolong these negotiations for another minute. "And *don't* tell Glaze I called," the woman said. Her speech was full of italics.

When Jodie hung up, she began to chew her thumbnail. She glanced up and saw her reflection in a window. She pulled her thumb away quickly; then she tried to smile at herself.

S H E   W A S   S E A T E D in what she considered a good spot near a window in the nonsmoking section when the woman entered the restaurant and was directed by the headwaiter to Jodie's table. The woman was twelve minutes late. Jodie leaned back and arranged her face into a temporary pleasantness. The stranger was pregnant and was walking with a slightly prideful sway, as if she herself were the china shop. Although she was sporting an attractive watercolor-hued peacock blue maternity blouse, she was also wearing shorts and sandals, apparently to show off her legs, which were deeply tanned. The ensemble didn't quite fit together, but it compelled attention. Her hair was carefully messed up, as if she had just come from an assignation, and she wore two opal earrings that went with the blouse. She was pretty enough, but it was the sort of prettiness that Jodie distrusted because there was nothing friendly about it, nothing settled or calm. She was the sort of woman whom other women instinctively didn't like. She looked like an aging groupie, a veteran of many beds, and she had the deadest eyes Jodie had ever seen, pale gray and icy.

"You must be Jodie," the woman said, putting one hand over her stomach and thrusting the other hand out. "I'm Gleinya Roberts." She laughed twice, as if her name itself was witty. When she stopped laughing, her mouth stayed open and her face froze momentarily, as more soundless laughter continued to emerge from her. Jodie found everything about her disconcerting, though she couldn't say why. "May I sit down?" the woman asked.

Feeling that she had been indeliberately rude, Jodie nodded and waved her hand toward the chair with the good view. The question had struck her as either preposterous or injured, and because she felt off-balance, she didn't remember to introduce herself until the right moment had passed. "I'm Jodie Sklar," she said.

"Well, I know *that*," Gleinya Roberts said, settling herself delicately into her chair. "You must be wondering if this baby is Glaze's. Don't worry. I can assure you that it's not," she said with a frozen half-grin, a grin that seemed preserved in ice. The thought of the baby's father hadn't occurred to Jodie until that moment. "I'm in my *fifth* month," the woman continued, "and the Little Furnace is certainly heating me up these days. Bad timing! It's much better to be pregnant in Minnesota in the winter. You can keep yourself warm that way. You don't have any children yourself, Jodie, do you?"

Jodie was so taken aback by the woman's prying and familiarity that she just smiled and shook her head. All the same, she felt it was time to establish some boundaries. "No, not yet," she said, after a moment. "Maybe someday." She paused for a second to take a breath and then said, "You know, I'm pleased to meet you and everything, but you must know that I'm . . . well, I'm really curious about why you're here. Why'd you call me?"

"Oh, don't let's rush it. In a minute, in a minute," Gleinya Roberts said, tipping her head and staring with her dead eyes at Jodie's hair. "I just want to establish a friendly basis." She opened her mouth and her face froze again as soundless laughter rattled its way in Jodie's direction. "Jodie, I just can't take my eyes off your hair. You have such beautiful black hair. Men must love it. Where do you get it from?"

"From? Where do I get it from? Well, my father had dark hair. It was quite glossy. It shone sometimes."

"Oh," the woman said. "I don't think women get their hair from their fathers. I don't think that's where that gene comes from. It's the mother, I believe. I'm a zoologist, an ornithologist, actually, so I'm not up on hair. But I do know you don't get much from your father except trouble. Sklar. What kind of name is that? Do Sklars have beautiful black hair?"

Before Jodie could answer, the waitress appeared and asked for their order. Gleinya Roberts reached for the menu, and while Jodie ordered a beer, the woman—Jodie was having trouble thinking of her as "Gleinya"—scanned the bill of fare with eyes slitted with skepticism and one eyebrow partially raised. "I'd *like* wine," Gleinya Roberts said, and just as the waitress was about to ask what kind, she continued, "but I can't have any because of the baby. What I *would* like is sparkling water but with no flavoring, no ice, and no sliced lemon or lime, please." The waitress wrote this down. "Are you ordering anything to eat?" Gleinya Roberts asked Jodie. "I am. Perhaps a salad. Do your salads have croutons?" The waitress said that they did. "Well, *please* take them out for me. I can't eat them. They're treated." She asked for the Caesar salad, explaining that she positively lived on Caesar salad these days. "But no additives of any kind, please," she said, after the waitress had already turned to leave. Apparently the waitress hadn't heard, because she didn't stop or turn around. If Jodie had been that waitress, she believed that she wouldn't have turned around, either. "I'm afraid I'm terribly picky," Gleinya Roberts announced. "You have to be, these days. It's the Age of Additives."

"I eat anything," Jodie said, rather aggressively. "I've always eaten anything." Gleinya Roberts patted her stomach and smiled sadly at Jodie but said nothing. "Now, Gleinya," she pressed on, "perhaps you can tell me why we're here."

Gleinya held her left hand out with the fingers straight and examined her wedding ring. It was a quick mean-spirited gesture, but it was not lost on Jodie. "It's about Glaze, of course," she said. "Maybe you can guess that I used to be with him. It ended two years ago, but we still talk from time to time." She took a long sip of her water, and while she did, Jodie allowed herself to wonder who called whom. And when: probably late at night. "Anyway," she went on, "that's how I know about you." She put down her water glass and smiled unpleasantly. "That's how I know about your *sleeping* porch. He's been spending some nights there. He's terribly in love with you," she said. "You're just *all* he talks about."

Jodie moved back in her chair, sat up straight, and said, "He's a wonderful guy."

"Yes," the other woman said, rather slowly, to affirm that Jodie had said what she had in fact said but not to agree to it. Suddenly, and quite unexpectedly, Gleinya Roberts half stood up, then sat down again and settled herself, flinging her elbows out, and before Jodie could ask why she had done so, though at this point the inquiry did seem rather pointless, Gleinya Roberts said, "It's so hard to get comfortable in your second term. All those little infant kicks." She patted her stomach again.

"They don't seem to have hurt you, exactly," Jodie said.

"No, but you have to be careful." She touched the base of her neck with the third finger of her right hand, tapping the skin thoughtfully. "You have to try to keep your looks up. You have to try to keep *yourself* up. Men get fickle. Of course, my husband, Jerry, says I'm still pretty, 'prettier than ever,' he says, a sweet lie, though I don't mind hearing it. He only says that to please me. It's just a love-lie. Still, I try to believe him when he says those things."

I bet you do, Jodie thought. I bet it's no effort at all. "You were going to tell me about Walton."

"Yes, I was," she said. The waitress reappeared, placed

Jodie's glass of beer, gowned in frost, in front of her, and Jodie took a long comforting gulp. All at once Gleinya Roberts' voice changed, going up half an octave. She had leaned forward, and her face was infected with old grudges and hatreds. "Jodie," she said, "I have to warn you. I have to do this, woman to woman. I want you to protect yourself. I know how suspicious this seems, coming from an old girlfriend, and I know that it must sound like sour grapes, but I have to tell you that what I'm saying is true, and I wouldn't say it unless I was worried for your safety. He likes fights. He likes fighting. You've seen how he favors his right foot, haven't you? That old injury?"

Jodie swallowed but could not bring herself to nod.

"He got it in a bar fight. Somebody kicked him in the ankle and shattered the bone. I mean, that's all right, men get into fights, but what you have to know is that he used to beat *me* up, and the girl before me, he beat her up, too. He'd get drunk and coked up and start in on me. Sometimes he did it carefully so it wouldn't show—"

"—He doesn't drink," Jodie said, her mouth instantly dry. "He doesn't do drugs."

"Maybe not *now*, he doesn't," Gleinya Roberts said, smiling for a microsecond and patting the tablecloth with little grace-note gestures. "But he has and probably will again. His sweet side is so sweet that it's hard to figure out the other side. He just explodes. He's such a good lover that you don't want to notice it. He's quite the dick artist. But then he just turns, and it's like a nightmare. He waits until you're really, really happy, and then he blows up. Once, months and months and months ago, I told him that someday I wanted to go out to the West Coast and sit on the banks of the Pacific Ocean and go whale watching. You know, see the whales go spouting by, on their migrations. We both had a vacation around the same time—"

"I don't think it's the 'banks' of the Pacific Ocean. That's for rivers. I think you mean 'shore,'" Jodie said.

Gleinya Roberts shrugged. "All *right*. 'Shore.' Anyway, we both had a vacation around the same time, and we drove out there . . . no, we flew . . . and then we rented a car. . . ."

She put her hand over her mouth, appearing to remember, but instead her eyes began to fill with dramatic, restaurant-scene tears; and at that moment Jodie felt a conviction that this woman was lying and was still probably in love with Walton.

"We rented a car," she was saying, "and we drove up from San Francisco toward Arcata, along there, along that coast. There are redwood forests a few miles back from the coastline, those big old trees. We'd stay in motels, and I'd make a picnic in the morning, and we'd go out, and Glaze would start drinking after breakfast, and by mid-afternoon he'd be silent and surly— he'd stop speaking to me—and by the time we got back to our motel, he'd be muttering, and I'd try to talk about what we had seen that day. I mean, usually when you go whale watching *there aren't any whales*. But there *are* always seals. You can hear the seals barking, down there on those rocks. I'd ask him if he didn't think the cliffs were beautiful or the wildflowers or the birds or whatever I had pointed out to him. But I always said something wrong. Something that was like a lighted match, and he'd blow up. And he'd start in on me. You ever been hit in the face?'

Jodie had turned so that she could see the sidewalk through the window. She was getting herself ready. It wasn't going to take much more.

"I didn't think so. It comes out of nowhere," Gleinya Roberts was saying, "and you're not ready for it, and then, boom, he lands the second one on you. The first time he beats you up, it's an initiation, and then he makes love to you to make up for it, but it makes the second one easier to do, because he's already done it. You don't expect it. Why *should* you? Why do you think he got thrown out of medical school? He hurt some-

body there. He broke two of my ribs. I had a shoulder separa-
tion from him. He got very practiced in the ways of apology
and remorse. He has a genius for remorse. And then of course
he's a demon under the sheets. The man can fuck, I'll give him
that, but, I don't know, after a while great sex is sort of a *gim-
mick*. It's like a 3-D movie, and you get tired of it. Well, maybe
you're not tired of it yet."

Jodie said nothing.

"I don't blame you. I wouldn't say anything either. I thought
he was Prince Charming, too. I've been there. And believe me,
I had to kiss a lot of frogs before I found the right guy. I had to
kiss them in every damn place they had. But he won't tell you.
He won't tell you about himself," she repeated. "Ask his father,
though. His father will tell you. Well, maybe he'll tell you. You
haven't met his father yet, have you?"

She speared a piece of her Caesar salad, chewed thoughtfully, then put down her fork.

"A woman has to tell another woman," she said, "in the case
of a man like this. I wanted to help you. I wouldn't want you to
be on daytime TV, one of those *afternoon* talk shows, in a body
cast on stage, warning other women about men like this. Jodie,
you can look in my eyes and see that what I'm telling you is
true."

Jodie looked. The eyes she saw were gray and blank, and for
a moment they reminded her of the blankness of the surface
of the ocean, and then the waters parted, and she saw a seemingly endless landscape of rancor, a desert of gray rocks and
black ashy flowers. Demons lived there. Then, just as quickly as
it had appeared, the desert was covered over again, and Jodie
knew that she had been right not to believe her.

"You're lying to me," Jodie said. She hadn't meant to say it,
only to think it, but it had come out, and there it was.

Gleinya Roberts nodded, acknowledging her own implausi-
bility. "You're just denying. You're gaga over him. Just as I was.

Taking a cruise on his pleasure ship. But Jodie, trust me, *that* cruise is going to end. Don't play the fool."

"What?"

"I said, 'Don't play the fool.'"

"I thought that was what you said."

Jodie, her head buzzing, and most of her cells on fire, found herself standing up. "You come in here," she said, "with your trophy wedding ring, and your trophy pregnancy, and your husband who says you're still pretty, and you tell me *this,* about Walton, spoiling the first happiness I've had in I don't know how long? Who the hell *are* you? *What* are you? You don't even look especially human." Gleinya Roberts tilted her head, considering this statement. Her face was unaccountably radiant. "I don't have to listen to you," Jodie said. "I don't have to listen to this nonsensical bullshit."

Her hands shaking, she reached into her purse for some money for the beer, and she heard Gleinya Roberts say, "Oh, I'll pay for it," while Jodie found a ten-dollar bill and flung it on the table. She saw that Gleinya Roberts' face was paralyzed into that attitude of soundless laughter—maybe it was just strain—and Jodie was stricken to see that the woman's teeth were perfect and white and symmetrical, and her tongue—her tongue!—was dark red and sensual as it licked her upper lip. Jodie leaned forward to tip over her beer in Gleinya Roberts' direction, careful to give the action the clear appearance of accident.

What was left of the beer made its dull way over to the other side of the table and dribbled halfheartedly downward.

"He's beautiful," Jodie said quietly, as the other woman gathered up the cloth napkins to sop up the beer, "and he makes sense to me, and I don't have to listen to you now."

"No, you don't," she said. "You go live with Glaze. You do that. But just remember: That man is like the kea. Ever heard of it? I didn't think so. It's a beautiful bright green New

Zealand bird. It's known for its playfulness. But it's a sheep killer. It picks out their eyes. Just remember the kea. And take this." From somewhere underneath the table she grasped for and then handed Jodie an audio cassette. "It's a predator tape. Used for attracting hawks and coyotes. It used to be his favorite listening. Just fascinated the hell out of him. It'll surprise you. *Women don't know about men.* Men don't let them."

Jodie had taken the tape, but she was now halfway out of the restaurant. Still, she heard behind her that voice coming after her. "Men don't want us to know. Jodie, they don't!"

IN A PURELY DISTANCED and distracted state, she took a bus over to Minnehaha Creek and walked down the path alongside the flowing waters to the bank of the Mississippi River. The air smelled rotten and dreary. Underneath a bush she found two bottle caps and a tuna fish can. She left them there.

SITTING ON THE BUS toward home, she tried to lean into the love she felt for Walton, and the love he said he felt for her, but instead of solid ground and rock just underneath the soil, and rock cliffs that comprised a wall where a human being could prop herself and stand, there was nothing: stone gave way to sand, and sand gave way to water, and the water drained away into darkness and emptiness. Into this emptiness, violence, like an ever-flowing stream, was poured—the violence of the kea, Walton's violence, Gleinya Roberts' violence, and finally her own. She traced every inch of her consciousness for a place on which she might set her foot against doubt, and she could not find it. Inside her was the impulse, as clear as blue sky on a fine summer morning, to acquire a pistol and shoot Gleinya Roberts through the heart. Her mind raced through the maze, back and forth, trying to find an exit.

Gleinya Roberts had lied to her. She was sure of that.

But it didn't matter. She was in fear of being struck. Although she had never been beaten by anyone, ever, in her life, the prospect frightened her so deeply that she felt parts of her psyche and her soul turning to stone. Other women might not be frightened. Other women would fight back, or were beaten and survived. But she was not them. She was herself, a woman mortally afraid of being violated.

THREE BLOCKS AWAY from her apartment, she bought, in a drugstore, a radio with a cassette player in it, and she took it with her upstairs; and in the living room she placed it on the coffee table, next to Walton's latest found treasures: a pleasantly shaped rock with streaks of red, probably jasper; a squirt gun; and a little ring through which was placed a ballpoint pen.

She dropped the predator tape Gleinya Roberts had given her into the machine, and she pushed the *play* button.

From the speaker came the scream of a rabbit. Whoever had made this tape had probably snapped the serrated metal jaws of a trap on the rabbit's leg and then turned on the recorder. It wasn't a tape loop: the rabbit's screams were varied, no two alike. Although the screams had a certain sameness, the clarifying monotony of terror, there existed, as in a row of corn, a range of distinctive external variety. Terror gave way to pain, pain made room for terror. The soul of the animal was audibly ripped apart, and out of its mouth came this shrieking. Jodie felt herself getting sick and dizzy. The screams continued. They went on and on. In the forests of the night these screams rose with predictable regularity once darkness fell. Though wordless, they had supreme eloquence and a huge claim upon truth. Jodie was weeping now, the heels of her hands dug into her cheekbones. The screams did not cease. They rose in frequency and intensity. The tape almost academically laid out at disarming length the necessity of terror. All things innocent and forsaken had their moment of expression, as the strong, following their nature, crushed themselves into their prey. Still it went on, this bloody fluting. Apparently it was not to be stopped.

Jodie reached out and pressed the *pause* button. She was shaking now, shivering. She felt herself falling into shock, and when she looked up, she saw Walton standing near the door— he had a key by now—with Einstein wagging her tail next to him, and he was carrying his daily gift, this time a birdhouse, and he said, "She found you, didn't she? That miserable, crazy woman."

HE PUTS DOWN the birdhouse and squats near her. From this position, he drops to his knees. Kneeling thus before her, he tries to smile, and his eyes have that pleasant fool quality they have always had. This man may never make a fortune. He may never amount to much. That would be fine. His dog pants behind him, like a backup singer emphasizing the vocal line and giving it a harmony. Walton's hands start at her hair and then slowly descend to her shoulders and arms. Before she can stop him, he has taken her into his embrace.

He is murmuring. Yes, he knew Gleinya Roberts, and, yes, they did own a predator tape *she* had found somewhere, but, no, he did not listen to it more than once. Yes, he had lived with her for a while, but she was insane (his father had been dead for a year; she had lied about that, too), and she was insanely jealous, hysterical, actually, and given to lies and lying, habitual lies, crazy bedeviling lies, and casual lies: lies about whether the milk was spoiled, lies about how many stamps were still in the drawer, lies about trivial matters and large ones, a cornucopia of lies, a feast of untruth. Gleinya Roberts was not married, for starters. He could prove that.

I'm just what I seem, he says. A modest man who loves you, who will love you forever. Did Gleinya tell you that I beat her up? Do you really think I am what that woman says I am? I used to get into barroom fights, but that's different. I never denied that. She's deluded. If what she said was true, would this dog be here with me?

Jodie looks at Walton and at his dog. Then she says, Raise your hand, fast, above Einstein's head. Look at her and raise your hand.

When he does what he is asked to do, Einstein neither cringes nor cowers. She watches Walton with her usual impassive interest, her tail still wagging. She has what seems to be a dog smile on her face. She approaches him, panting. She wants to play. She sits down next to where he kneels. She is the fool's dog. She looks at Walton—there is no mistaking this look—with straightforward dog love.

Jodie believes this dog. She believes this dog more than the woman.

Let me explain something, Walton is saying. You're beautiful. I started with that the first time I saw you. He does a little inventory: You lick your fingers after opening tin cans, you wear hats at a jaunty angle, you have a quick laugh like a bark, you move like a dancer, you're funny, you're great in bed, you love my dog, you're thoughtful, you have opinions. It's the whole package. How can I not love you?

And if I *ever* do to you what that woman says I did, you can just walk.

ONE DAY he will present her with an engagement ring, pretending that he found it in an ashtray at Clara's Country Kitchen Café. The ring will fit her finger, and it will be a seemingly perfect ring, with two tiny sapphires and one tiny diamond, probably all flawed, but flawless to the naked eye. They will be walking under a bridge on the south end of Lake of the Isles, and when they are halfway under the bridge, he will show her the ring and ask her to marry him.

Then she will sit for a few more days on the sleeping porch, considering this man. She won't be able to help it that when he moves suddenly, she will flinch. She will be distracted, but with the new radio on, she will from time to time do her best to read some of the books she never got around to reading before. Literature, however, will not help her in this instance. She will take out her tarot cards and place them in their proper order on the table.

This covers him.

This crosses him.

This crowns him.

This is beneath him.

This is behind him.

But the future will not unveil itself. The newspapers of the future are all blank. She will in exasperation throw all the tarot cards into the dumpster. She will buy a copy of the Rolling Stones' album *Beggars' Banquet.* She will listen to "Gimme Shelter," the song Walton had quoted, but now she hears two lines slurred hysterically and almost inaudibly in the background—lines she had never heard before.

> Rape, murder, are just a kiss away,
> Kiss away, kiss away, kiss away.

She will throw away the album, also, into the dumpster.

Once upon a time, happily ever after. She will look occasionally for the hideous fat man at the breakfast counter on Hennepin Avenue, but of course he will have vanished. When you are awarded a wish, you must specify the conditions under which it is granted. Everyone knows that. The fat man could have told her this simple truth, but he did not. Women are supposed to know such things. They are supposed to arm themselves against the infidelities of the future.

She will feel herself getting ready to leap, to say *yes*.

And just before she does, just before she agrees to marry him, she will buy a recording of Granados' piano suite *Goyescas*. Again and again she will listen to the fourth of the pieces, "Quejas ó la Maja y el ruiseñor," the story in music of a maiden singing to her nightingale. Every question the maiden sings, the bird sings back.

One Sunday night around one o'clock she will hear the distant sound of gunshots, or perhaps a car backfiring. She will then hear voices raised in anger and agitation. Sirens, glass breaking, the clatter of a garbage can rolled on pavement: city sounds. But she will fall back to sleep easily, her hands tucked under her pillow, drowsy and calm.

Reincarnation

WE HAD REACHED that part of the dinner when all the guests, smoothed out with wine and the meal, the first and second helpings, sit back and speak their minds. "Hearts," I would once have said, "sit back and speak their *hearts.*" I used to think that this was the basis of civilization, such conversations. Late spring, and the last of the light flowed through the west windows over the radiators, and over the boards on the radiators, and the houseplants on the boards. Lyric light, after-dinner light, alcoholic light. That kind. We were sitting in Ryan and Alicia's house on the west side of town, and we had eaten the dinner they had served. We were there, my wife and I, and Kyle and Brant, who had been together for six years and might as well have been married.

In houses like this one where all the furniture is worn out, the fabric frayed by use or scratched and shredded by the cats and children, the music stand knocked over, the butter plate on the piano keys, the flute on the mantel, and the sheet music for flute jammed in underneath the scattered trash on the coffee table, you feel an atmosphere of the *OK, so-what?* domestic life, a sort of aggressive familial complacency, a relaxed tattered permission that Ryan and Alicia are happy to give you. You wouldn't have that permission if you hadn't been invited in the first place, but the hint of squalor really lets you go. Let's get direct and personal, you think, while keeping up your end of the conversation.

Alicia had taken her shoes off. She was sitting next to me, and she was wearing a white cotton dress, and her legs were crossed and glowing in that room at that moment. She is a pretty woman with rust-colored hair and warm, intelligent brown eyes that go sleepy when she's amused, and she's a close listener who watches you as you talk and remembers your gestures and gives them back to you, though not exactly in a mocking way. Of course I was in love with her a little. Quite a few of us were. But it was friendly and comfortable, this love, and didn't have an emergency feeling to it. That's what I was thinking. We had slept together years ago, we were almost kids then, it was almost harmless, but sometimes she still turns up in my dreams. We've just finished making love in these dreams and we're lying on our backs in bed and talking about everything that matters, and then I wake up and think of calling her, but I never do. She is an anthropologist and a semiprofessional musician who has given up anthropology for a year or two of motherhood.

The talk had turned to reincarnation. Was this bourgeois, this topic? Sure. Of course. If that needs to be acknowledged, I will acknowledge it.

"In my previous life," I said, "I was a hedgehog." I nodded, agreeing with myself. "A hedgehog, nosing around under the hedges, eating grubs."

"What kind of grubs?" Brant asked. "It makes a difference."

"No," I said, "it doesn't make any difference. But since you ask, the grubs I ate, as a hedgehog, were larvae, beetle larvae. That's a fact."

"Funny to be saying that just after dinner," my wife said. "Why do people talk about things they don't actually believe in? Could you explain that to me?"

"Me? No, I couldn't. But why don't you play along? This time? For example, what were you," I asked her, "in your previous life?"

"I didn't have a previous life," my wife said. "Why don't you ask Ryan over there? Maybe he had a previous life. He might know. Or else we could talk about things that really matter."

"Okay, Ryan," I said. "What's your opinion?"

Ryan is an incredible—actually, preposterously—handsome accountant who works for the city. When you're walking with him, women and men turn helplessly to gaze in his direction. He's baffled by his own good looks and doesn't know what to do with them. I don't think he likes looking the way he does. His handsomeness is like a freak accident. And it causes other accidents. He's a bit dull, though, as handsome people often are. *They* never have to say anything. He doesn't have a clue about conversation. As the genial dull host, he was sitting back and smiling at us, his arms crossed, leaning back in his chair. "In my previous life," Ryan said, "I was a swan."

"Ryan," my wife said, "you *are* a swan."

"No," he said, "I was a swan, I'm not a swan now. I'm an ex-swan."

"Maybe you mean swain," my wife said. "But if you mean swan, I've always been curious about this: What do swans eat?"

Ryan, quite nonplused by my wife's question, raised his arms and touched his brow, as if he were thinking. You couldn't expect smart remarks from him. He didn't even know what an epigram was. The light was disappearing from the living room and the dining room, as if leached out by the window facing the street. Alicia and Ryan's children were making a racket downstairs.

I noticed that Kyle and Brant were keeping pretty quiet. They might have been squirming; I couldn't tell in that light. So I rushed in. "What were *you?*" I asked, directing the question to Brant, who's funnier and more talkative than Kyle usually is. Kyle doesn't always make eye contact, even when he's speaking to someone. This particular evening, he was playing with his water glass.

"I was a shrink," Brant said. "I listened to people talk all day. I got rich."

"Where?"

"In Des Moines," Brant said. "I had very little competition with other shrinks. The trouble was, all I ever got were run-of-the-mill neuroses. I waited for the big ones, but I never got any. It drove me to drink, listening to that whining bullshit all day. Run-of-the-mill neuroses drove me to a run-of-the-mill addiction. As a therapist I had no compassion and I died in my swimming pool. I drowned or something."

"You would have been revived," Kyle said, looking up, "if the ambulance hadn't been stopped by that swan crossing the road."

"I never did that," Ryan said, shaking his head. "I never crossed the road in front of an ambulance. I would never do that. It's not swanlike."

My wife had taken her sandals off now, down there under the table somewhere, half in imitation of Alicia, half not. Why do women do that? They just make you look.

"God, this is a desperately empty conversation," Kyle said. He has a pleasingly melancholic delivery, a great FM voice, and, in fact, works at the local NPR station. His friendliness is always a bit condescending, but I don't mind that. Today his nose was sharper. He was a bit too thin, I thought. It was worrisome.

"It's a dinner party," Alicia said. "What do you expect? If

you just hold on, we'll get to something shameful, and there'll be a big mess we'll all remember. The night is young. We're all such good friends that we're, like, *resources* for each other. You've got to wade through the personal shrapnel. For example, nobody asked me what I was, in my previous life. I was famous."

"You were famous?" Ryan asked, and reached down to touch his wife in a husbandly way on her ankle. He was just catnip to her. That's why she married him. I noticed Brant and Kyle noticing his gesture. "You?"

"Yes, I was."

"Well, who were *you?*" Brant asked her. "What name did they give you?"

"That would be telling," Alicia said. "But I was beautiful. There was this thing that I did, this endearing little turning-of-the-head, kind of a shy pout thing. It broke hearts. Men wanted to put their mouths on me."

"Alicia, honey," Brant said, sort of grinning, "you do that *now*, that shy pout thing."

"Do not."

"You were Marie Antoinette," Ryan half-whispered to her. "You told the rest of us to eat cake."

My wife drank what remained of her wine and raised her arms in an exasperated stretch. She's class-conscious and generally doesn't like whimsy in any of its forms, especially this kind. "Marie Antoinette! Jesus. Why do middle-class people like us talk so much about incarnation and reincarnation? We should be talking about our lives right now. I just don't understand it. No, maybe I do understand it. It just seems vain to me. Actually, no, it doesn't seem vain so much as habitual." She stretched again, and her beauty, her earnest small-town integrity and physical grace, flared up in that one movement. I could tell she was going to start something. "I'm sure about one thing," she said. "When I'm dead, I'll be dust. No more of me anywhere. I'll be among the happy dead. I don't want to go around this routine one more time. No thanks. Once is enough. It's more than enough. You know what I saw today?"

"Katherine," I said. "Honey."

"This is what I saw," Katherine continued, ignoring me. Alicia was nodding in her direction and pouring more wine. "What I saw was couples, or I mean a couple, in Ridgeway Park down by the reservoir. I was hurrying home. Speeding to pick up the kids. So there was this couple. And, of course, they were beautiful. She was beautiful and he was beautiful and they were being beautiful together. They had a blanket and a picnic basket and of course it was a warm day so it was all very Renoir and like that. She was wearing a dress like yours, Alicia, oh, no she wasn't, it was a pair of blue jeans. How could I forget? Blue jeans. So was he. His hair was longer than hers, and more blond. They were sort of nestled together and you got the feeling that soon it wouldn't be Renoir, it would be one of those other guys, Degas, where the woman has her clothes off and the man is looking right at you and he's going to make a move in a minute or two, just as soon as he finishes his sandwich."

"That's not Degas. I thought you claimed you were driving by," I said.

"They were staring into each others' eyes and they were kissing and it was love, love, love on the blanket in Ridgeway Park, and the perpetuation of the species. So I gave them a wave. Also, I honked. I don't know if the girl saw me. Their kissing— you know how you always notice this?—it was pretty slow, exploratory. I might have been speeding by in my station wagon, but I could tell that, at least. Right out there in public they were doing that. And it set me to thinking. Why do people, when they're feeling like that, insist on being happy in public places? You see these damn couples out on the sidewalks and in the coffee shops and they're just slobbering over each other, and you think, well, they sure could have some consideration for others, people who aren't in love anymore. They're just making it a lot worse for the rest of us. So anyway, I saw these two, and you know what I felt like doing?"

"Yes," Kyle said. He was quite well read. "You felt like standing up in the movie theater and shouting, 'Don't do it! It's not to late to change your minds, both of you.'"

Alicia interrupted at that point. She was rather good at interrupting in such a way that you would never notice that she was interrupting. "Brant," she said, "I can't get it out of my head what you said a minute or two ago." She stopped and inserted a little interim of silence into the evening so that we could all get our breath. "Those run-of-the-mill neuroses that you listened to, when you were a shrink. What sort of neuroses were they? You never said."

"I couldn't tell you."

"Why not?" Alicia was gently imitating Brant's head motions.

"I couldn't tell you," Brant said, "because it would violate the privacy of the doctor's consultation room."

"But it's over," I said, recovering myself somewhat. "You're dead, and the Des Moines patients are dead, so you can tell us now."

"Yes, I'm dead," Brant said, "but I try not to remember the bad things in my previous lives." He was sounding huffy. "I try to remember only the good things."

"Oh, now *that's* an exaggeration," Kyle said, touching Brant on the arm.

"Well, I can tell you that they masturbate a lot," Brant said.

Ryan was pouring the wine, making his handsome and pleasingly dull presence known. "Oh, I doubt it," he said. "I don't think therapy patients masturbate all that often." Then he stopped as if he had thought of something. "They don't have to. They talk instead."

"I wasn't talking about the patients," Brant said. "I meant the shrinks."

"What *do* the people do out there?" I asked. "In Des Moines? I don't think I've been there."

"Oh, them? Well, they get into land auctions, and fights, and bankruptcy hearings, and they farm and farm and farm, and then they sell insurance. How should I know? All I heard about was their troubles, and then I died. Oh, listen: I just remembered." He drank what was left of his wine, and instantly Ryan poured more. "Here's a story I remember. This isn't run-of-the-mill. This is a story you'll all like.

"We had a neighbor when I was a kid, a really nice guy to the neighborhood children, very kind and all that. He was the father of two daughters, and they were about age ten or something. He was so nice, and everybody *said* he was so nice, that, after a while, he became the sort of guy who can't discover himself doing anything wrong. It's like Elizabeth Taylor coming to believe she's Elizabeth Taylor. And what this man did was, he fell terribly in love with a woman who lived down the block and across the street. Whose name, if you can believe it, was Claire Carlson. The guy's name was Jimmy Palantier. Anyway, this guy, Jimmy, fell in love with Claire Carlson, the neighbor, and she must have been touched by him because they had an affair. That's not an interesting part of the story. No one would care about the story if that was all there was to it.

"No, the interesting part of the story has to do with Jimmy. And the fact that he thought he was a nice guy and could not discover, I guess you'd say, a flaw in himself. Here he was, in love, and married to someone else. He couldn't feel guilty. He knew he was supposed to, but he couldn't. And what he did—this is where the story begins—was to become friends, or better friends, with Claire Carlson's husband, whom everybody called J. T. I can't remember what the initials stood for. He wanted to be friends with the husband of the woman he was sleeping with. Maybe he thought that he would get closer to her that way. Or that he'd keep everything on this positive social level. I don't know what he thought.

"So Jimmy would call up this big, burly guy, J. T., or somehow arrange to borrow a shovel or a power tool, and they would chat. The thin guy and the burly guy would talk. They were both ex-Navy men. They had that in common. The important feature of this story is that J. T. would chat *back*. Like the family man he was. Like the family men they were. Straight men are quite a puzzle. Anyway, they started doing householder whatnot together. They'd give each other help on repair projects, chopping and sawing down dead trees in the yard, that sort of thing. Sometimes they needed a tool, a gizmo, and they'd go off together, and you can imagine Claire's surprise when she saw her lover and her husband hunkering down inside her husband's truck, dusting up the driveway, doing various errands. It terrified her, seeing this. Seeing this—what?—this *guy* thing happening.

"Meanwhile, she and Jimmy were sleeping with each other whenever it could be arranged. The usual intrigues. She probably asked him to stop being friendly with her husband and he probably refused."

"How do you know this," I interrupted, "if you were a child at the time?"

Brant took off his glasses, pulled out his shirt from his trousers, and polished the lenses on the shirt flap. I noticed a food stain on the fabric. "Don't ask me how I know," he said. "I just know, that's all. Where was I in my story?" Brant sighed. "Oh, yes. Jimmy and J. T. out in the truck, passing a bait and tackle shop. They discovered that they both liked to fish. They stopped and bought some new line and lures. Guy equipment. It turned out that Jimmy had a boat with an outboard motor. They bought fishing licenses. One day, one summer day, let's say in mid-July, they went fishing. They left Claire behind, of course. I don't know what Jimmy's wife was doing. She's not part of this story.

"So the lover and the husband stepped into the boat with their fishing poles and lines and out they went into the bay of Henryson Lake, about fifteen miles west of here. It's a good lake for fishing, particularly on the west side, I'm told. Pike and bass, so they say. How would I know? You won't catch me catching fish. So they're out on the boat. Whenever I think about this, I think of the air, the *largeness* of the sun and the air and the sky, and the wind, you know, causing the water to lap against the boat. I think about these things. I even think of the strength of the fishing line they were using, and if it broke. I think of those two guys in the boat, fishing. It just amazes me to think about them, sitting there."

"You weren't there," Katherine said.

"No, I wasn't there."

"So you're making this up. So this is all academic."

Brant put his glasses back on. "No, it is not academic. Not at all. I keep thinking about the water and the wind, and sometimes I wonder if there was a smell of inland lake water vegetation, you know, one of those heavy green smells."

"So they're out on the boat," my wife said.

"Yeah, " Ryan said, leaning back, so that a bit of light from the west window rushed across his face, streaking it. "Which guy killed the other guy?"

"I keep forgetting that I'm in America," Brant said. "That's surprising, because I'm an American and I've never been out of the country. I keep forgetting about the necessities of violence in the U.S.A. Well, if you were expecting violence, you'll be disappointed. Something else happened."

"Brant, don't be coy," Kyle said. "Just tell the story. You always tell it so well."

"All right," Brant said. He leaned forward, instead of back, and he put his elbows on the dinner table, and he grinned suddenly and unexpectedly. "J. T. caught something. The line pulled and the reel sang, and he yanked and pulled in a tremendous fish, and together they brought it in. Jimmy scooped the fishnet down into the water and pulled the monster into the boat and then they put it on the what-do-you-call-it, the . . . "

"The fish pail," I said.

"No, not the fish pail. The stringer. They looped its gills and put it back into the water to keep it fresh and alive, and they laughed over their luck with the fish, and in the laughter that followed this catch, this triumph, with J. T. smiling and Jimmy smiling, in that moment of camaraderie and fellowship occasioned by the catching of the enormous fish, J. T. turned to Jimmy, and he said, quietly and suddenly clear as day, clear as a shiny knife, *'I know what you're doing.'"*

Brant sat back in his chair, crossed his arms, and looked at all of us with satisfaction.

"That's what he said?" I asked. "'I know what you're doing'?"

"That's it."

Alicia, who was still sitting next to me, moved her chair back away from the table and she tapped the wood floor with her bare foot impatiently. "I don't get it. That's your story? That's what it leads up to?"

"Yes." Brant was apparently pleased that his story's success had been wasted on us. "Two people in a boat. One man has a secret, he thinks, and is cheating the other man. But the other man knows. The other man says, 'I know what you're doing.' And that's the end of the story. That's all the story has to tell. Because it's enough to know that one of them recognizes what the other one is up to."

"Men don't act that way," Alicia said.

"They don't? How do they act? Tell me about men."

"I don't know. They just don't act *that* way. More wine, anybody?" She held up the bottle.

"They go into rages, do you think?" Kyle said. He hadn't said much until now, and I had been considering, and not for the first time, how gray he sometimes seemed. "They fight, or they're silent and dangerous? They don't settle for *knowing*. Is that the idea? Actually, that's an untrue story. That's always been an untrue story, B. You heard that story from your mother, and she got the facts wrong or she remanufactured them. That story doesn't come thirdhand. It comes fifth-hand." He was picking at something on his face as he said this.

Brant raised his hand slyly and then pretended to toss away an invisible ball the hand had held. "Doesn't matter *where* the story comes from, or who got it. It doesn't even matter if it's true. The topic of conversation was run-of-the-mill troubles."

"No," I said, "we were talking about reincarnation."

"Well, it's about that, too."

"It does matter if it's true," Ryan said, standing up, motioning us away from the dinner table. "It matters if it happened. If those guys were in the boat."

Brant looked at him, one of those searching looks when there's too much intensity in the gaze. "No, it doesn't matter if they were in the boat. It only matters if you think it could have happened. I think it could have. Maybe you don't think so. Do you think it could have happened? Come on, Ryan. Give us your view. Give us the swan perspective."

Ryan was walking into the kitchen. I don't know what he had in mind to get there. Without turning around, he said, "All right. Yes. It could have happened."

Alicia leaned toward me. She said, "It's not enough to know something. You have to tell somebody that you know. Your knowledge has to be known."

"What happens then?" I asked.

"Then the wind dies and you're out in the boat together," she said.

* * *

AN HOUR LATER, we had all stepped into the backyard in the semidark with one small floodlight, attached to a motion detector, aimed toward the trees. The floodlight was also on a bad switch, so the bulb kept going on and off. What Ryan and Alicia had built out there was something of a wooden platform without railings where you could squat or stand or sit while you contemplated the stars or the darkness of the woods beyond the floodlight. Boom: Something moved. Boom: The light went on. Then calm, and after half a minute, the light went off. There were chairs, a few. Like the rest of the house, it wasn't quite enough of anything to be festive. The boards were sagging inwardly, and the deck gave the impression of being in remission from an attack of the natural, organic sort. Ryan and Alicia were looking after the drinks, and Brant and Kyle were gazing up at a tree house that Ryan's son from his first marriage had built. The talk had slowed down and evolved into mutters and one-liners and half-lit nodding in the interrupted dark.

"Incarnation," I said, my words aimed straight into the largely empty sky. "I happen to know one thing about it. I saw it once. It happened in New Jersey."

From behind me, I heard Kyle saying, "No one ever got reincarnated in New Jersey. Can't happen."

"I didn't say 'reincarnated.' I said, 'incarnated.' Do you want to hear this story or not?" I asked, irritable in my most sociable manner. "This story actually happened because I saw it. I had been in Philadelphia and had gone over to Camden, New Jersey. Not a lively place, except crimewise. I was about a block away from the Campbell Soup factory, which smelled that particular day, as I remember it, of chili beef soup, and I was on my way to Walt Whitman's house on Mickle Street. I just wanted to visit the place. I was in town anyway, and it was a spring day, and I knew it was there in Camden, New Jersey, and I found it right there on Mickle Street because I knew the ad-

dress. I was fortunate that I knew the address because the his-
torical marker plate had been unscrewed from the front of the
house, and stolen."

"And probably," Brant said, "boiled down to make shoes, for
metal feet."

"Probably so," I said. "I went to the house and rang the bell.
A very beautiful woman answered the door. I said that I was an
admirer of Walt Whitman's poetry and wished to see the house.
She was quite obliging. That was her job, I suppose. She was an
African-American lady, and she spoke about Walt Whitman as
if he were, or had been, a close relative. Just as if he were her
crackpot uncle. She told stories and jokes about him and then
she'd start laughing. She took me to the deathbed. She showed
me his rocking chair and the highboy. Several handwritten letters were stashed in display cases. I saw his hairbrush and his
comb. She took me all around. I signed my name in the register.
I was the first visitor in three days, and the last visitors had
been from Japan."

"So what was incarnated?" Alicia asked. "You didn't see his
ghost, did you?"

"No," I said. "Of course not." I was telling this story, but I
was looking off toward the woods beyond the yard, and I
thought I saw a raccoon there, getting curious about the potato
chips we had left behind when we'd been out there having
drinks before dinner. The floodlight went on for a few seconds.
The animal scurried away. "That's creepy," I said. "That light. It
scares away the critters.

"Anyway," I said, "after the tour, the bed and the hairbrushes
and the highboy and the rocking chair, I thanked the lady and
stepped out the door onto Mickle Street. And as I watched, an
alley cat crossed the street, and as my eye followed this cat, I
saw what was across the street. I hadn't noticed it before. Right
there, right across from Walt Whitman's house, the man who

wrote, well, *Leaves of Grass,* there's a new county prison. Yellow
brick with slit windows. There's American ingenuity for you.
Whitman on one side of the street, a prison on the other. It
was as ugly as men can make it. Barbed wire and concertina
wire were around it, like decorations. It was so ugly they didn't
need barbed wire, but they had it anyway.

"I looked up at the slit windows and I saw a young man
there, looking back out. We exchanged glances, but I sure
wasn't the person this kid was waiting for. And I figured that
this place must be one of those holding prisons, one of those
places where they hold kids and adults until their trials come
up. So there's this kid standing there at the window—an ordinary pimply blond-haired kid—and he's got a sign that he's put
in the window and the sign is in capital letters and it says HI
DAD. So, I figured his dad was coming along, and, sure
enough, while I was standing there, literally at the stoop of
Walt Whitman's house, along comes one of those airport lim-
ousines. It's not a limousine, it's a van. A van for taking people
to the Philly airport. And it stops and parks and this big guy
gets out, this big Italian-looking guy.

"And this guy runs out into the middle of the street, into the
middle of traffic, though there isn't too much in Mickle Street
because it was a residential street until they built the prison
there. I guess this guy, this father, doesn't have time to visit his
son, or it's not visiting hours, or something. Anyway, he stands
there in the middle of the street and he waves at his son, and
his son waves back at him.

"And then the kid sort of jiggles or shakes the HI DAD
sign, and the father, this big guy, acknowledges it by nodding
and smiling, and then he starts holding up his hands, all ten fingers, and then one hand, four fingers, and the kid seems to understand because he moves the HI DAD sign up and down. I
figured it meant that the kid had fourteen days until trial. Any-

how, the kid nodded, too. I couldn't tell if he was a nice-look-
ing kid or a mean one or anything—you can't tell about things
like that from a distance.

"And, at last, the father looks up at his son and he presses
both of his hands with the palms inward to his lips, and then
he throws his son a kiss with both hands. Standing in the middle of the street, he throws a kiss to his son. Do you understand this? He's standing there in the middle of Mickle Street
with his hands flung out in the air, and then he turns around
and gets back into the airport van, and he starts it and drives
away. The kid removes the HI DAD sign from the window, and
that's the last I ever saw of him."

I sat back, momentarily tired out by my own story.

"THAT'S A GOOD ONE," Katherine, my wife, said. "You
never told me that one." She scratched at her scalp. "But you
said it was about incarnation. I don't get that part."

I almost didn't hear her question, because I could see the
raccoon more clearly now. Its movements were causing the
motion detector to turn the lights on every two minutes or so.
They stayed on for thirty seconds, then went off. Raccoons are
shy animals but courageous at night, and no one can deny the
intelligence visible in their eyes.

"See that raccoon?" I asked, pointing. Kyle and Brant said
that they saw it, but no one else apparently did. "Oh," I said,
"the incarnation part is about Whitman. Whitman's poetry is
about love you don't have to earn. It's about love that you just
have or that you just get or you give but not the kind that you
did something to earn. It's not Protestant love. It's love for
being itself. If you're a father, you love your kid, no matter
what. In jail or out. That's what I meant."

"That kid had earned his father's love," Ryan said. "He
earned it by being his father's son."

"That's not *earning*," I said. "He didn't have to do anything right or wrong. There wasn't any test his father had given him that he'd failed or passed. He just was. He just *was* that kid. That's what Whitman talks about."

"No, that's not Whitman, that's being a parent," Katherine said, "about which many people know nothing. You love your kids because they're your kids. You don't love other people that way. You don't love Arab terrorists that way. You don't love Afghan tribespeople that way. You wouldn't want to."

"I need a drink," Brant said. "I could use a *digestif*. Just a spot of brandy for the road. Ryan, I don't mean to bully you in your host duties or anything, but you got any brandy? I could sure use some."

S O M E H O W , my Mickle Street story had created the wrong tone or put some element into the air that the other guests were forced to ponder. A silence without depth or extension drifted down over us like an invisible black fabric. You would have thought that I had committed a terrible social blunder, courageous in its rudeness. The night sky was dimly visible overhead, and I had had too much to drink, so that when I looked up, the stars appeared to be swirling, or blindly racing some sickening stellar soapbox derby, right to left, right to left.

"There's no such thing as unearned love," Katherine said, stubbornly, out of the dark. Then she took my hand. "You should know that. You earned mine. You have it. I'll never give it up." Then, appearing to remember that we were in some sense in public, she said, "I love this guy. I love the sight of him."

Ryan was back with the bottle of brandy and the tray, and the brandy glasses he'd once bought at the discount store. The signs, as opposed to the essence, of civilization in the Midwest can be quite hasty and contingent. He had already poured it out, and we took glasses and drank in silence together. He had turned the floodlight on in order not to stumble and now turned it off again. I didn't like the way the light kept going on and off.

"I love *him,* too," Alicia said, "that guy." She angled her head in Ryan's direction. "And not because he looks the way he does. If he looked like a bowling ball with hair he wouldn't have caught my attention in the first place, but he doesn't look a bit like that. You know what I love about him? He cleans up. He does the dishes. I make these messes, and he cleans them all up. How can you not love that?"

Kyle and Brant were listening to all this but not saying anything.

"Right," Ryan said. "I know about cleaning up the messes. I do that. But sometimes, sometimes in the middle of love you just want all of it, all those attachments, to go away. You think it would be a fine idea if the whole thing just . . . stopped. A great burning shell of flames. And took itself up to . . . I don't know what I'm saying."

"Yes, you do," Katherine said.

"Yes, I do. I do know. What if you could get beyond attraction? Being drawn by people? Don't you ever get tired of affection? The lust stuff? All these prickled nipples and the sweat and the erections and the rest of it? Don't you?"

"No," somebody said. "You don't." I don't remember who said that.

"Anybody want to hear some music?" Alicia asked. "I'll play something." She went into the living room, found her flute, and brought it back out.

WITH THE FLOODLIGHTS still off, Alicia sat down and began to play. She was first chair in a local semiprofessional orchestra. Even in the dark, I could see the eyes of some animal, that raccoon or maybe a skunk, watching us. Alicia played Debussy's "Syrinx"—she told us what it was—and then she played it a second time. It takes two and a half minutes to play.

The nymph Syrinx was pursued by Pan and disappeared into a reed bed, where she was transformed into a reed. Once, after waking from a nightmare, I felt as if I had been turned into a piece of wood, like Pinocchio, and for ten or fifteen seconds I could not remember how to move my limbs. Years ago, during the summer between my junior and senior year in high school, I worked in a geriatrics ward, where one old woman who always wore pink bedroom slippers told me with great seriousness that she was a queen of the Indies, and one old man with a bright gray mustache believed that he might be—he whispered this to me—a box turtle. He said that he was a turtle because he moved so slowly and there was a weight on his back, either his shell or death. I asked him how it was, being a turtle, and he said it was okay once you got used to it.

Maybe he was joking, in his old man's way.

A breeze from the south moved through the plant life in Alicia and Ryan's backyard. Of all of us, Alicia and Kyle had known each other the longest. Before we had sat down to dinner, Kyle, who had brought over a little wooden train for Janey, Alicia and Ryan's older daughter, had been upstairs chatting with her. You could hear them laughing and giggling from downstairs.

At that moment, sitting there with the breeze going through the apple trees, and Alicia playing her flute, and, in the dark, Katherine taking my hand in an emotion like happiness, but not identical to it, a *hopeful* feeling or sensation, I felt as if maybe I too would be transformed somehow. I would explode or levitate or turn slowly into another thing. I felt *as if* that, but not exactly that. Sometimes in these situations you sense as if you're going to go crazy or float off into space, but you never do. I waited on Alicia and Ryan's half-completed back deck to see what would happen next.

The raccoon turned around and lumbered away.

"MOM?" It was Janey, calling down from her upstairs bedroom window. "Mom? I can't sleep when you're playing!" I looked up. Her silhouette stood there studying the lot of us.

Alicia's notes stopped in mid-phrase. I could hear her putting down her flute.

"All right," she called. "Go back to bed."

"I will," Janey said. Then her voice faded as she said, "Just don't play any more."

"Now there's a motto," Kyle said.

It was so dark that I couldn't tell where anyone was except by voice. The stars were still unpleasantly racing from right to left. "Kyle," I said, "you've been pretty quiet all evening. What's new?"

"When we expire," Kyle said, after a moment, "where do you suppose we go?"

The wind continued to flow through those same trees. Its sound filled up the quiet and apparently empty moments. "Oh," Ryan said, "I'll bet we float."

"Float?"

"Yeah, float. Float between worlds, maybe."

"You think it's painful?" Kyle asked.

"No," Katherine said. "I don't think it would be."

"Why not?"

"Because you've done all that by then," my wife said. "You've done pain. You don't need to do it, after you've done it."

"Nice to think so," Kyle said. "Nice to think *you* could get past it."

"Yes, isn't it?" my wife asked. "It might even be true."

"Yes, it could be. I went to the doctor this week. Those people certainly think about pain a lot. And then they talk about it, but not so you'd know that that's what they're talking about. They just keep you confused."

"They mention it sometimes," I said. "Not very often."

"But they don't call it *pain*," Kyle said. "Not as often as they should." Where was Brant? He hadn't said anything, not a word, during all this. "Not as often as they will. Pain every goddamn where."

"What does that mean?" Alicia asked.

"What does that mean? I know what you're doing," Kyle said. "You're all holding hands, the lot of you. You're all dancing on the lawn. Slow two-steps. You're all going home. You're not today, you're in tomorrow. You're all soldiers of the future! You're all fine."

"And I know what you're doing," Ryan said, out of the dark. "You're—"

"—No, you *don't* know what I'm doing," Kyle informed him, informed us, more loudly now. I could hear a few crickets and that same persistent wind. "You don't know what I'm doing. You, with your party manners? You, with your shipshape attitudes? *You haven't heard a word I've said all evening.* The lucky deaf! You know that I'm sitting here, but what you don't know is that Brant's hand is on my face, and his thumb is caressing my cheek, back and forth, just a caress, that's all. And you don't know that his hand is wet. How would *you* know that, you, a swan? If the hawk dies in the forest, would you see it? And the water on my hands, by the way, isn't from his body, it's from mine." He waited. "All this fluid came out of my eyes."

A few minutes later—minutes of pure backyard dark—the floodlight went back on, and when it did, Brant's hand was still there, where Kyle had said it was, and still wet. I know because I looked.

The Next Building
I Plan to Bomb

I N   T H E   P A R K I N G   L O T next to the bank, Harry Edmonds saw a piece of gray scrap paper the size of a greeting card. It had blown up next to his leg and attached itself to him there. Across the top margin was some scrabby writing in purple ink. He picked it up and examined it. On the upper lefthand corner someone had scrawled the phrase: THE NEXT BUILDING I PLAN TO BOMB. Harry unfolded the paper and saw an inked drawing of what appeared to be a sizable train station or some other public structure, perhaps an airport terminal. In the drawing were arched windows and front pillars but very little other supporting detail. The building looked solid, monumental, and difficult to destroy.

He glanced around the parking lot. There he was in Five Oaks, Michigan, where there were no such buildings. In the light wind other pieces of paper floated by in an agitated manner. One yellow flyer was stuck to a fire hydrant. On the street was the usual crowd of bankers, lawyers, shoppers, and students. As usual, no one was watching him or paying much attention to him. He put the piece of paper into his coat pocket.

All afternoon, while he sat at his desk, his hand traveled down to his pocket to touch the drawing. Late in the day, half as a joke, he showed the paper to the office receptionist.

"You've got to take it to the police," she told him. "This is dangerous. This is the work of a maniac. That's LaGuardia there, the airport? In the picture? I was there last month. I'm sure it's LaGuardia, Mr. Edmonds. No kidding. Definitely La-Guardia."

So at the end of the day, before going home, he drove to the main police station on the first floor of the City Hall. Driving into the sun, he felt his eyes squinting against the burrowing glare. He had stepped inside the front door when the waxy bureaucratic smell of the building hit him and gave him an immediate headache. A cop in uniform, wearing an impatient expression, sat behind a desk, shuffling through some papers, and at that moment it occurred to Harry Edmonds that if he showed what was in his pocket to the police he himself would become a prime suspect and an object of intense scrutiny, all privacy gone. He turned on his heel and went home.

AT DINNER, he said to his girlfriend, "Look what I found in a parking lot today." He handed her the drawing.

Lucia examined the soiled paper, her thumb and finger at its corner, and said, "'The next building I plan to bomb.'" Her tone was light and urbane. She sold computer software and was sensitive to gestures. Then she said, "That's Union Station, in Chicago." She smiled. "Well, Harry, what are you going to do with this? Some nut case did this, right?"

"Actually, I got as far as the foyer in the police station this afternoon," he said. "Then I turned around. I couldn't show it to them. I thought they'd suspect me or something."

"Oh, that's so melodramatic," she said. "You've never committed a crime in your life. You're a banker, for Chrissake. You're in the trust department. You're harmless."

Harry sat back in his chair and looked at her. "I'm not that harmless."

"Yes, you are," she laughed. "You're quite harmless."

"Lucia," he said, "I wish you wouldn't use that word."

"'Harmless?' It's a compliment."

"Not in this country, it isn't," he said.

On the table were the blue plates and matching napkins and the yellow candles that Lucia brought out whenever she was proud of what she or Harry had cooked. Today it was Burmese chicken curry. "Well, if you're worried, take it to the cops," Lucia told him. "That's what the cops are there for. Honey," she said, "no one will suspect you of anything. You're handsome and stable and you're my sweetie, and I love you, and what else happened today? Put that awful creepy paper back into your pocket. How do you like the curry?"

"It's delicious," he said.

AFTER HARRY had gotten up his nerve sufficiently to enter the police station again, he walked in a determined manner toward the front desk. After looking carefully at the drawing and the inked phrase, and writing down Harry Edmonds' name and address, the officer, whose badge identified him as Sergeant Bursk, asked, "Mr. Edmonds, you got any kids?"

"Kids? No, I don't have kids. Why?"

"Kids did this," Sergeant Bursk told him, waving the paper in front of him as if he were drying it off. "My kids could've done this. Kids do this. Boys do this. They draw torture chambers and they make threats and what-have-you. That's what they do. It's the youth. But they're kids. They don't mean it."

"How do you know?"

"Because I have three of them," Sergeant Bursk said. "I'm not saying that you should have kids, I'm just saying that I have them. I'll keep this drawing, though, if you don't mind."

"Actually," Harry said, "I'd like it back."

"Okay," Sergeant Bursk said, handing it to him, "but if we hear of any major bombings, and, you know, large-scale serious death, maybe we'll give you a call."

"Yeah," Harry said. He had been expecting this. "By the way," he asked, "does this look like any place in particular to you?"

The cop examined the picture. "Sure," he said. "That's Grand Central. In New York, on Forty-second Street, I think. I was there once. You can tell by the clock. See this clock here?" He pointed at a vague circle. "That's Grand Central, and this is the big clock that they've got there on the front."

"THE FUCK IT IS," the kid said. The kid was in bed with Harry Edmonds in the Motel 6. They had found each other in a bar downtown and then gone to this motel, and after they were finished, Harry drew the drawing out of his pants' pocket on the floor and showed it to him. The kid's long brown hair fell over his eyes and, loosened from its ponytail, spread out on the pillow. "I know this fucking place," the kid said. "I've, like, traveled, you know, all over Europe. This is in Europe, this place, this is fucking Deutschland we're talking about here." The kid got up on his elbows to see better. "Oh, yeah, I remember this place. I was there, two summers ago? Hamburg? This is the Dammtor Bahnhof."

"Never heard of it," Harry Edmonds said.

"You never heard of it 'cause you've never been there, man. You have to fucking be there to know about it." The kid squinched his eyebrows together like a professor making a difficult point. "A *bahnhof,* see, is a train station, and the Dammtor

Bahnhof is, like, one of the stations there, and this is the one that the Nazis rounded up the Jews to. And, like, sent them off from. This place, man. Absolutely. It's still standing. This one, it fucking deserves to be bombed. Just blow it totally the fuck away, off the face of the earth. That's just my opinion. It's evil, man."

The kid moved his body around in bed, getting himself comfortable again after stating his opinions. He was slinky and warm, like a cat. The kid even made back-of-the-throat noises, a sort of satisfied purr.

"I THOUGHT we were finished with that," Harry's therapist said. "I thought we were finished with the casual sex. I thought, Harry, that we had worked through those fugitive impulses. I must tell you that it troubles me that we haven't. I won't say that we're back to square one, but it is a backwards step. And what I'm wondering now is, why did it happen?"

"Lucia said I was harmless, that's why."

"And did that anger you?"

"You bet it angered me." Harry sat back in his chair and looked directly at his therapist. He wished she would get a new pair of eyeglasses. These eyeglasses made her look like one of those movie victims killed within the first ten minutes, right after the opening credits. One of those innocent bystanders. "Bankers are not harmless, I can assure you."

"Then why did you pick up that boy?" She waited. When he didn't say anything, she said, "I can't think of anything more dangerous to do."

"It was the building," Harry said.

"What building?"

"I showed Lucia the building. On the paper. This paper." He took it out of his pocket and handed it to his therapist. By now the paper was becoming soft and wrinkled. While she studied the picture, Harry watched the second hand of the wall clock turn.

"You found this?" she asked. "You didn't draw this."

"Yes, I found it." He waited. "I found it in a parking lot six blocks from here."

"All right. You showed Lucia this picture. And perhaps she called you harmless. Why did you think it so disturbing to be called harmless?"

"Because," Harry said, "in this country, if you're harmless, you get killed and eaten. That's the way things are going these days. That's the current trend. I thought you had noticed. Perhaps not."

"And why do you say that people get killed and eaten? That's an extravagant metaphor. It's a kind of hysterical irony."

"No, it isn't. I work in a bank and I see it happen every day. I mop up the blood."

"I don't see what this has to do with picking up young men and taking them to motels," she said. "That's back in the country of acting out. And what I'm wondering is, what does this mean about your relationship to Lucia? You're endangering her, you know." As if to emphasize the point, she said, "It's wrong, what you did. And very very dangerous. With all your thinking, did you think about that?"

Harry didn't answer. Then he said, "It's funny. Everybody has a theory about what that building is. You haven't said anything about it. What's your theory?"

"This building?" Harry's therapist examined the paper through her movie-victim glasses. "Oh, it's the Field Museum, in Chicago. And that's not a theory. It is the Field Museum."

ON TUESDAY NIGHT, at 3 A.M., Harry fixed his gaze on the bedroom ceiling. There, as if on a screen, shaped by the light through the curtains luffing in the window, was a public building with front pillars and curved arched windows and perhaps a clock. On the ceiling the projected sun of Harry's mind rose wonderfully, brilliantly gold, one or two mind-wisp cumulus clouds passing from right to left across it, but not so obscured that its light could not penetrate the great public building into which men, women, and children—children in strollers, children hand in hand with their parents—now filed, shadows on the ceiling, lighted shadows, and for a moment Harry saw an explosive flash.

Harry Edmonds lay in his bed without sleeping. Next to him was his girlfriend, whom he had planned to marry, once he ironed out a few items of business in his personal life and got them settled. He had made love to her, to this woman, this Lucia, a few hours earlier, with earnest caresses, but now he seemed to be awake again. He rose from bed and went down to the kitchen. In the harsh fluorescence he ate a cookie and on an impulse turned on the radio. The radio blistered with the economy of call-in hatred and religion revealed to rabid-mouthed men who now gasped and screamed into all available microphones. He adjusted the dial to a call-in station. Speaking from Delaware, a man said, "There's a few places I'd do some trouble to, believe me, starting with the Supreme Court and moving on to a clinic or two." Harry snapped off the radio.

NOW HE SITS in the light of the kitchen. He feels as dazed as it is possible for a sane man to feel at three-thirty in the morning. I am not silly, nor am I trivial, Harry says to himself, as he reaches for a pad of paper and a no. 2 pencil. At the top of the pad, Harry writes, "The next place I plan to bomb," and then very slowly, and with great care, begins to draw his own face, its smooth cleanshaven contours, its courteous half-smile.

When he perceives his eyes beginning to water, he rips off the top sheet with his picture on it and throws it in the wastebasket. The refrigerator seems to be humming some tune to him, some tune without a melody, and he flicks off the overhead light before he recognizes that tune.

IT IS MIDDAY in downtown Five Oaks, Michigan, the time for lunch and rest and conversation, and for a remnant, a lucky few, it may be a time for love, but here before us is Harry Edmonds, an officer in the trust department at Southeastern Michigan Bank and Trust, standing on a street corner in a strong spring wind. The wind pulls at his tie and musses his hair. Nearby, a recycling container appears to have overturned, and sheets of paper, hundreds of them, papers covered with drawings and illustrations and words, have scattered. Like a flock of birds, they have achieved flight. All around Harry Edmonds they are gripped in this whirlwind and flap and snap in circles. Some stick to him. There are glossy papers with perfumed inserts, and there are yellowing papers with four-color superheroes, and there are the papers with attractive unclothed airbrushed bodies, and there are the papers with bills and announcements and loans. Here are the personals, swirling past, and there a flyer for home theater big-screen TV. Harry Edmonds, a man uncertain of the value of his own life, who at this moment does not know whether his life has, in fact, any importance at all, or any future, lifts his head in the wind, increasing in volume and intensity, and for a moment he imagines himself being blown away. From across the street, the way he raises his head might appear, to an observer, as a posture of prayer. God, it is said, resides in the whirlwind, and certainly Harry Edmonds' eyes are closed and now his head is bowed. He does not move forward or backward, and it is unclear from the expression on his face whether he is making any sort of wish. He remains stationary, on this street corner, while all about him the papers fly first toward him, and then away.

A moment later he is gone from the spot where he stood. No doubt he has returned to his job at the bank, and that is where we must leave him.

Time Exposure

E ARLIER IN THE EVENING, while searching on the bathroom floor for her reading glasses, Irene Glad-felter had noticed a spidery damp spot on the wall under the sink. She would have to take care of it herself; her husband was out, having a beer a few blocks away in the neighborhood bar, the Shipwreck.

On her hands and knees, she'd worried at the plaster—Walt could patch it up later—with a screwdriver and a chisel, making a small neat hole. Then she had remembered that the maintenance guy, Aldo, should be performing such work. This wasn't her property, and the leak was really none of her business.

But she had found the pipe, rotted away with rust at one of its connection points. The water dripped down onto a heap of razor blades, a small secretive pyramidal scrapyard. Snaggling the flashlight's beam inward, she saw the piles of . . . edges, not all of them lying flat. A few stood propped against each other like sentries. This mound of blue blades had been inserted one by one through the old medicine cabinet's razor slot by Walt and by the unit's previous renters down through the millennia of shaving. The blades had rusted into a soft metallic brown. She unsettled herself just by looking at them. You thought something as simple as a morning shave wouldn't leave a trace, but then it did.

She hated the look of the dull blue metal. It made her shy.

Back in the bedroom, she found her reading glasses on the bedside table, inside a green box of tissues. Inanimate things liked to hide. She had noticed this again and again. She undressed, turned on the TV, and got under the covers, spreading her catalogues around her in friendly disarray.

Thursday was her husband's night out. At around eleven-thirty he would return home from the Shipwreck pleased with himself, ripe with cigarette smoke and beer. Knowing his habits, she always left a single breath mint out for him on the kitchen counter, and the stove's fluorescent light burning, so he could find his way in.

With the cat snoring at her feet, she sat propped up in bed reading her catalogues and watching a TV movie with the sound muted. Drawer organizers, peg-and-dowel wood wine racks: a physical pleasure that began at her spine and spread upward toward her forehead like a sunflower filled her whenever she gazed at objects she did not need or want. They were her suitors, and she brushed them away.

She liked these occasional evenings alone, these little shallow pools of rest and emptiness. Here was a glossy photo of a swivel bookstand, there a typewriter table. The sunflower bloomed again. She glanced at the TV set. When she was in bed by herself, she had a queenly indifference to the details of stories. She didn't have to explain the plots to Walter, her usual task whenever they watched television together. Tonight she checked the screen now and then to see, first, a roadster bursting off a cliff into a slow arc of explosive death, and then a teenager fitting a black shoe sensuously on a woman's foot. Ap-

parently this movie was some sort of violent update of Cin-
derella. Now a man dressed like an unsuccessful investment
broker was inching his way down a back alley. The walls of the
alley were coated with sinister drippings.

She bathed in the movies more satisfactorily when they
didn't make any sense. Tomorrow, at work, during her break,
she could reconstruct what the sense was, but she usually didn't
bother.

When she looked up from her furniture catalogue, hearing
Walt unlock the front door and trudge toward the bedroom,
she knew the evening had gone badly, just from the labored
slush of his walk. When he stood in the doorway, his gray hair
poking through his oil-stained cap, she forgot to ask him if
he'd taken his breath mint. He had a peevish expression. First
he examined the television, then the bedroom window, as if he
didn't know what to look at. "Walter," she said. "Now what
is it?"

A garage mechanic, in late middle age having trouble with
his knees and back, he could no longer stand straight. His
upper body seemed to perch out at an angle from his waist like
a permanently bent metal beam. And he had pockmarks on his
face from an attack of shingles. His spiky hair was his last spirited feature.

"The guy upstairs," he said. "Burt Mink. It beats anything.
The guy upstairs is a damn criminal."

She didn't ask Walter any questions. Burt Mink? The upholsterer? Him? The more awful the story, the better. But it could
always wait. It would have to. With Walt, a person exercised pa-
tience. When you rushed Walt, he lost his thoughts' thread, and
he became a meaningless old guy who could not make himself
understood. He came from a family of reluctant speakers: even
his mother had never been able to manage more than about
twenty words a minute. His father and two uncles had been laconic farmers in western Michigan, where every word spoken

was begrudged, like a mortgage payment. Irene watched as he shambled off irritably into the bathroom.

She understood the slow procession of his moods and knew how to time them. And she had grown used to his fumes, the oil fumes at least. With their two sons grown and out of the house, the mechanic's smell made her think of her two boys when they'd been younger, teenagers dismantling cars in the garage, surly and sweatily handsome grease monkeys. That was when they'd all been living in the house on Mackenzie Street, before the boys had become men and left, and she and Walter had moved to this apartment building north of Detroit to save money for their retirement. They hadn't saved any money. Selling that house had been a terrible idea. Once they sold it, she recognized that she had poured her feelings into every floorboard, every ceiling corner.

She heard Walt brushing his teeth and spitting. When he came out of the bathroom he still had his street clothes on. "There's a mess on the floor in there," he said. "Hole in the wall."

"I made it," she said. "I noticed a dampness."

He shrugged the information off with a somewhat alarming indifference. "I don't feel like getting into bed," he told her. "I don't feel like sleeping. I don't feel like any of that."

"You have to sleep. You'll have to go to work tomorrow."

He walked over to the wall facing the bed and adjusted a tilted photograph of their younger son in uniform. "I can go to work," he said. "I've done it before. I can work without sleep. I can't sleep thinking about Burt Mink."

"What about Burt Mink?"

He turned, not answering, and went into the living room. She heard him sit down in the reclining chair. It always sighed when people sat down in it. She heard him shuffling a pack of cards.

She fell asleep to the sound of the cards.

* * *

AT 4 A.M. she put on her bathrobe. In the living room, playing cards were scattered evenly on the floor like snow. To get to her chair, she had to step on the jack of diamonds, the two of spades, and the six of hearts. Walter was sitting there like a sentry, his hands on his knees, eyes wide open.

"So," she said, almost cheerfully. "What'd Burt Mink say? What'd he do?" She was a lapsed Jehovah's Witness. She usually expected things to turn out badly. It once excited her, how things turned out badly, but not now, not anymore.

"You shouldn't hear," Walter said.

"I shouldn't?"

"Pigeon, you shouldn't hear a story like this," he said.

"Tell me anyway."

THE GUY UPSTAIRS, down the hall, Burt Mink, said he had killed a child and was maybe going to do it again.

He'd been completely drunk when he admitted this. His mouth'd been open and his words slurred, and his whole face was a mess, going every which way. He sounded like a man asleep but talking, one of those still functioning zombies. His head hung down and his nose got itself to within two inches of the bar.

They'd been talking about fishing, then cars. The guy'd already been drinking too much, and his voice got like a radio that was losing a station. The son of a bitch had been muttering about traffic, then about school buses, like he was interested in school buses. Nobody is interested in school buses. But this son of a bitch was. School buses, for Chrissake. With little kids on them.

Somehow this creep admitted he had lured an eight-year-old boy into his car and then done things to him and buried him out at the edge of the county near an apple orchard. The kid had been wearing a yellow shirt. He was buried near an apple tree, what was left of him.

It hadn't taken very long.

He didn't say if he had learned the kid's name. The kid looked like an angel. He actually said that.

Nobody knows who I am, Burt Mink said. No one ever sees inside anyone else.

Dead drunk but not sorry, this guy, like he'd been discussing the price of nails at the hardware store.

He worked upholstering furniture, after all. You'd never guess this other thing about him.

THE LIVING ROOM froze for a half a moment, then came to life again. Irene could feel her breath coming back.

"But that's a movie," she said when Walter was finished. "They ran that movie on TV last month. Remember? Maybe you were asleep. This boy in a yellow shirt was abducted, and the man buried the body in a grove of apple trees. It was the movie-of-the-week. The villain said that nobody knew who he really was. Everyone went around saying, 'Yellow shirt, yellow shirt.' I didn't like that movie," she said, almost as an afterthought. "Dina Merrill was in it. She played a psychologist. Wore a pink scarf. You just heard a plot summary."

"What?"

"It's a movie, Walter," she said. "He's telling you about a thing they broadcast last week. You didn't see it. But I did. He's confused."

"No. He told me he did it. He didn't say about movies. He said he killed an angel. That was our exact conversation."

Walt stood up and walked to the window, where he stood gazing out in a speculative posture, though bent as always. "Someone's got to right the balance."

"Don't you do it," she said. "Drop that thought. Burt Mink

just thinks he was a character in a TV show, that's all. He's telling you about the movie. That's his business, what he thinks when he's drunk, I guess. Nobody got hurt. I'd watch him, maybe, but a plot summary, that's what he was telling you. My God, Walt, people do worse than that, telling you about movies they think they were in."

She stood up and felt on her back that Walt was staying put, aimlessly thinking.

From the bedroom, she heard Walt say, "I believed him. That's the bad part."

AT SEVEN-THIRTY she put some bread out on the ledge for the birds and dropped a peanut or two on the front sidewalk for the chipmunk. A fine fall day, the air so crisp you could see the Renaissance Center in Detroit if you looked straight south from the bus stop. One of her boys worked in Detroit, and she worried about him sometimes, worried that he'd become part of the daily feast, but he was a big strong kid, a peaceful furry bear, knew his work and didn't go looking for trouble.

She wished she had brought along her new point-and-shoot camera. She had a particular sugar maple in mind for a picture that she planned to send to Ed Oskins' weather show on Channel 4. They showed a weather picture every day, usually a landscape, and she thought she had a good chance with this tree right here in Ferndale, growing on the boulevard across from the collision shop. Bright burning red leaves rose from its branches, stopping traffic. It glorified that city block.

She couldn't imagine violent death on a day like this. It had to wait patiently for gloom and shadow, a few hours after dinnertime. Just like the movies, it had to have darkness, or it didn't happen.

The bus arrived, hesitated in a jovial roar of diesel exhaust, and Mrs. Gladfelter hoisted herself up.

* * *

ALTHOUGH THE BUS was not especially crowded, she sat down next to a sensibly dressed woman in a light tan overcoat. Her straight brown hair was braided down one side. Her eyes were alert, more the exception than the rule on these buses. Mrs. Gladfelter liked to sit with other women if she could: less chance of funny business that way.

In the public tone she used with strangers, she said, "They've taken the flowers out." She pointed to a circular area in the median, the marigold spot. "Have you noticed how they put them in to form an F? The marigolds? An F for Ferndale?"

The woman in the tan overcoat turned to Mrs. Gladfelter. She said that she had noticed that, yes. They spoke for two more minutes before they turned back to their own thoughts. Mrs. Gladfelter exhaled. Normal people were sometimes hard to find on the bus. Frequently all you saw were people in various stages of medication. But today no lost souls were visible on either side of the aisle.

CONSIDERING THE TIMES, she felt pleased to have her job, checking out food; it was steady, and the manager was a kind man, and though the ceiling lights were too bright, like a toothache, and she had to be on her feet all day, the job had compensations, especially now that management had installed laser scanners. She could talk to customers, briefly, if they initiated it, and sometimes she chatted with Shirley, her best friend among the other cash-out girls.

The regularity soothed her. Food, processing, payment, bagging. The work's rhythms occupied just enough of her mind so that she didn't have to think about anything she didn't want to think about. She kept track of the prices. She wrote down the numbers of the check-cashing cards on the checks. She had no responsibility for judgment calls. It was like being an elevator operator.

At two in the afternoon, she saw Burt Mink in her checkout line, two carts back. Looking hungover, one eye seemingly glazed and the other with a drooping lid, he was pushing a cart loaded with no-brand frozen dinners and precut vegetables from the salad bar. He wore a flannel shirt with a hardly noticeable pale white stain. His wet stringy hair was combed over the bald spot at the top of his head, and he had a narrow rodent-like face with protruding teeth, but when he saw Mrs. Gladfelter, he smiled and waved, and the effect was so startling that she felt herself go dizzy for a moment before she waved back and continued bagging the groceries of a very young and very pregnant young woman who had paid for her chocolates and eggs and ice cream with cash.

Well, after all, she thought, he's been here before. I've checked him through before, and we're neighbors. There's that.

"Here you are," she said to the pregnant woman, handing her her change. "Take care of yourself, honey. You must be due any day now."

"A week," the woman said, tottering out, and Burt Mink advanced in the line. She checked through the woman ahead of him while he scanned the headlines of *Weekly World News*. Coffee cups had been found orbiting in space. The surface of Mars had been photographed; Graceland, complete with swimming pool, had turned up in the pictures. Earthlings were being teleported to other locales in the galaxy. This was common knowledge.

"Mr. Mink," she said, smiling. "Good afternoon."

He unloaded his cart with all the frozen dinners in front, and he said grimly, "Yeah, but I had too much last night. I got to watch that." He smelled unclean.

"Yes," she said, checking his items through. The frozen dinners chilled her fingers. She thought of him eating the frozen food, putting it into his mouth.

"I like to come here," he said. "A familiar face, you know."

"Well, we're neighbors, of course."

"Yeah," he said sourly. "You're downstairs. But I see more of your husband than I do of you."

"Hmm," she said. "Bars aren't for me. He tells me about it."

Burt Mink nodded. "Not much to see anyway. Not much to do but drink."

She nodded. "I'm better off at home. He tells me what people say." Burt Mink did not react, not a twitch or a glimmer, as he wrote his check. He had dandruff on his ears and another stain on his frayed gray pants. Even for an upholsterer, he was unpresentable. She couldn't imagine a woman who would have him. "Time alone, you know. Good for all of us. I'll have to see your check-cashing card."

He extracted his wallet from his trousers and with his scarred fingers began to flip through it. Next to the check-cashing card, in its plastic divider, was a photograph of a child, a boy, a school photograph, rather worn by now, an amazingly unattractive boy with an overbite and a narrow ratlike face, unmistakably Burt Mink himself. Did adults carry their own photos, as children, around with them? This adult did, anyway.

She felt a curious queasy sensation, seeing the rat-faced boy in the photo. She didn't recognize this sensation and wouldn't be able to say what it was. She wrote down his number on the back of the check. After saying goodbye and lifting his two bags of groceries, Burt Mink disappeared out of the store like all the other customers.

A harmless and ugly man, she decided, who worked upholstering furniture and who, after hours, imagined himself as a dangerous character in the movies. The movies were getting into everything now. They spread over everybody like the flu.

*   *   *

AFTER TAKING THE BUS home, she carried her new camera to the corner of the sugar maple and the collision shop. She struggled to frame the tree in the viewfinder properly so that the wisps of vapor trails were visible against the dark blue of the background, and after several tries, Mrs. Gladfelter believed that she had managed it.

She had a simple dinner planned, beef stew, already in the refrigerator. She strolled over to the city park, two blocks west of their apartment.

Perched on the last building before the park entrance, a billboard asked "How Tropical Can You Be?" The billboard showed tuxedoed men and sequined women dancing on the deck of a cruise ship. Underneath the picture was an 800-number for a travel agency. The men and women appeared, to Mrs. Gladfelter, to be imaginary. They possessed impossible honey-colored skin. Somebody had spray-painted the word FIRB over one of the women's faces.

Carrying her camera, Mrs. Gladfelter strolled into the park.

A man wearing a Hawaiian shirt, and army camouflage trousers, and flip-flops sat on the first bench, dozing but still giving off an air of violence and moonshine. He clutched in his right hand a copy of the Ferndale *Shopper's Gazette*. She walked past him quietly, wearing her smile-armor.

Kids were kissing on the next bench. They looked about fifteen years old, the two of them, and optimistic, the way people did when they were stuck on each other, their tongues in each other's mouths. Making her way to a little rise in the park's center, Mrs. Gladfelter placed the camera on a bench for steadiness, pointed it toward the west gate and pressed the super night button, a feature that held the aperture open for two seconds. Then she put the camera in her pocket and headed toward home.

Just before she passed the man in flip-flops it occurred to her that if you were flying over this park at just the right altitude, the whole assembly, including the trees and the bearded man and the lovers and herself, might look like something—a face, or a letter, or a symbol like the F arranged in the marigolds in the middle of Woodward Avenue. But it might look like something else, something terrible and perplexing. She put that thought away and scuttled toward her building.

A FEW DAYS LATER, when she picked up the developed film, she was delighted to see that the photograph of the sugar maple was good enough to frame. The super night shot, however, was terribly blurred in it: streaks of light crossed the sky, like meteors, and the west gate of the park had the appearance of fiery brown gelatin.

She put the sugar-maple photograph out on the dining room table near the place setting for Walt's fork and knife. For the last several days, he had been quieter than usual, losing the thread of conversation, frowning into corners. She thought the photographs might cheer him up, now that autumn was here, the gray skies and soul gloom of winter about to unfold.

That night, a Wednesday, he trundled himself in from work and showered as he usually did, and had his beer and watched the local news, saying very little. She tried not to provoke him. When dinner was served, he sat down and began eating. Then he saw her photograph.

"What's this?" he asked. "This is your picture? You took this?"

She smiled proudly. "I'm sending it into the weather show."

"It's nice," he said. "Real good. They should appreciate it."

He ate everything. He sopped up the gravy with a piece of bread, and when he finished, he placed his fork carefully in the middle of the plate and said, "I'm not going to the Shipwreck tomorrow. I believe I'll stay home."

"Okay with me," she said, although it wasn't. She would miss her catalogues and the expressive solitary quiet. "But I'll bet Burt Mink'll expect you."

"Don't think so. He's had a thing happen to him."

"What thing?"

"Accident. Car accident." Walt rubbed his jaw with his fist. "He's banged up. Could have died."

"What?" she asked. "Where? How'd you find this out?"

"I heard," he said, not explaining. He shrugged for her benefit. "Then I called the hospital. He's in there all right. But they said it wasn't critical or anything of that nature. Just a few bones broken. He wasn't wearing a seat belt. That part didn't surprise me."

"A few bones broken!" She showed her teeth. "Like saying a little fire claimed your house. Walter, what happened exactly?"

"Something went out in his car, brakes I guess. He hit a lamp pole, but not one of the breakaway kind." He examined his fork carefully. "I heard he was speeding."

"Oh, Walter," she said. From the street a car honked. The chipmunk on the kitchen ledge scrabbled back and forth. "Walter, it was just a story! He never did anything."

"What? What are you saying?"

"You know what I'm saying. What did you do to his car?"

"Let's wash these dishes," he said. "Let's make some coffee and we'll clean up here."

She would not move. "I know you," she said. "I know your mind, and don't say I don't. Now answer me, Walter. What did you do?"

He sat up, as straight as he could with his bent back. He said, "I'm a mechanic. You can't ask me such a thing as that. Besides, it's technical."

"You could have killed him," she cried out, "and him with his only sin being ugliness!"

"No." He stood, but he still would not look at her. "No. He was drunk and he admitted his crime, and he got away with it. I couldn't stand it. I wouldn't tolerate it when I imagined him doing harm like that to our boys when they were youngsters, and I drew a line."

"What line?" she asked. "He's a crazy man! Just another damn crazy person like you and I see every day on the job. Ferndale's full of them, and Detroit's worse. He saw a story on TV. All he did was repeat it! And who are you to judge, and go and do such a thing to him and his car?"

"The only judge he has," Walter said to her, gazing at her face at last. She raised her hand to cover up the wrinkles. "Hell, I'd do it again. He shouldn't have talked that way. It was so ugly, it kept me awake. Imagine saying those things. I went and thought about it. It stayed with me, Irene. Stayed and stayed. Replacing brake pads, changing oil, there's in my head that boy in the yellow shirt. What kind of story is that, and him wanting to be in it, as the star?"

"You kept it going, Walter. It could've ended with him."

Picking up his plate and taking it to the kitchen, Walter said, "Wasn't meant to kill him, exactly, what I did. Paralyze him, maybe. That was all. Put him out of that hobby of his." He rinsed the plates in the sink. "I'm not a vigilante. One night while you were asleep, I fiddled with his Chevy. I'm a good mechanic. I know what to do. Anyway," he said, smiling now, "I wasn't sleeping, thanks to him, and now I am."

"It was just a story!" she said, lifting her hands involuntarily. "Like that's just a photograph!" She pointed toward the sugar maple.

"Some stories you shouldn't tell," Walter said, "if you're in them. From where I sat, he had guilt all over him. True or not, I wouldn't abide it."

Suddenly Irene said, "Why do you people do these things to each other? Why do you?"

"What people are you talking about, Irene?"

"You," she said. "You guys. You gibber and gabber and then you just go after each other, fists and guns out, all because of the tales you tell, to make yourselves so big."

"No, we don't," he said. "Where did you ever hear it before?"

He walked past her, apparently at ease with himself for now, and headed toward the reclining chair, to finish the sports page. The chair sighed when he sat in it.

"I shouldn't have said anything," he muttered. "I should have kept you in the dark. It would've been better all around that way."

THAT NIGHT she stood at the window in her bathrobe and slippers, sipping tap water from a glass with a scoop of vanilla ice cream in it, for her nerves. She was thinking of Burt Mink in the hospital, and of how, years ago, she herself had left the Jehovah's Witnesses, "defellowshipped," as they called it, after she had met Walter.

She had encountered Walter in all his salty early handsomeness when she and her father had been going door to door with copies of *The Watchtower* and *Awake!* Walter had been up on a ladder, cleaning gutters, and somehow found out her name before she'd reached the end of the block. He called her that night.

He replaced the wild beast 666 in her imagination with four-barrel carburetors and timing lights. Before Walter had come into her life, she could gaze at the bedroom ceiling and see Armageddon happening right up there, all the panic and terror. The truth had been explained. God was hungry for vengeance, thirsty for it. The clouds on Irene's ceiling boiled blood. She felt herself uplifted and groomed in all this bedlam.

Then Walter took her for rides in his reconditioned Olds

convertible. He showed her how to clean fish and how to swing a baseball bat. He said he loved her and repeated it so often she had to believe him.

After three months of Walter, Armageddon lost interest for her. Could an angel turn into a demon, out of jealousy? No. Did angels kill other angels? Probably not. Someone had made it all up.

And after her boys were born, she just didn't care to imagine the death of anything. All that prized calamity was just another story.

Men often puzzled her. A world war wasn't big enough for them. No, they had to have a universe war, and give it a fancy name that most adults couldn't even spell. This end-of-the-world story they could recount until they were blue in the face, going onto strangers' front porches, all dressed up out of respect for the bloodshed to come.

A strange appetite, like something in the *Weekly World News,* and she had once shared it. You certainly have to believe a lot of things to get through a lifetime.

She stood at the window and sipped her tap water and ice cream.

The soul calms down in middle age, she thought, but it does take some doing, getting it there.

"PIGEON, HONEY," Walter called from the bedroom. His voice faded and swelled as if someone were manipulating a volume control. "Where are you?"

"Here," she said. "I'll be back in a minute."

She was thinking that she'd call the hospital tomorrow and find out how Burt Mink was, maybe even talk to him. Just because he had a smile that made babies wail and cry didn't mean you couldn't ask after him. As she was toying with these courtesies, she saw a taxi pull up to the curb in front of the building, and there he was, the subject of her thinking, getting to his feet behind the opened car door, as if her mind had given birth to him—Burt Mink—coming out, wrapped in a raincoat and up on crutches. He looked like a bat in splints.

The cabbie carried his overnight bag to the door, and Burt Mink hobbled his way forward. He glanced up, gave Irene a smile that would freeze dogs and cats to stone, and then he was gone, upstairs. After he'd disappeared from view, she waved at him.

TWO DAYS LATER around sunset she put a cooked chicken on a tray and walked upstairs. She knocked at Burt Mink's door, and for the longest duration she heard the sound of crutches being gathered, and slippers whispering along the carpeting. After the door opened and she saw the full distemper of his face, she wanted, rather desperately, to run away. Instead she said, "Hi. I brought you this." She handed the tray toward him.

"Can't take it," he grumbled. "I got my crutches."

"Well, maybe I can carry it inside."

"Guess so," he said. When he exhaled, he sounded as if he were quietly gargling. "Thank you." The words came out dutifully. "I'm much appreciative. You can put that in the kitchen there."

The apartment smelled of burnt lamb shank and curdled milk. The kitchen had few cleared areas: a careless convalescent man's eating space, marked by food spillage and catastrophe. She laughed to let the tensions loose. Then she peered into the living room. "Anywhere here?"

"Anywhere," he said. "I gotta sit down. My bones is all broken."

She tiptoed nervously into the living room. Burt Mink sat in a chair in front of a TV set tuned to a news station. The maladjusted color made the announcers appear to be marmalade orange. She heard the bubbling of a tropical aquarium and turned to look at it. The aquarium rested on an aluminum stand near a large ashtray filled with chewing-gum wrappers. At the bottom of the tank, a small metal deep-sea diver produced air bubbles that rose to the surface. The diver's arms were thrust out as if in self-defense. Only two or three fish swam back and forth in the water, their eyes perpetually staring, astonished and frightened. They made panic-stricken veerings around the stones and seaweed.

"Sit down if you want," he said. "The news is on."

"Everybody's mixed up," she told him. "The color needs adjusting."

"Not for me," he said. He pointed at his eyes. "Colorblind. Rare form, the blues and the golds." Just then the screen flashed on her weather photo, the sugar maple she had taken such care to photograph. On the screen, the autumn leaves were a lush purple.

"I wanted to say something." Irene held herself upright against the living room wall. "I wanted to say how sorry I was. How sorry I was and am about all of this. I'm sorry about your accident. I'm just so sorry. I can't stop saying it."

"Well, thank you." He examined her with the fixed gaze of someone who may be making some sort of plan, or is considering an idea he has no intention of articulating publicly. With repellent politeness, Burt Mink said, "Go over there and look at those fish. You might like them. I got some neon tetras in there that're still alive."

She walked closer to the fish tank and was pretending to be interested in them when she heard Burt Mink say, "Jesus has a plan for me."

"He has a plan for all of us," she said, on the other side of the tank. Through the water, fish darting in front of it, Burt Mink's face had a viscous shimmering irregularity.

"That's not what I meant," Burt Mink said. "He told me I should despair."

"That can't be right," Mrs. Gladfelter said, as the air in the room suddenly took on the smell of aquarium water.

"You arguing with Jesus?" Burt Mink asked. "That'd be something."

Mrs. Gladfelter noticed some plastic dusty flowers in a chipped vase on top of the TV set. Next to the vase was a bright red apple made out of glass. "I have to go now," she said. "I hope you're feeling better soon, Mr. Mink."

He shrugged from his chair. "I'm in Hell. That's a certainty. I could make you a map. But thank you for the chicken. I'm much appreciative."

"Oh," she said, reaching out to pat him on the shoulder. Even as she did it, she saw how pointless gestures of kindness were in this room—how they went nowhere, and stopped right where they happened. Then a thought occurred to her. "You're colorblind? You've never seen a yellow shirt, have you? You've only heard about them. They're just news to you."

He didn't even bother to shrug. He gazed at her for a moment with a face so emptied of expression that it seemed like one of those contemporary sculptures she'd seen in museums, so blandly abstract that it didn't stand for anything. He seemed completely absorbed again in the TV set, studying it, as if for a test.

Walking out, her skin puckering from an icy airy chill that might have originated in the room or might have been in her own mind, Mrs. Gladfelter turned around for a quick last glance. The room looked like a cell inside someone's head, not her own, but someone else's, someone who had never thought of a pleasantry but who sat at the bottom of the ocean, feeling the crushing pressure of the water. An ocean god had thought this room and this man up. That was an odd idea, the sort of idea she had never had before.

She closed the door behind her. She had to stop in the hall-way to get her breath. Behind the walls the razor blades stood up at full attention.

But in her mind's eye the boy in the yellow shirt appeared before her. His brown hair uncombed, child-debris all over him, a real kid stinking of sweat and mud, maybe a real brat, nobody's close friend. Who would trust him? What d'you want, lady? he asked her. Some respect, she said. OK, he muttered, OK, Mrs. Gladfelter, not so sarcastic now, sorry. What're you doin' here?

Just run now, she said, past that apple tree, do it, someone's after you, and she pointed, and the boy took off, arms and legs pumping, scabby knees and all, past the grove until he was a small vanishing point near the horizon, alive this time, free of murder, and she inhaled fully, taking the stairs one by one, thinking: *He's gone now, I saved him.*

Saul and Patsy
Are in Labor

T H E M O O N L I G H T on the sheets is as heavy as damp cotton, and Patsy, pregnant in her ninth month with a child who does not care to be born, sits up in bed to glare at whatever is still visible. The moonlight falls on the red oak bedroom floor, the carved polar bear on the bedside table, and her husband, Saul, under his electric blanket. Sleeping, Saul is always cold. His dreams, he has reported, are Arctic. Moonlit, he seems a bit blue. But it soothes her, having him there: his quiet groans and his exhaling supply the rhythms of Patsy's waking nights.

She pulls back the covers, walks to the window, and sheds her nightgown.

Brown-haired, athletic, with a runner's body, she is ordinarily a slender woman, but now her breasts and belly are swollen, the skin stretched taut, her fingers and feet thickened with water. She finds herself tilting backward to balance herself against her new frontal weight. She feels like a human rain forest: hot, choked with life, reeking with reproduction.

Out in the yard the full-faced moon shines through two pine trees this side of the garage and on Saul's motorcycle parked in the driveway. Beyond the garage she sees a single deer passing silently through the field.

Patsy leans toward the desk in front of the window and permits the moon to gaze on her nakedness. She soaks up the moonlight, bathes in it. As she turns, she clasps her hands behind head. She's had it with pregnancy; now she wants the labor, the full-blast finality of it. When she looks at the desk she sees the ampersand key on the upper row of the typewriter keyboard, the & above the 7. It's shaped like herself, distended and full: the big female *and:* &. The baby gives her a sleepy kick.

Hey, she says to the moonlight, *put me in labor. Pull this child into the world. Help me out here.*

Three hours later, just before dawn, her water breaks.

The labor room: Between contractions and the blips of the fetal monitor, she is dimly aware of Saul. He's donned his green hospital scrubs. They wouldn't let him wear his Detroit Tigers baseball cap in here. He's holding her hand and his eyes are anxious with nervous energy. He thinks he's coaching her. But he keeps miscounting the breaths, and she has to correct him.

After two hours of this, she is moved into the huge circular incandescence of the delivery room. She feels as if she's about to expel her entire body outward in a floorflood. With her hair soaked with sweat and sticking to the back of her neck, she can feel the universe sputtering out for an instant into two flattened dimensions. Everything she sees is suddenly painted on a wall. She screams. Then she swears and loosens her hand from Saul's—his touch maddens her—and swears again. The pain blossoms and blossoms, a huge multicolored floral sprouting of it. When the nurses smile, the smiles—full of professionalism and complacency from the other world—make her furious. The seconds split.

"Okay, here's the head. One last push, please."

Patsy backstrokes through the pain. Then the baby girl presents herself in a mess of blood and fleshy wrappings. After the cord is cut, Patsy hears her daughter's cry and a thud to her right: Saul, on the floor, passed out, gone.

"Can someone see to the dad?" the obstetrician asks, rather calmly. "He's fainted." Then, as an afterthought, she says, "No offense, Patsy, but he looked like the fainting type."

After a moment, during which Patsy feels plumbed out and vacant, they give the baby an Apgar test. While they weigh her, a nurse squats down next to Saul and takes his pulse. "Yes, he's coming back," she says. "He'll be fine." His eyes open, and underneath the face mask he smiles sheepishly. The papery cotton over his mouth crinkles upward. It's typical of Saul, Patsy thinks, to have somebody make a fuss over him at the moment of his daughter's birth. He steals scenes.

"Is my husband okay?" she asks. She can't quite find him. Turning back to herself, she can see, blurred, in the salty recession of this birth, the paint of her toenails through her thin white cotton socks. Saul had painted those toenails when she had grown too wide to bend down and do the job herself.

"Here's the baby," the nurse says. The world has recovered itself and accordioned out into three dimensions again. The nurse's smile and her daughter's ancient sleepy expression sunspot near Patsy's heart, and the huge overhead delivery room light goes out, like a sigh.

Someone takes Patsy's hand. Who but Saul, unsteady but upright? Cold sweat drips down his forehead. He kisses Patsy through his face mask, a sterile kiss, and he informs her that they're parents now. Hi, Mom, he says. He apologizes for his cold sweat and the sudden bout of unconsciousness. Patsy

raises her hand and caresses Saul's face. Oh, don't worry, the
nurse says, apparently referring to Saul's fainting fit. She pats
him on the back, as if he were some sort of good dog.

THEY NAME THEIR DAUGHTER Mary Esther Carlson-
Bernstein. While making dinner, one of his improvised stir-
fries, Saul says that he's been having second thoughts: Mary
Esther is burdened with a lot of name, a lot of Christianity and
Judaism mixed in there. Possibly another name would be better.
Jayne, maybe, or Liz. Direct, futuristic American monosylla-
bles. As he theorizes and chops carrots and broccoli before
dropping the bamboo shoots and water chestnuts into the pan,
Patsy can see that he's so tired that he's only half-awake. His
socks don't match, his jeans are beltless, and his hair has gone
back to its customary anarchy.

Last night, between feedings, Saul claimed that he didn't
know if he could manage it, *it* being the long haul of fatherhood. But that was just Saul-talk. Right now, Mary Esther is
sleeping upstairs. Fingering the pages of her magazine, Patsy
leans back in the alcove, still in her bathrobe, watching her husband cook. She wonders what she did with the breast pump
and when the diaper guy is going to deliver the new batch.

Standing there, Saul sniffs, adds a spot of peanut oil, stirs
again, and after a minute he ladles out dinner onto Patsy's plate.
Then with that habit he has of reading her thoughts and re-
wording them, he turns toward her and says, "You left the
breast pump upstairs." And then: "Hey, you think I'm sleep-
walking. But I'm not. I'm conscious."

THEY LIVE IN a rented house on a dirt road outside of
Five Oaks, Michigan, and for the last few months Saul has

glimpsed an albino deer, always at a distance, on the fringes of their property. After work or on weekends, he walks across the unfarmed fields up to the next property line, marked by rusting fence posts, or, past the fields, into the neighboring woods of silver maple and scrub oak, hoping to get a sight of the animal. It gives him the shivers. He thinks this is the most godforsaken locale in which he's ever found himself, certainly worse than Baltimore, and that he feels right at home in it, and so does that deer. It is no easy thing to be a Jew in the Midwest, Saul thinks, where all the trees and shrubs are miserly and soul-shriveled, and where fate beats on your heart like a baseball bat, but he has mastered it. He is suited for brush and lowland under-growth and the antipicturesque. The fungal smell of wood rot in the culverts strengthens him, he believes.

Clouds, mud, wind. Joy and despair live side by side in Saul with very few emotions in between. Even his depressions are thick with lyric intensity. In the spiritual mildew of the Midwest all winter he lives stranded in an ink drawing. He himself is the suggested figure in the lower righthand corner.

He makes his way back to the house, mud clutching fast to his boots. He has a secret he has not told Patsy, though she probably knows it: he does not have any clue to being a parent. He does not love being one, though he loves his daughter with a newfound intensity close to hysteria. To him, fatherhood is one long unrewritable bourgeois script. Love, rage, and tender-ness disable him in the chairs in which he sits, miming calm, holding Mary Esther. At night, when Patsy is fast asleep, Saul kneels on the landing and beats his fists on the stairs.

ON THE MORNING when Mary Esther was celebrating her birthday—she was four weeks old—they sat at the breakfast table with the sun in a rare appearance blazing in through the east window and reflecting off the butter knife. With one hand Patsy fed herself cornflakes. With the other hand she held Mary Esther, who was nursing. Patsy was also glancing down at the morning paper on the table and was talking to Saul about his upcoming birthday, what color shirt to get him. She chewed her cornflakes thoughtfully and only reacted when Mary Esther sucked too hard. A deep brown, she says. You'd look good in that. It'd show off your eyes.

Listening, Saul watched them both, rattled by the domestic sensuality of their pairing, and his spirit shook with wild bruised jealous love. He felt pointless and redundant, an ambassador from the tiny principality of irony. His heart, that trapped bird, flapped in its cage. Behind Patsy in the kitchen the spice rack displaced its orderly contents. A delivery truck rumbled by on Whitefeather Road. He felt specifically his shallow and approximate condition. In broad daylight, night enfolded him.

He went off to work feeling superfluous and ecstatic and horny, his body glowing with its confusions.

THIS SEMESTER Saul has been taken off teaching American history and has been assigned remedial English for learning-disabled students in the junior high. The school claims it cannot afford a specialist in this area, and because Saul has loudly been an advocate of the rights of the learning-disabled, and because, he suspects, the principal has it in for him, he has been assigned a group of seven kids in remedial writing, and they all meet in a converted storage room at the back of the school at eight-thirty, following the second bell.

Five of them are pleasant and sweet-tempered and bewildered, but two of them hate the class and appear to hate Saul. They sit as far away from him as possible, close to the brooms, whispering to each other and smiling malevolently. Saul has tried everything with them—jokes, praise, discipline—and nothing has seemed to work.

He thinks of the two boys, Gordy Himmelmann and Bob Pawlak, as the Child Cossacks. Gordy apparently has no parents. He lives with siblings and grandparents and perhaps he coalesced out of the mud of the earth. He wears tee-shirts spotted with blood and manure. His boots are scuffed from the objects he has kicked. On his face there are two rashes, one of acne, the other of blankness. His eyes, on those occasions when they meet Saul's, are cold and lunar. If you were dying on the side of the road in a rainstorm, Gordy's eyes would pass over you and continue on to the next interesting sight.

He has no sense of humor. Bob Pawlak does. He brags about killing animals, and his laughter, describing how he has killed them, rises from chuckles to a sort of rhythmic squeal. His smile is the meanest one Saul has ever seen on an ex-child. It is also visible on the face of Bob Pawlak's father. About his boy, this father has said, "Yeah, he is sure a hell-raiser." He shook his dismayed parental head, smiling meanly at Saul in the school's front office, his eyes glittering with what Saul assumed was Jew-hatred.

Saul can hardly stand to look at Gordy and Bob. There are no windows in the room where he teaches them, and no fan, and after half an hour of everyone's mingled breathing, the air in the room is foul enough to kill a canary.

Yesterday Saul gave the kids pictures clipped from magazines. They were supposed to write a one-sentence story to accompany each picture. For these ninth-graders, the task is a challenge. Now, before school starts, his mind still on Patsy and Mary Esther, Saul begins to read yesterday's sentences. Gordy and Bob have as usual not written anything: Gordy tore his picture to bits, and Bob shredded and ate his.

It is dangerous to dive into a pool of water without the nolige of the depth because if it is salow you could hit your head that might creat unconsheness and drownding.

Quite serprisingly the boy finds among the presents rapings which are now discarded into trash a model air plan.

Two sentences, each one requiring ten minutes' work. Saul stares at them, feeling himself stumbling in the usual cognitive limp. The sentences are like glimpses into the shattered mind of God.

Like the hourse a cow is an animal and the human race feasts on its meat and diary which form the bulky hornd animal.

The cold blooded crecher the bird will lay an egg and in a piriod of time a new bird will brake out of it as a storm of re-production.

Saul looks up from his desk at the sputtering overhead lights and the grimy acoustic tile. It is in the storm of reproduction—mouths of babes, etc.—that he himself is currently being tossed.

He looks down at the floor again and spots a piece of paper with the words *your a kick* close to the wastebasket. Finally, a nice compliment. He tosses it away.

THE NEIGHBORS bring food down Whitefeather Road, indented with the patterned tire-tracked mud of spring, to Saul and Patsy's house. They've read Mary Esther's birth announcement in *The Five Oaks Gazette*, but they might know anyway. Small-city snooping keeps everyone informed. With the gray March overcast behind her, Mrs. O'Neill, beaming fixedly with her brand of insane charity, offers them a plate of the cookies for which she has gained local notoriety. They look like molasses blasted in a kiln and crystallized into teeth-shattering candied rock. Anne McPhee gives Patsy a gallon of homemade potato salad preserved in pink translucent Tupperware. Laurie Welch brings molded green Jell-O. Mad Dog Bettermine hauls a case of discount no-name beer into the living room, roaring approval of the baby. In return, Saul gives Mad Dog a cigar, and together the two men retire to the back porch, lighting up and drinking, belching smoke. Back in town, Harold, Saul's barber, gives Saul a free terrible haircut. Charity is everywhere, specific and ungrudging. Saul can make no sense of it.

They all track mud into the nursery. Fond wishes are expressed. Dressed in her sleep suit, Mary Esther lies in the rickety crib that Saul himself assembled, following the confusing and contradictory instructions enclosed in the shipping box. Above the crib hangs a mobile of cardboard stars and planets. Mary Esther sleeps and cries while the mobile slowly turns in the small breezes caused by the visitors as they bend over the baby.

ONE NIGHT, when Mary Esther is eight weeks old and the smell of spring is pouring into the room from the purple lilacs in the driveway, Patsy awakens and finds herself alone in bed. The clock says that it's three-thirty. Saul has to be up for work in three hours. From downstairs she hears very faintly the sound of groans and music. The groans aren't Saul's. She knows his groans. These are different. She puts on her bathrobe.

In the living room, sitting in his usual overstuffed chair and wearing his blue jeans and tee-shirt, Saul is watching a porn film on the VCR. His head is propped against his arm as if he were listening attentively to a lecture. He glances up at Patsy, flashes her a guilty wave with his left hand, then returns his gaze to the movie. On the TV screen, two people, a man and a woman are having showy sex in a curiously grim manner inside a stalled freight elevator, as if they were under orders.

"What's this, Saul?"

"Film I rented."

"Where'd you get it?"

"The store."

Moans have been dubbed onto the soundtrack. The man and the woman do not look at each other. For some reason, a green ceramic poodle sits in the opposite corner of the elevator. "Not very classy, Saul," she says.

"Well," Saul says, "they're just acting." He points at the screen. "She hasn't taken her shoes off. That's pretty strange. They're having sex in the elevator and her shoes are still on. I guess the boys in the audience don't like feet."

Patsy studies the TV screen. Unexpected sadness locates her and settles in, like a headache. She rests her eyes on the Matisse poster above Saul's chair: naked people dancing in a ring. In this room the human body is excessively represented, and for a moment Patsy has the feeling that everything in life is probably too much, there is just too much to face down.

"Come upstairs, Saul."

"In a minute, after this part."

"I don't like to look at them. I don't like you looking at them."

"It's hell, isn't it?"

She touches his shoulder. "This is sort of furtive."

"That's marriage-driven rhetoric you're using there, Patsy."

"Why are you doing this, Saul?"

"Well, I wanted a real movie and I got this instead. I was in the video place and I went past the musicals into the sad private room where the Xs were. There I was, me, full of curiosity."

"About what?"

"Well, we used to have fun. We used to get hot. So this . . . anyway, it's like nostalgia, you know? Nostalgia for something. It's sort of like going into a museum where the exhibits are happy, and you watch the happiness, and it isn't yours, so you watch more of it."

"This isn't like you, Saul. Doesn't it make you feel like shit or something?"

He sits in his chair, thinking. Then he says, "Yup, it does." He clicks off the TV set, rises, and puts his arms around Patsy, and they stand quietly there for what seems to Patsy a long time. Behind Saul on the living room bookshelf are volumes of history and literature—Saul's collections of Dashiell Hammett and Samuel Eliot Morison—and the Scrabble game on the top shelf. "Don't leave me alone back here," Patsy says. "Don't leave me alone, okay?"

"I love you, Patsy," he says. "You know that. Always have."

"That's not what I'm talking about."

"I know."

"You don't get everything now," she says. "You need to diversify."

They stand for a few moments longer, swaying slightly together.

TWO NIGHTS LATER, Saul finishes diapering Mary Esther and then walks into the upstairs hallway toward the bathroom. He brushes against Patsy, who is heading downstairs. Under the ceiling light her eyes are shadowed with fatigue. They do not speak, and for ten seconds, she is a stranger to him. He cannot remember why he married her, and he cannot remember his desire for her. He stands there, staring at the floor, angry and frightened, hoarding his injuries.

WHEN SAUL ENTERS his classroom the next day, Gordy and Bob greet his arrival with rattled throat noises. On their foreheads they have written MAD IN THE USA, in pencil. "Mad" or "made," misspelled? Saul doesn't ask. Seated in their broken desks and only vaguely attentive, the other students fidget and smile politely, picking at their frayed clothes uniformly one or two sizes too small.

"Today," Saul says, "we're going to pretend that we're young again. We're going to think about what babies would say if they could talk."

He reaches into his jacket pocket for his seven duplicate photographs of Mary Esther, in which she leans against the back of the sofa, her stuffed gnome in her lap.

"This is my daughter," Saul says, passing the photographs out. "Mary Esther." The four girls in the classroom make peculiar cooing sounds. The boys react with nervous laughter, except for Gordy and Bob, who have suddenly turned to stone. "Babies want to say things, right? What would she say if she could talk? Write it out on a sheet of paper. Give her some words."

Saul knows he is testing the Cossacks. He is screwing up their heads with his parental love. At the back of the room, Gordy Himmelman studies the photograph. His face expresses nothing. All his feelings are bricked up; nothing escapes from him.

His is the zombie point of view.

Nevertheless, he now bends down over his desk, pencil in hand.

At the end of the hour, Saul collects the papers, and his students shuffle out into the hallway. Saul has noticed that poor readers do not lift their feet off the floor. You can hear them coming down the hallway from the slide and scrape and squeal of their shoes.

He searches for Gordy Himmelman's paper. Here it is, mad in America, several lines of scrawled writing.

They thro me up in to the air. Peopl come in when I screem
and thro me up in to the air. They stik my face up. They never
catch me.

The next lines are heavily erased.

> her + try it out . You ink

Saul holds up the paper to read the illegible words, and now
he sees the word *kick* again, next to the word *lidle*.

His head randomly swimming, Saul holds the photographs
of his daughter, the little kike thoughtfully misspelled by Gordy
Himmelman, and brings the photos to his chest absentmindedly. From the hallway he hears the sound of lively laughter.

THAT NIGHT, Saul, fortified with Mad Dog's no-brand
beer, reads the want ads, deeply interested. The want ads are
full of trash and leavings, employment opportunities and the
promise of new lives amid the advertised wreckage of the old.
He reads the personals like a scholar, checking for verbal nu-
ance. Sitting in his overstuffed chair, he scans the columns
when his eye stops.

BEEHIVES FOR SALE—Must sell. Shells, frames, extractor.
Also incl. smoke and protective hat tools and face covering.
Good condition. Any offer considered. Eager to deal. $$$ po-
tential. Call after 7 p.m. 890-7236.

Saul takes Mary Esther out of her pendulum chair and holds
her as he walks around the house, thick with plans and vision.
In the vision, he stands proudly—regally!—in front of Patsy,
holding a jar of honey. Sunlight slithers through its glass and
transforms the room itself into pure gold. Sweetness is every-

where. Honey will make all the desires right again between them. Gordy Himmelman, meanwhile, will have erased himself from the planet. He will have caused himself to disappear. Patsy accepts Saul's gift. She can't stop smiling at him. She tears off their clothes. She pours the honey over Saul.

Gazing at the newspapers and magazines piling up next to the TV set as he holds Mary Esther, Saul finds himself shaking with a kind of excitement. Irony, his constant companion, is asleep, or on vacation, and in the heady absence of irony Saul begins to imagine himself as a beekeeper.

HE DOES NOT ACCUSE Gordy of anti-Semitism, or of anything else. He ignores him, as he ignores Bob Pawlak. At the end of the school year they will go away and fall down into the earth and the dirt they came from and become one with the stones and the inanimate all-embracing horizon.

On a fine warm day in April, Saul drives out to the north side of town, where he buys the wooden frames and the other equipment from a laconic man named Gunderson. Gunderson wears overalls and boots. Using the flat of his hand, he rubs the top of his bald head with a farmer's gesture of suspicion as he examines Saul's white shirt, pressed pants, ten-day growth of beard, and brown leather shoes. "Don't wear black clothes around these fellas," Gunderson advises. "They hate black." Saul pays him in cash, and Gunderson counts the money after Saul has handed it over, wetting his thumb to turn the bills.

With Mad Dog's pickup, Saul brings it all back to White-feather Road. He stores his purchases behind the garage. He takes out books on beekeeping from the public library and studies their instructions with care. He takes notes in a yellow notebook and makes calculations about placement. The bees need direct sunlight, and water nearby. By long-distance telephone he buys a hive of bees, complete with a queen, from an apiary in South Carolina, using his credit card number. When the bee box arrives in the main post office, he receives an angry call from the assistant postal manager telling him to come down and pick up this damn humming thing.

As it turns out, the bees like Saul. He is calm and slow around them and talks to them when he removes them from the shipping box and introduces them into the shells and frames, following the instructions that he has learned by heart. The hives and frames sit unsteadily on the platform Saul has laid down on bricks near two fence posts on the edge of the property. But the structure is, he thinks, steady enough for bees. He gorges them with sugar syrup, sprinkling it over them, before letting them free, shaking them into the frames. Some of them settle on his gloved hand and are so drowsy that, when he pushes them off, they waterfall into the hive. When the queen and the other bees are enclosed, he replaces the frames inside the shell, being careful to put a feeder with sugar water nearby.

The books have warned him about the loud buzzing sound of angry bees, but for the first few days Saul never hears it. Something about Saul seems to keep the bees occupied and unirritated. He is stung twice, once on the wrist and once on the back of the neck, but the pain is pointed and directed and so focused that he can manage it. It's unfocused pain that he can't stand.

Out at the back of Saul's property, a quarter mile away from the house, the hives and the bees won't bother anyone, Saul thinks. "Just don't bring them in here," Patsy tells him, glancing through one of his apiary books. "Not that they'd come. I just want them and me to have a little distance between us, is all." She smiles. "Bees, Saul? Honey? You're such a literalist."

And then one night, balancing his checkbook at his desk, with Mary Esther half asleep in the crook of his left arm, Saul feels a moment of calm peacefulness, the rarest of his emotions. Under his desk lamp, with his daughter burping up on his

Johns Hopkins sweatshirt, he sits forward, waiting. He turns around and sees Patsy, in worn jeans and a tee-shirt, watching him from the doorway. Her arms are folded, and her breasts are outlined perfectly beneath the cloth. She is holding on her face an expression of sly playfulness. He thinks she looks beautiful and tells her so.

She comes into the room, her bare feet whisking against the wood floor, and she puts her arms around him, pressing herself against him.

"Put Mary Esther into her crib," she whispers. She clicks off the desk lamp.

As they make love, Saul thinks of his bees. Those insects, he thinks, are a kind of solution.

SPRING MOVES into summer, and the mud on White-feather Road dries into sculpted gravel. Just before school ends, Saul tells his students about the bees and the hives. Pride escapes from his face, radiating it. When he explains how honey is extracted from the frames, he glances at Gordy Himmelman and sees a look of dumb animal rage directed back at him. The boy looks as if he's taking a bath in lye. What's the big deal? Saul wonders before he turns away.

One night in early June, Patsy is headed upstairs, looking for the Snugli, which she thinks she forgot in Mary Esther's room, when she hears Saul's voice coming from behind the door. She stops on the landing, her hand on the banister. At first she thinks he might be singing to Mary Esther, but, no, Saul is not singing. He's sitting in there—well, he's probably sitting, Saul doesn't like to stand when he speaks—talking to his daughter, and Patsy hears him finishing a sentence: ". . . was never very happy."

Patsy moves closer to the door.

"Who explains?" Saul is saying, apparently to his daughter. "No one."

Saul goes on talking to Mary Esther, filling her in on his mother and several other mysterious phenomena. What does he think he's doing, discussing this stuff with an infant? "I should sing you a song," he announces, interrupting himself. "That's what parents do."

To get away from Saul's song, Patsy retreats to the window for a breath of air. Looking out, she sees someone standing on the front lawn, bathed in moonlight, staring in the direction of the house. He's thin and ugly and scruffy, and he looks a bit like a clod, but a dangerous clod.

"Saul," she says. Then, more loudly, "Saul, there's someone out on the lawn."

He joins her at the window. "I can't see him," Saul says. "Oh, yeah, there." He shouts, "Hello? Can I help you?"

The boy turns around. "Sure, fuckwad. Yeah, you bet, shit-bird." He gets on a bike and races away down the driveway and onto Whitefeather Road.

Saul does not move. His hands are planted on the windowsill. "It's Gordy Himmelman," he groans. "That little bastard has come on our property. I'm getting on the phone."

"Saul, why'd he come here? What did you do to him?" She holds her arms against her chest. "What does he have against us?"

"I was his teacher. And we're Jewish," Saul says. "And, uh, we're parents. He never had any. I showed those kids the baby pictures. Big mistake. Somebody must've found Gordy somewhere in a barrel of brine. He was not of woman born." He tries to smile. "I'm kidding, sort of."

"Do you think he'll be back?" she asks.

"Oh yes." Saul wipes his forehead. "They always come back, those kind. And I'll be ready."

* * *

IT HAS BEEN a spring and summer of violent weather, and
Saul has been reading the Old Testament again, looking for
clues. On Thursday, at four in the afternoon, Saul has finished
mowing the front lawn and is sitting on the porch drinking the
last bottle of Mad Dog's beer when he looks to the west and
feels a sudden cooling of the air, a shunting of atmospheres.
Just above the horizon a mass of clouds begins boiling. Clouds
that look like breasts and handtools—he can't help thinking the
way he thinks—advance over him. The wind picks up.

"Patsy," he calls. "Hey Patsy."

Something calamitous is happening in the atmosphere. The
pressure is dropping so fast that Saul can feel it in his elbows
and knees.

"Patsy!" he shouts.

From upstairs he hears her calling back, "What, Saul?"

"Go to the basement," he says. "Close the upstairs window
and take Mary Esther down there. Take a flashlight. We're
going to get a huge storm."

Through the house Saul rushes, closing windows and
switching off lights, and when he returns to the front door to
close it, he sees out in the yard the tall and emaciated apparition
of Gordy Himmelman, standing fixedly like an emanation
from the dirt and stone of the fields. He has returned. Toward
Saul he aims his vacant stare. Saul, who cannot stop thinking
even in moments of critical emergency, is struck into stillness
by Gordy's presence, his authoritative malevolence standing
there in the just mown grass. The volatile ambitious sky and the
forlorn backwardness of the fields have together given rise to
this human disaster, who, even as Saul watches, yells toward the
house, "Hey, Mr. Bernstein. Guess what. Just guess what. Go
take a look at your bees."

Feeling like a commando, Saul, who is fast when he has to
be, catches up to Gordy who is pumping away on his broken

and rusted bicycle. Saul tears Gordy off. He throws and kicks the junk Schwinn into the ditch. In the rain that has just started, Saul grabs Gordy by the shoulders and shakes him back and forth. He presses his thumbs hard enough to bruise. Gordy, violently stinking, smells of neglect and seepage, and Saul nearly gags. Saul cannot stop shaking him. He cannot stop shaking himself. With violent rapid horizontal jerking motions the boy's head is whipped.

Saul wants to see his eyes. But the eyes are as empty as mirrors.

"Hey, stop it," Gordy says. "It hurts. You're hurting. You're hurting him."

"Hurt who?" Saul asks. Thunder rolls toward him. He sees himself reflected in Gordy Himmelman's eyes, a tiny figure backed by lightning. *Who, me?*

"Stop it, don't hurt him." Patsy's voice, repeating Gordy's words, snakes into his ear, and he feels her hand on his arm, restraining him. She's here, out in this rain, less frightened of the rain than she is of Saul. The boy has started to sag, seeing the two of them there, his scarecrow arms raised to protect himself, assuming, probably, that he's about to be killed. There he squats, the child of attention deficit, at Saul's feet.

"Stay there," Saul mumbles. "Stay right there." Through the rain he begins walking, then running, toward his bees.

THE STORM, empty of content, tucks itself toward the east and is being replaced even now by one of those insincere Midwestern blue skies.

Mary Esther begins to cry and wail as Patsy jogs toward Saul. Gordy Himmelman follows along behind her.

When she is within a hundred feet of Saul's beehives, she sees that the frames have been knocked over, scattered, and kicked. Saul lies, face down, where they once stood. He is touching his tongue to the earth momentarily, where the honey is, for a brief taste. When he rises, he sees Patsy. "All the bees swarmed," he says. "They've left. They're gone."

She holds Mary Esther tightly and examines Saul's face. "How come they didn't attack him? Didn't they sting him?"

"Who knows?" Saul spreads his arms. "They just didn't."

Gordy Himmelman watches them from a hundred yards away, and with his empty gaze he makes Patsy think of the albino deer Saul has insisted he has seen: half blind, wandering these fields day after day without direction.

"Look," Saul says, pointing at Mary Esther, who stopped crying when she saw her father. "Her shoe is untied." He wipes his face with his sleeve and shakes off the dirt from his jeans. Approaching Patsy, he gives off a smell of dirt and honey and sweat. In the midst of his distractedness, he ties Mary Esther's shoe.

His hair is soaked with rain. He glances at Patsy, who, with some difficulty, is keeping her mouth shut. She not only loves Saul but at this moment is in love with him, and she has to be careful not to say so just now. It's strange, she thinks, that she loves him, an odd trick of fate: He is fitful and emotional, a man whose sense of theater begins completely with himself. What she loves is the extravagance of feeling that focuses itself into the tiniest actions of human attention, like the tying of this pink shoe. It's better to keep love a secret for a while than to talk about it all the time. It generates more energy that way. He finishes the knot. He kisses them both. Dirt is attached to his lips.

At a distance of a hundred yards, the boy, Gordy, watches all this, and from her vantage point Patsy cannot guess what that expression on his face may mean, those mortuary eyes. Face it: He's a loss. Whatever they have to give away, they can only give him a tiny portion, and it won't be enough, whatever it is. All the same, he will stick around, she's pretty sure of that. They will have to give him something, because now, like it or not, he's following them back, their faithful zombie, made, or mad, in America, and now he's theirs.

Well, maybe we're missionaries, Patsy thinks, as she stumbles and Saul holds her up. We're the missionaries they left behind when they took all the religion away. On the front porch of the house she can see the empty bottle of Saul's no-brand beer still standing on the lip of the ledge, and she can see the porch swing slowly rock back and forth, as if someone were sitting there, waiting for them.

Flood Show

I N   L A T E   M A R C H , at its low flood stage, the Chaska
River rises up to the benches and the picnic areas in the
Eurekaville city park. No one pays much attention to it
anymore. Three years ago, Conor and Janet organized a flood
lunch for themselves and their three kids. They started their
meal perched crosslegged on an oilcloth they had draped over
the picnic table. The two adults sat at the ends, and the kids sat
in the middle, crowding the food. They had had to walk
through water to get there. The water was flowing across the
grass directly under the table, past the charcoal grilles and the
bandstand. It had soaked the swing-seats. It had reached
the second rung of the ladder on the slide.

After a few minutes, they all took off their shoes, which
were wet anyway, and they sat down on the benches. The waters slurred over their feet pleasantly, while the deviled eggs
and mustard-ham sandwiches stayed safe in their waxed paper
and Tupperware. It was a sunny day, and the flood had a peace-
able aspect. The twins yelled and threw some of their food into

the water and smiled when it floated off downriver. The picnic tables, bolted into cement, served as anchors and observation platforms. Jeremy, who was thirteen that spring, drew a picture, a pencil sketch, the water suggested by curlicues and subtle smearings of spit.

Every three years or so, Eurekaville gets floods like this. It's the sort of town where floods are welcome. They spill over the top banks, submerge the baseball diamond and the soccer field, soak a basement or two along Island Drive, and then recede. Usually the waters pass by lethargically. On the weekends, people wade out into it and play flood-volleyball and flood-softball. This year the Eurekaville High School junior class has brought bleachers down from the gym and set them up on the paved driveway of the park's northwest slope, close to the river itself, where you can get a good view of the waterlogged trash floating by. Jeremy, who is Conor's son from his first marriage and who is now sixteen, has been selling popcorn and candy bars to the spectators who want to sit there and chat while they watch the flotsam. He's been joined in this effort by a couple of his classmates. All profits, he claims, will go into the fund for the fall class trip to Washington, D.C.

By late Friday afternoon, with the sun not quite visible, thirty people had turned out to watch the flood—a social event, a way to end the day, a break from domestic chores, especially on a cloudy spring evening. One of Jeremy's friends had brought down a boom box and played Jesus Jones and Biohazard. There was dancing in the bleachers, slowish and tidal, against the music's frantic rhythms.

CONOR'S DREAMS these days have been invaded by water. He wakes on Saturday morning and makes quiet closed-door love to his wife. When he holds her, or when they kiss, and his eyes close, he thinks of the river. He thinks of the rivers inside both of them, rivers of blood and water. Lymphatic pools. All the fluids, the carriers of their desires. Odors of sweat, odors of salt. Touching Janet, he almost says, *We're mostly water.* Of course everyone knows that, the body's content of liquid matter. But he can't help it: that's what he thinks.

After his bagel and orange juice, Conor leaves Janet upstairs with the twins, Annah and Joe, who conspire together to dress as slowly as they possibly can, and he bicycles down to the river to take a look. Conor is a large bearish man with thick brown hair covered by a beret that does not benefit his appearance. He knows the beret makes him a bit strange-looking, and this pleases him. Whenever he bikes anywhere there is something violent in his body motions. Pedaling along, he looks like a trained circus bear. Despite his size, however, Conor is mild and kindhearted—the sort of man who believes that love and caresses are probably the answer for everything—but you wouldn't know that about him unless you saw his eyes, which are placidly sensual, curious—a photographer's eyes, just this side of sentimental, belonging to someone who quite possibly thinks too much about love for his own good.

The business district of Eurekaville has its habitual sleepy aura, its morning shroud of mist and fog. One still-burning streetlight has its orange pall of settled vaporish dampness around its glass globe. Conor is used to these morning effects; he likes them, in fact. In this town you get accustomed to the hazy glow around everything, and the sleepiness, or you leave.

He stops his bicycle to get a breath. He's in front of the hardware store, and he leans against a parking meter. Looking down a side street, he watches several workmen moving a huge wide-load steel platform truck under a house that has been loosened from its foundation and placed on bricks. Apparently they're going to truck the entire house off somewhere. The thought of moving a house on a truck impresses Conor, technology somehow outsmarting domesticity.

He sees a wren in an elm tree and a grosbeak fluttering overhead.

An hour later, after conversation and coffee in his favorite café, where the waitress tells him that she believes she's seen Merilyn, Conor's ex-wife, around town, and Conor has pretended indifference to this news, he takes up a position down at the park, close to the bleachers. He watches a rattan chair stuck inside some gnarly tree branches swirl slowly past, legs pointing up, followed by a brown broom, swirling, sweeping the water.

Because the Chaska River hasn't flooded badly—destructively—for years, Eurekaville has developed what Conor's son Jeremy describes as a goof attitude about rising waters. According to Jeremy's angle on it, this flooding used to be a disaster-thing. The townspeople sandbagged and worried themselves sick. Now it's a spectator-thing. The big difference, according to Jeremy, is sales. "It's . . . it's like, well, not a drowning occasion, you know? If it ever was. It's like one of those Prozac disasters, where nothing happens, except publicity? It's cool and stuff, so you can watch it. And eat popcorn? And then you sort of daydream. You're into the river, right? But not?"

As early as it is, Jeremy's already down here, watching the flood and selling popcorn, which at this time of morning no one wants to buy. Actually, he is standing near a card table, flirting with a girl Conor doesn't quite recognize. She's very pretty. It's probably why he's really here. They're laughing. At this hour, not quite mid-morning, the boom box on the table is playing old favorites by Led Zeppelin. The music, which sounded sexy and feverish to Conor years ago, now sounds charming and quaint, like a football marching band. Jeremy keeps brushing the girl's arms, bumping against her, and then she bumps against Jeremy and stabilizes herself by reaching for his hip. A morning dance. Jeremy's on the basketball team, and something about this girl makes Conor think of a cheerleader. Her smile goes beyond infectiousness into aggression.

Merilyn is nowhere in sight.

The flood has made everybody feel companionable. Conor waves to his son, who barely acknowledges him with a quick head-flick. Then Conor gets back on his bicycle and heads down to his photography studio, checking the sidewalks and the stores to see if he can spot Merilyn. It's been so long, he's not sure he'd recognize her.

BECAUSE IT'S SATURDAY, he doesn't have many appointments, just somebody's daughter, and an older couple, who have recently celebrated their fiftieth anniversary and who want a studio photo to commemorate it. The daughter will come first. She's scheduled for nine-thirty.

When she and her mother arrive at the appointed time, Conor is wearing his battery-operated lighted derby and has prepared the spring-loaded rabbit on the table behind the tripod. When the rabbit flips up, at the touch of a button, the kids smile, and Conor usually gets the shot.

The girl's mother, who says her name is Romola, has an errand to run. Can she leave her daughter here for ten minutes? She looks harried and beautiful and professionally religious, somehow, with a pendant-cross, and Conor says sure.

Her daughter appears to be about ten years old. She has an odd resemblance to Merilyn, who is of course lurking in town somewhere, hiding out. They both have a way of pinching their eyes halfway shut to convey distaste. Seated on a stool in front of the backdrop, the girl asks how long this'll take. Conor's adjusting the lights. He says, "Oh, fifteen minutes. The whole thing takes about fifteen minutes. You could practice your smile for the picture."

She looks at him carefully. "I don't like you," she says triumphantly.

"You don't know me," Conor points out. He checks his camera's film, the f-stop, refocuses, and says, "Seen the flood yet?"

"We're too busy. We go to church," the girl says. Her name is Sarah, he remembers. "It's a nothing flood anyway. In the old days the floods drowned sinners. You've got a beard. I don't like beards. Anyway, we go to church and I go to church school. I'm in fourth grade. The rest of the week is chores."

Conor turns on the little blinking lights in his derby hat, and the girl smiles. Conor tells her to look at the tin foil star on the wall, and he gets his first group of shots. "Good for you," Conor says. To make conversation, he says, "What do you learn there? At Bible school?"

"We learned that when he was up on the cross Jesus didn't pull at the nails. We learned that last week." She smiles. She doesn't seem accustomed to smiling. Conor gets five more good shots. "Do you think he pulled at the nails?"

"I don't know," Conor says. "I have no opinion." He's working to get the right expression on the girl's face. She's wearing a green dress, the color of shelled peas, that won't photograph well.

"I think maybe he did. I think he pulled at the nails."

"How come?" Conor asks.

"I just do," the girl says. "And I think they came out, because he was God, but not in time." Conor touches the button, the rabbit pops up, and the girl laughs. In five minutes her mother returns, and the session ends; but Conor's mood has soured, and he wouldn't mind having a drink.

THE NEXT DAY, Sunday, Conor stands in the doorway of Jeremy's bedroom. Jeremy is dressing to see Merilyn. "Just keep it light with her," he says, as Jeremy struggles into a sweatshirt at least one size too large for him. "Nothing too serious." The boy's head, with its ponytail and earrings, pokes out into the air with a controlled thrashing motion. His big hands never do emerge fully from the sleeves. Only Jeremy's calloused fingertips are visible. They will come out fully when they are needed. Hands three-quarters hidden: *youthful fashion-irony,* Conor thinks.

After putting his glasses back on, Jeremy gives himself a quick appraisal in the mirror. Sweatshirt, exploding-purple Bermuda shorts, sneakers, ponytail, earrings. Conor believes that his son looks weird and athletic, just the right sixteen-year-old pose: menacing; handsome; still under construction. As if to belie his appearance, Jeremy does a pivot and a layup near the door frame. It's hard for him to pass through the doors in this house without jumping up and tapping the lintels, even in the living room, where he jumps and touches the nail hole— used for mistletoe in December—in the hallway.

Satisfied with himself, Jeremy nods, one of those private gestures of self-approval that Conor isn't supposed to notice but does. "Nothing too earnest, okay?"

"Daad," Jeremy says, giving the word a sitcom delivery. Most of the time he treats his father as if he were a sitcom dad: good-natured, bumbling, basically a fool. Jeremy's right eyebrow is pierced, but out of deference to the occasion he's left the ring out of it. He shakes his head as if he had a sudden neck pain. "Merilyn's just another mom. It's not a big puzzle or anything, being with her. You just take her places. You just talk to her. Remember?"

"Remember what?"

"Well, you were married to her, right? Once? You must've talked and taken her places. That's what you did. Except you guys were young. So that's what I'll do. I'm young. We'll just talk. Stuff will happen. It's cool."

"Right," Conor says. "So where will you take her?"

"I don't know. The flood, maybe. I bet she hasn't seen a flood. This guy I know, he said a cow floated down the river yesterday."

"A cow? In the river? Oh, Merilyn would like that, all right."

"She's my mom. Come on, Dad. Relax. Nothing to it."

Jeremy says he will drive down to the motel where Merilyn is staying. After that, they will do what they are going to do. At the back stairs, playing with the cat's dish with his foot and biting his fingernail, Jeremy hesitates, smiles, and says, "Well, why don't you loosen up and wish me luck?" and Conor does.

FIVE DAYS BEFORE Merilyn left, fourteen years ago, Conor found a grocery list in green ink under the phone in the kitchen. "Grapefruit, yogurt," the list began, then followed with, "cereal, diapers, baby wipes, wheat germ, sadness." And then, the next line: "Sadness, sadness, sadness."

IN THOSE DAYS, Merilyn had a shocking physical beauty: startlingly blue eyes, and a sort of compact uneasy voluptuousness. She was fretful about her appearance, didn't like to be looked at—she had never liked being beautiful, didn't like the attention it got her—and wore drab scarves to cover herself.

For weeks she had been maintaining an unsuccessful and debilitating cheerfulness in front of Conor, a stagy display of frozen failed smiles, and most of what she said those last few evenings seemed memorized, as if she didn't trust herself to say anything spontaneously. She half-laughed, half-coughed after many of her sentences and often raised her fingers to her face and hair as if Conor were staring at them, which he was. He had never known why a beautiful woman had agreed to marry him in the first place. Now he knew he was losing her.

She worked as a nurse, and they had met when he'd gone up to her ward to visit a friend. The first time he ever talked to her, and then the first time they kissed—after a movie they both agreed they disliked—he thought she was the meaning of his life. He would love her, and that would be the point of his being alive. There didn't have to be any other point. When they made love, he had to keep himself from trembling.

Women like her, he thought, didn't usually allow themselves to be loved by a man like him. But there she was.

When, two and a half years later, she said that she was leaving him, and leaving Jeremy behind with him, and that that was the only action she could think of taking that wouldn't destroy her life, because it wasn't his fault but she couldn't stand to be married to anybody, that she could not be a mother, that it wasn't personal, Conor had agreed to let her go and not to follow her. Her desperation impressed him, silenced him.

She had loaded up the Ford and a trailer with everything she wanted to go with her. The rain had turned to sleet, and by the time she had packed the books and the clothes, Merilyn had collected small flecks of ice on her blue scarf. She'd been so eager to go that she hadn't turned on the windshield wiper until she was halfway down the block. Conor had watched her from the front porch. From the side, her beautiful face—the meaning of his life—looked somehow both determined and blank. She turned the corner, the tires splashed slush, the front end dipped from the bad shocks, and she was gone.

HE HAD A TRUNK in the attic filled with photographs he had taken of her. Some of the shots were studio portraits, while others were taken more quickly, outdoors. In them, she is sitting on stumps, leaning against trees, and so on. In the photographs she is trying to look spontaneous and friendly, but the photographs emphasize, through tricks of angle and lighting, her body and its voluptuousness. All of the shots have a painfully thick and willful artistry, as if she had been mortified, in her somewhat involuntary beauty, under a glaze.

She had asked him to destroy these photographs, but he never had.

N O W , having seen Jeremy go off to find his mother somewhere in Eurekaville and maybe take her to the flood, Conor wanders into the living room. Janet's sprawled on the floor, reading the Sunday comics to Annah. Annah is picking her nose and laughing. Joe, over in the corner, is staging a war with his plastic mutant men. The forces of good muscle face down evil muscle. Conor sits on the floor next to his wife and daughter, and Annah rumbles herself backward into Conor's lap.

"Jeremy's off?" Janet asks. "To find Merilyn?"

Conor nods. Half consciously, he's bouncing his daughter, who holds on to him by grasping his wrist.

Janet looks back at the paper. "They'll have a good time."

"What does that mean?"

She flicks her hair back. "'What does that mean?'" she repeats. "I'm not using code here. It means what it says. He'll show her around. He'll be the mayor of Eurekaville. At last he's got Merilyn on his turf. She'll be impressed."

"Nothing," Conor says, "ever impressed Merilyn, ever, in her life."

"Her life isn't over."

"No," Conor says, "it isn't. I mean, nothing has impressed her so far."

"How would you know? You didn't follow Merilyn down to Tulsa. There could be all sorts of things in Tulsa that impress Merilyn."

"All right," Conor says. "Maybe the oil wells. Maybe something. Maybe the dust bowl and the shopping malls. All I'm saying is that nothing impressed her here."

A little air pocket of silence opens between them, then shuts again.

"Daddy," Annah says, "tip me."

Conor grasps her and tips her over, and Annah gives out a little pleased shriek. Then he rights her again.

"I wonder," Janet says, "if she isn't getting a little old for that."

"Are you getting too old for this, Annie?" Annah shakes her head. "She's only five." Conor tips her again. Annah shrieks again, and when she does, Janet drops the section of the newspaper that she's reading and lies backward on the floor, until her head is propped on her arm, and she can watch Conor.

"Mom!" Joe shouts from the corner. "The plutonium creatures are winning!"

"Fight back," Janet instructs. "Show 'em what you've got." She reaches out and touches Conor on the thigh. "Honey," she says, "you can't impress everybody. You impress me sometimes. You just didn't impress Merilyn. No one did. Marriage didn't. What's wrong with a beautiful woman wanting to live alone? It's her beauty. She can keep it to herself if she wants to."

Conor shrugs. He's not in the mood to argue about this. "It's funny to think of her in town, that's all."

"No, it's not. It's only funny," Janet says, "to think of her in town if you still love her, and I'd say that if you still love her, after fourteen years, then you're a damn fool, and I don't want to hear about it. It's Jeremy, not you, who could use some attention from Merilyn. It's his to get, being her son and all. She left him more than she left you. But I'll be damned if I'm going to go on with this conversation one further sentence more."

Both Annah and Joe have stopped their playing to listen. They are not watching their parents, but their heads are raised, like forest animals who can smell smoke nearby.

"All I ever wanted from her was a reason," Conor says. "I just got tired of all that enigmatic shit."

"Hey," Janet says. "I told you about that one further sentence." Annah gets out of her father's lap and snuggles next to Janet. "All right," Janet says. "Listen. Listen to this. Here's something I never told you. One night Merilyn and I were working the same station, we were both in pediatrics that night, third floor, it was a quiet night, not many sick kids that week. And, you know, we started talking. Nursing stuff, women stuff. And Merilyn sort of got going."

"About what?"

"About you, dummy, she got going about you. Herself and you. She said you two had gone bowling. You'd dressed in your rags and gone off to Colonial Lanes, the both of you, and you'd been bowling, and she'd thrown the ball down the lane and turned around and you were looking at her, appreciating her, and of course all the other men in the bowling alley were looking at her, too, and what was bothering her was that you were looking at her the way they did, sort of a leer, I guess, as if you didn't know her, as if you weren't married to her. Who could blame you? She looked like a cover girl or something. Perfect this, perfect that, she was perfect all over, it would make anybody sweat. So she said she had a sore thumb and wanted to go home. You were staring at your wife the way a man looks at a woman walking by in the street. Boy, how she hated that, that guy stuff. You went back home, it was cold, a cold blister night, she got you into bed, she made love to you, she threw herself into it, and then in the dark you were your usual gladsome self, and you know what you did?"

"No."

"You thanked her. You two made hot love and then you thanked her, and then in the dark you went on staring at her, you couldn't believe how lucky you were. There she was in your arms, the beauteous Merilyn. I bet it never occurred to you at the time that you aren't supposed to thank women after you make love to them and they make love to you, because you know what, sweetie? They're not doing you a favor. They're doing it because they want to. Usually. Anyway, that was the night she got pregnant with Jeremy and it was the same night she decided she would leave you, because you couldn't stop looking at her, and thanking her, and she hated that. For sure she hated it. She lives in Tulsa, that's how much."

Conor is watching Janet say this, focusing on her mouth, watching the lips move. "Son-of-a-bitch," he says.

"So she told me this," Janet says, "one night, at our nursing station. And we laughed and sort of cried when we had coffee later, but you know what I was thinking?" She waits. "Do you? You don't, do you?"

"No."

"I was thinking," Janet says, "that I'm going to get my hands on this guy, I am going to get that man come hell or high water. I am going to get him and he is going to be mine. Mine forever. And do you know why?"

"Give me a clue."

"To hell with clues. I wanted a man who looked at me like that. I wanted a man who would work up a lather with me in bed and then thank me. No one had ever thanked me before, that was for goddamn certain sure. And you know what? That's what happened. You married another nurse. Me, this time. And it was me you looked at, me you thanked. Heaven in a bottle. Are you listening to me? Conor, pay attention. I'm about to do something."

Conor follows her gaze. A living room, newspaper on the floor, Sunday morning, the twins playing, a family, a house, a life, sunlight coming in through the window. Janet walks over to Conor, unties her bathrobe, pulls it open, drops it at his feet, lifts her arms up and pulls her nightgown over her head. In front of her children and her husband, she stands naked. She is beautiful, all right, but he is used to her.

"I'm different from Merilyn," she says. "You can look at me any time you want."

NOW, on Sunday afternoon, Conor cleans out his pickup, throwing out the bank deposit slips. When he's finished, with his binoculars around his neck and his telephoto lens attached to his camera, the 400 millimeter one that he uses for shots of birds beside him on the seat, he drives down to the river, hoping for a good view of an osprey, or maybe a teal.

He parks near a cottonwood. He is on the opposite side from the park. Above him are scattered the usual sparrows, the usual crows. He gets out his telephoto lens and frames an ugly field sparrow flittering and shivering in the flat light. A grackle, and then a pigeon, follow the sparrow into his viewfinder. It is a parade of the common, the colorless, the drear. The birds with color do not want to perch anywhere near the Chaska River, not even the swallows or swifts. He puts his camera back in his truck.

He's standing there, searching the sky and the opposite bank with his binoculars, looking for what he thought he saw here last week, a Wilson's snipe, when he lowers the lenses and sees, at some distance, Jeremy and Merilyn. Merilyn is sitting on a bench, watching Jeremy, who has taken off his sweatshirt and is talking to his mother. Merilyn isn't especially pretty anymore. She's gained weight. Conor had heard from Jeremy that she'd gained weight but hadn't seen it for himself. Now, through the binoculars, Merilyn appears to be overweight and rather calm. She has that loaf-of-bread quality. There's a peaceful expression on her face. It's the happy contentment of someone who probably doesn't bother about very much anymore.

Jeremy stands up, throws his hands down on the ground, and begins walking on his hands. He walks in a circle on his hands. He's very strong and can do this for a long time. It's one of his parlor tricks.

Conor moves his binoculars and sees that Jeremy has brought a girl along, the girl he saw yesterday at the flood show, the one who was dancing with him. Conor doesn't know this girl's name. She's standing behind the bench and smiling while Jeremy walks on his hands. It's that same aggressive smile.

Goddamn it, Conor thinks, *they're lovers, they've been sleeping together, and he didn't tell me.*

He moves the binoculars back to Merilyn. She's still watching Jeremy, but she seems only mildly interested in his display. She's not smiling. She's not pretending to be impressed. Apparently that's what she's turned into. That's what all these years have done to her. She doesn't have to look interested in anything if she doesn't want to.

To see better, Conor walks down past his truck to the bank. He lifts the binoculars to his eyes again, and when he gets the group in view, Merilyn turns her head to his side of the river. She sees Conor. Conor's large bearlike body is recognizable anywhere. And what she does is, she raises her hand and seems to wave.

From where he is standing, Conor thinks that Merilyn has invited him over to join their group. Through the binoculars a trace of a smile, Conor believes, has appeared on Merilyn's face. This smile is one that Conor recognizes. In the middle of her pudginess, this smile is the same one that he saw sixteen years ago. It's the smile he lost his heart to. A little crow's foot of delight in Conor's presence. A merriment.

And this is why Conor believes she is asking him to join them, right this minute, and to be his old self. And this is why he steps into the river, smiling that smile of his. It's not a wide river after all, no more than sixty or seventy feet across. Anyone could swim it. What are a few wet clothes? He will swim across the Chaska to Merilyn and Jeremy and Jeremy's girl-friend, and they will laugh, pleased with his impulsiveness and passion, and that will be that.

He is up to his thighs in water when the shocking coldness of the river registers on him. This is a river of recently melted snow. It isn't flowing past so much as biting him. It feels like cheerful party icepicks, like happy knives. Without meaning to, Conor gasps. But once you start something like this, you have to finish it. Conor wades deeper.

The sun has come out. He looks up. A long-billed marsh wren is in a tree above the bank. He cannot breathe, and he dives in.

Conor is a fair swimmer, but the water is putting his body into shock and he has to remember to move his arms. Having dived, he feels the current taking him downriver, at first slowly, and then with some urgency. He is hopeless with cold. Tiny bells, the size of gnats, ring on every inch of his skin. He thinks, *This is crazy*. He thinks, *It wasn't an invitation, that wave*. He thinks, *I will die*. The river's current, which is now the sleepy hand of his death waking up, reaches into his chest and feels his heart. Conor moves his arms back and forth but he can't see the bank now and doesn't know which way he's going. Of course, by this time he's choking on water, and the bells on his skin are beginning to ring audibly. He is moving his arms more slowly. Flashcard random pictures pop up delightedly in his mind, and he sees the girl in his studio the day before, and she says, "I don't like you."

He doesn't want to die a comic death. It occurs to him that the binoculars are pulling him toward the river bottom, and he reaches for them and takes them off of his neck.

He swirls around like a broom.

He pulls his arms. It seems to him that he is not making any progress. It also seems to him that he cannot breathe at all. But he has always been a large easygoing man, incapable of panic, and he does not panic now. His sinking will take its time.

THE TOUCH of the shore is silt. The graspings of hands on his elbow are almost unfriendly, aggressive. Jeremy is there, pulling, and what Conor hears, through his own coughing and spitting, is Jeremy's voice.

"Dad! What the fuck are you doing? What in the fucking . . . Daddy! Are you okay? Jesus. Are you . . . what the fuck is this? Shit! Jesus. Daddy!"

Conor looks at his son and says, "Watch your language."

"What? What! Get out of there." Conor is being pulled and pushed by his son. Pulled and pushed also, it seems, by his son's girlfriend. Perhaps she is simply trying to help. But the help she is giving him has been salted with violence.

"What do you think?" Conor asks, turning toward her. "Do you think he pulled at the nails?"

Conor's trousers are dripping water on the grass. Water pours out of his shirt. It drains off his hands. Now in the air his ears register their pain on him; his eardrums are in pain, a complex aching inside the ravine of his head. And Merilyn, the source, the beneficiary of his grand gesture, is simply saying, with her nurse's voice, "He's in shock. Get him into the car."

"Merilyn," he says. He can't see her. She's behind him.

"What?"

"I couldn't help it. I never got over it." He says it more loudly, because he can't see her. He might as well be talking to the air. "I never got over it! I never did."

"Daddy, stop it," Jeremy says. "For God's sake shut up. Please. Get in the car."

Jeremy opens the door of the old clunker Buick he bought on his sixteenth birthday for four hundred dollars, and Conor, without thinking, gets in. Before he is quite conscious of the sequence of one event after another, the car's engine has started, and the Buick moves slowly away—away from Merilyn: Conor remembers to look. She grows smaller with every foot of distance between them, and Conor, pleased with himself, pleased with his inscribed fate as the unhappy lover, tries to wipe his eyes with his wet shirt.

"I won't tell anybody about this if you don't," Jeremy says.

"Okay."

"I'll tell them you fell into the river. I'll say that you slipped on the mud."

"Thanks."

"That can happen. I mean really." Jeremy is enthusiastic now, creating a cover story for his father. "You were taking pictures and stuff, and you got too close to the river, and, you know, bang, you slipped, and like that. Just don't ever tell Mom, okay? We'll just . . . holy shit! What's that?"

The Buick has been climbing a hill, and near the top, where a slight curve to the right banks the road toward the passenger side, there comes into view an amazing sight that has cut Jeremy into silence: an old wooden two-story house on an enormous platform truck, squarely in the middle of the road, blocking them. The house on the truck is moving at five or ten miles an hour. Who knows what its speed is, this white clapboard monument, this parade, a smaller truck in front, and one in back, with flashing lights, and a WIDE LOAD sign? No one would think of measuring its speed. Conor looks up and sees what he knows is a bedroom window. He imagines himself in that bedroom. He is dripping water all over his son's car, and he is beginning now to shiver, as the truck, carrying the burden it was made to carry, struggles up the next hill.

The Cures for Love

ON THE DAY he left her for good, she put on one of his caps. It fit snugly over her light brown hair. The cap had the manufacturer's name of his pickup truck embossed above the visor in gold letters. She wore the cap backward, the way he once had, while she cooked dinner. Then she kept it on in her bath that evening. When she leaned back in the tub, the visor hitting the tiles, she could smell his sweat from the inside of the headband, even over the smell of the soap. His sweat had always smelled like freshly broiled white-fish.

WHAT HE OWNED, he took. Except for the cap, he hadn't left much else behind in the apartment. He had what he thought was a soulful indifference to material possessions, so he didn't bother saving them. It hadn't occurred to her until later that she might be one of those possessions. He had liked having things—quality durable goods—around for a little while, she thought bitterly, and then he enthusiastically threw them all out. They were there one day—his leather vest, his golf clubs—and then they were gone. She had borrowed one of his gray tee-shirts months ago to wear to bed when she had had a cold, and she still had it, a gray tee in her bottom dresser drawer. But she had accidentally washed it, and she couldn't smell him on the fabric anymore, not a trace of him.

HER CAT NOW yowled around five-thirty, at exactly the time when he used to come home. She—the cat—had fallen for him the moment she'd seen him, rushing over to him, squirming on her back in his lap, declawed paws waving in the air. The guy had had a gift, a tiny genius for relentless charm, that caused anything—women, men, cats, trees for all she knew—to fall in love with him, and not calmly, either, but at the upper frequencies.

Her clocks ached. Time had congealed. For the last two days, knowing he would go, she had tried to be busy. She had tried reading books, for example. They couldn't preoccupy her. They were just somebody's thoughts. Her wounded imagination included him and herself, but only those two, bone hurtling against bone.

She was not a romantic and did not like the word *romance*. They hadn't had a romance, the two of them. Nothing soft or tender, like that. They had just, well, driven into each other like reckless drivers at an intersection, neither one wanting to yield the right-of-way. She was a classicist recently out of graduate school, and for a job she taught Latin and Greek in a Chicago private school, and she understood from her reading of Thucydides and Catullus and Sophocles and Sappho, among others, how people actually fought, and what happened when they actually fell in love and were genuinely and almost immediately incompatible. The old guys told the truth, she believed, about love and warfare, the peculiar combination of attraction and hatred existing together. They had told the truth before Christianity put civilization into a dream world.

AFTER SHE GOT out of the bathtub, she put herself into bed without drying herself off first. She removed the baseball cap and rolled around under the covers, dampening the sheets. *It's like this*, she said to herself.

SHE THOUGHT of herself as "she." At home she narrated her actions to herself as she performed them: "Now she is watering the plants." "Now she is feeding the cat." "Now she is staring off into space." "Now she is calling her friend Ticia, who is not at home. She will not leave a message on Ticia's machine. She doesn't do that."

She stood naked in front of the mirror. She thought: I am the sexiest woman who can read Latin and Greek in the state of Illinois. She surveyed her legs and her face, which he had praised many times. I look great and feel like shit and that's that.

THE NEXT MORNING she made breakfast but couldn't eat it. She hated it that she had gotten into this situation, loaded down with humiliating feelings. She wouldn't tell anyone. Pushing the scrambled eggs around on the plate, making a mess of them, the buttered wheat toast, and the strawberry jam, her head down on her arm, she fell into speculation: *Okay, yes, right, it's a mistake to think that infatuation has anything to do with personality, or personal tastes. You don't, uh,* decide *about any of this, do you?* she asked herself, half-forming the words on her lips. Love puts anyone in a state outside the realm of thought, like one of those

Eleusinian cults where no one ever gets permission to speak of the mysteries. When you're not looking, your mouth gets taped shut. You fall in love with someone not because he's nice to you or can read your mind but because, when he kisses you, your knees weaken, or because you can't stop looking at his skin or at the way his legs, inside his jeans, shape the fabric. His breath meets your breath, and the two breaths either intermingle and create a charge or they don't. Personality comes later; *personality*, she thought, reaching for the copy of Ovid that was about to fall off the table, *is the consolation prize of middle age.*

She put the breakfast dishes in the sink. She turned on the radio and noticed after five minutes that she hadn't listened to any of it. She snapped it off and glanced angrily in the direction of the bedroom, where all this trouble had started.

She and he had ridden each other in that bed. She glowered at it, framed in the doorway of the bedroom, sun pouring in the east window and across the yellow bedspread. They had a style, but, well, yes, almost everyone had a style. For starters, they took their time. Nothing for the manuals, nothing for the record books. But the point wasn't the lovemaking, not exactly. What they did started with sex but ended somewhere else. She believed that the sex they had together invoked the old gods, just invited them right in, until, boom, there they were. She wondered over the way the spirit-gods, the ones she lonesomely believed in, descended over them and surrounded them and briefly made them feel like gods themselves. She felt huge and powerful, together with him. It was archaic, this descent, and pleasantly scary. They both felt it happening; at least he said he did. The difference was that, after a while, he didn't care about the descent of the old gods or the spirits or whatever the hell he thought they were. He was from Arizona, and he had a taste for deserts and heat and golf and emptiness. Perhaps that explained it.

He had once blindfolded her with her silk bathrobe belt during their lovemaking and she had still felt the spirit coming down. Blindfolded, she could see it more clearly than ever.

OVID. AT the breakfast table she held onto the book that had almost fallen to the floor. Ovid: an urbane know-it-all with a taste for taking inventories. She had seldom enjoyed reading Ovid. He had a masculine smirking cynicism, and then its opposite, self-pity, which she found offensive.

And this was the *Remedia amoris,* a book she couldn't remember studying in graduate school or anywhere else. The remedies for love. She hadn't realized she even owned it. It was in the back of her edition of the *Ars amatoria.* Funny how books put themselves into your hands when they wanted you to read them.

Because spring had hit Chicago, and sunlight had given this particular Saturday morning a light fever, and because her black mood was making her soul sore, she decided to get on the Chicago Transit Authority bus and read Ovid while she rode to the suburbs and back. Absentmindedly, she found herself crying while she stood at the corner bus stop, next to the graffitied shelter, waiting. She was grateful that no one looked at her.

After the bus arrived in a jovial roar of diesel fumes and she got on, she found a seat near a smudgy semi-clean window. The noise was therapeutic, and the absence on the bus of businessmen with their golf magazines relieved her. No one on this bus on Saturday morning had a clue about how to conduct a life. She gazed at the tattered jackets and gummy spotted clothes of the other passengers. No one with a serious relationship with money rode a bus like this at such a time. It was the fuck-up express. Hollow and stoned and vacant-eyed people like herself sat there, men who worked in carwashes, women who worked in diners. They looked as if their rights to their own sufferings had already been revoked months ago.

Over the terrible clatter, trees in blossom rushed past, dogwood, and lilacs, and like that. The blossoms seemed every bit as noisy as the bus. She shook her head and glanced down at her book.

> *Scripta cave relegas blandae servata puellae:*
> *Constantis animos scripta relecta movent.*
> *Omnia pone feros (pones invitus) in ignes*
> *Et dic 'ardoris sit rogus iste mei.'*

Oh, right. Yeah. Burn the love letters? Throw them all in the flames? And then announce, "This is the pyre of my love"? Hey, thanks a lot. What love letters? He hadn't left any love letters, just this cap—she was still wearing it—with "Chevy" embossed on it in gold.

> *Quisquis amas, loca sola nocent: loca sola caveto;*
> *Quo fugis? in populo tutior esse potes.*
> *Non tibi secretis (augent secreta furores)*
> *Est opus; auxilio turba futura tibi est.*

Riding the CTA bus, and now glimpsing Lake Michigan through a canyon of buildings, she felt herself stepping into an emotional lull, the eye of the storm that had been knocking her around. In the storm's eye, everyone spoke Latin. The case endings and the declensions and Ovid's I-know-it-all syntax and tone remained absolutely stable, however, no matter what the subject was. They were like formulas recited from a comfortable sofa by a banker who had never made a dangerous investment. The urbanity and the calm of the poem clawed at her. She decided to translate the four lines so that they sounded heartbroken and absentminded, jostled around in the aisles.

The lonely places
　　are the worst. I tell you,
　　　　when you're heart-
　　sick, go
where the pushing and shoving
　　　　crowd gives you
　　some nerve. Don't be
　　　　alone, up in your
burning room, burning—
　　trust me:
　　　　get knocked
down in public,
　　　　you'll be helped up.

All right: so it was a free translation. So what? She scribbled it on the back of a deposit slip from the Harris Bank and put it into her purse. She wouldn't do any more translating just now. Any advice blew unwelcome winds into her. Especially advice from Ovid.

Now they were just north of the Loop. This time, when she looked out of the window, she saw an apartment building on fire: firetrucks flamesroof waterlights crowdsbluesky smokesmoke. There, and gone just that rapidly. Suffering, too, probably, experienced by someone, but not immediately visible, not from here, at forty miles per hour. She thought: *Well, that's corny, an apartment fire as seen from a bus. Nothing to do about that one.* Quickly she smelled smoke, and then, just as quickly, it was gone. To herself, she grinned without realizing what she was doing. Then she looked around. No one had seen her smile. She had always liked fires. She felt ashamed of herself, but momentarily cheerful.

She found herself in Evanston, got out, and took the return bus back. She had observed too much of the lake on the way. Lake Michigan was at its most decorative and bourgeois in the northern suburbs: whitecaps, blue water, waves lapping the shore, abjectly picturesque.

BY AFTERNOON she was sitting in O'Hare Airport, at gate 23A, the waiting area for a flight to Memphis. She wasn't going to Memphis—she didn't have a ticket to anywhere—and she wasn't about to meet anyone, but she had decided to take Ovid's advice to go where the crowds were, for the tonic effect. She had always liked the anonymity of airports anyway. A businessman carrying a laptop computer and whose face had a WASPy nondescript pudgy blankness fueled by liquor and avarice was raising his voice at the gate agent, an African-American woman. Men like that raised their voices and made demands as a way of life; it was as automatic and as thoughtless as cement turning and slopping around inside a cement mixer. "I don't think you understand the situation," he was saying. He had a standby ticket but had not been in the gate area when they had called his name, and now, the plane being full, he would have to take a later flight. "You have no understanding of my predicament here. Who is your superior?" His wingtip shoes were scuffed, and his suit was tailored one size too small for him, so that it bulged at the waist. He had combed strands of hair across his sizable bald spot. His forehead was damp with sweat, and his nose sported broken capillaries. He was not quite first class. She decided to eat a chili dog and find another gate to sit in. Walking away, she heard the gate agent saying, "I'm sorry, sir. I'm sorry."

You couldn't eat a chili dog in this airport sitting down. It was not permitted. You had to stand at the plastic counter of Here's Mr. Chili, trying not to spill on the polyester guy reading *USA Today,* your volume of Publius Ovidius Naso next to you, your napkin in your other hand, thinking about Ovid's exile to the fringe of the Roman empire, to Tomis, where, broken in spirit, solitary, he wrote the *Tristia,* some of the saddest poems written by anyone anywhere, but a—what?—male sadness about being far from where the action was. There was no action in Tomis, no glamour, no togas—just peasants and plenty of mud labor. On the opposite side of Here's Mr. Chili was another gate where post-frightened passengers were scurrying out of the plane from Minneapolis. A woman in jeans and carrying a backpack fell into the arms of her boyfriend. They had started to kiss, the way people do in airports, in that depressing public style, all hands and tongues. And over here a chunky Scandinavian grandma was grasping her grandchildren in her arms like ships tied up tightly to a dock. You should go where people are happy, Ovid was saying. You should witness the high visibility of joy. You should believe. In . . . ?

> *Si quis amas nec vis, facito contagia vites*
> Right, right: "If you don't
>   want to love,
>   don't expose yourself to
> the sight
>   of love, the contagion."

Evening would be coming on soon; she had to get back.

She was feeling a bit light-headed, the effect of the additives in the chili dog: the Red concourse of O'Hare, with its glacially smooth floors and reflecting surfaces, was, at the hour before twilight, the scariest manmade place she'd ever seen. *This airport is really manmade,* she thought, *they don't get more manmade than this.* Of course, she had seen it a hundred times before, she just hadn't bothered looking. If something hadn't been hammered or fired, it wasn't in this airport. Stone, metal, and glass, like the hyperextended surfaces of eternity, across which insect-people moved, briefly, trying before time ran out to find a designated anthill. Here was a gate for Phoenix. There was a gate for Raleigh-Durham. One locale was pretty much like another.

People made a big deal of their own geographical differences to give themselves specific details to talk about. Los Angeles, Cedar Rapids, Duluth. What did it matter where anyone lived—Rome, Chicago, or Romania? All she really wanted was to be in the same room with her as-of-yesterday ex. Just being around him had made her happy. It was horrible but true. She had loved him so much it gave her the creeps. He wasn't worthy of her love but so what. Maybe, she thought, she should start doing an inventory of her faults, you know, figure the whole thing out—scars, bad habits, phrases she had used that he hadn't liked. Then she could do an inventory of his faults. She felt some ketchup under her shoe and let herself fall.

She looked up.

Hands gripped her. Random sounds of sympathy. "Hey, lady, are you all right?" "Can you stand?" "Do you need some help?" A man, a woman, a second man: Ovid's public brigade of first-aiders held her, clutched at her where she had sprawled sort of deliberately, here in the Red concourse. Expressions of fake concern like faces painted on flesh-colored balloons lowered themselves to her level. "I just slipped." "You're okay, you're fine?" "Yes." She felt her breast being brushed against, not totally and completely unpleasantly. It felt like the memory of a touch rather than a touch itself, no desire in it, no nothing. There: She was up. Upright. And dragging herself off, Ovid under her arm, to the bus back to the Loop and her apartment. Falling in the airport and being lifted up: okay, so it happened as predicted, but it didn't make you feel wonderful. Comfortably numb was more like it. She dropped the *Remedia amoris* into a trash bin. Then she thought, uh oh, big mistake, maybe the advice is all wrong but at least he wants to cheer me up, who else wants to do that? She reached her hand into the trash bin and, looking like a wino grasping for return bottles, she pulled out her soiled book, smeared with mustard and relish.

* * *

"KIT?"

A voice.

"Yes?" She turned around. She faced an expression of pleased surprise, on a woman she couldn't remember ever seeing before.

"It's me. Caroline."

"Caroline?" As if she recognized her. Which she didn't. At all.

"What a coincidence! This is too amazing! What are you doing here?"

"I'm, um, I was here. Seeing someone off. You know. To . . . ah, Seattle."

"Seattle." The Caroline-person nodded, in a, well, professional way, one of those therapeutic nods. Her hair had a spiky thickness, like straw or hay. Maybe Caroline would mention the traffic in Seattle. The ferries? Puget Sound? "What's that?" She pointed at the haplessly soiled book.

"Oh, this?" Kit shrugged. "Ovid."

More nodding. Blondish hair spiked here and there, arrows pointing at the ceiling and the light fixtures and the arrival-and-departure screens. The Caroline-person carried—no, actually pulled on wheels—a tan suitcase, and she wore a business suit, account executive attire, a little gold pin in the shape of the Greek lambda on her lapel. Not a very pretty pin, but maybe a clue: lambda, lambda, now what would that . . . possibly mean? Suitcase: This woman *didn't* live here in Chicago. Or else she *did.*

"You were always reading, Kit. All that Greek and Latin!" She stepped back and surveyed. "You look simply fabulous! With the cap? Such a cute retro look, it's so street-smart, like . . . who's that actress?"

"Yeah, well, I have to . . . it's nice to see you, Caroline, but I'm headed back to the Loop, it's late, and I have to—"

"—Is your car here?" A hand wave: Caroline-person wedding ring: tasteful diamond of course, that's the way it goes in the Midwest, wedding rings everyfuckingwhere.

"Uh, no, we took, I mean, he and I took the taxi out." Somehow it seemed important to repeat that. "We took a taxi."

"Great! I'll give you a ride back. I'll take you to your place. I'll drop you right at the doorstep. Would you like some company? Come on!"

She felt her elbow being touched.

DOWN THE LONG corridors of O'Hare Airport shaped like the ever-ballooning hallways of eternity, the Caroline-person pulled her suitcase, its tiny wheels humming behind her high-heeled businesslike stride; and easily keeping up in her jogging shoes, in which she jogged when the mood struck her, Kit tried to remember where on this planet, and in this life, she'd met this person. Graduate school? College? She wasn't a parent of one of her students, that was certain. *You were always reading.* Must've been college. "It's been so long," the woman was saying. "Must be . . . what?" They edged out of the way of a beeping handicap cart.

Kit shook her head as if equally exasperated by their mutual ignorance.

"Well, I don't know either," Caroline-person said. "So, who'd you see off?"

"What?"

"To Seattle."

"Oh," Kit said.

"Something the matter?"

"It was Billy," Kit said. "It was Billy I put on the plane."

"Kit," she said, "I haven't seen you in years. Who's this Billy?" She gave her a sly girlish smile. "Must be somebody special."

Kit nodded. "Yeah. Must be."

"Oh," Caroline said, "you can tell me."

"Actually, I can't."

"Why not?"

"Oh, I'd just rather not."

A smile took over Caroline's face like the moon taking over the sun during an eclipse. "But you can. You can tell me."

"No, I can't."

"Why?"

"Because I don't remember you, Caroline. I don't remember the first thing about you. I know a person's not supposed to admit that, but it's been a bad couple of days, and I just don't know who you are. Probably we went to college together or something, classics majors and all that, but I can't remember." They had stopped near a Buick display, and Kit wondered for a moment how the GM people got the car, a large midnight blue Roadmaster, into the airport. People rushed past them and around them. "I don't remember you at all."

"You're kidding," the woman said.

"No," Kit said, "I'm not. I can't remember seeing you before."

The woman who said her name was Caroline put her hand on her forehead and stared at Kit with a what-have-we-here? shocked look. Kit knew she was supposed to feel humiliated and embarrassed, but instead she felt shiny and new and fine for the first time all day. She didn't like to be tactless, but that seemed to be the direction, at least right now, this weekend, where her freedom lay. She'd been so good for so long, she thought, so loving and sweet and agreeable, and look where it had gotten her. "You're telling me," the woman said, "that you don't remember our—"

"—Stop," Kit said. "Don't tell me."

"Wait. You don't even want to be reminded? You're . . . but

why? Now I'm offended," the woman told her. "Let's start over. Let's begin again. Kit, I feel very hurt."

"I know," Kit said. "It's been a really strange afternoon."

"I just don't think . . ." the woman said, but then she was unable to finish the sentence. "Our ride into the city . . ."

"Oh, that's all right," Kit said. "I couldn't take up your offer. I'll ride the bus back. They have good buses here," she added.

"No," she said. "Go with me."

"I can't, Caroline. I don't remember you. We're strangers."

"Well, uh, goodbye then," the woman muttered. "You certainly have changed."

"I certainly have. But I'm almost never like this. It's Billy who did this to me." She gazed in Caroline's direction. "And my vocabulary," she said, not quite knowing what she meant. But she liked it, so she repeated it. "My vocabulary did this to me."

"It's that bad?" the woman said.

Standing by the Buick Roadmaster in O'Hare Airport, where she had gone for no good reason except that she could not stand to be alone in her apartment, she felt, for about ten seconds, tiny and scaled-down, like a model person in a model airport as viewed from above, and she reached out and balanced herself on the driver's side door handle and then shook her head and closed her eyes. If she accepted compassion from this woman, there would be nothing left of her in the morning. Sympathy would give her chills and fever, and she would start shaking, and the shaking would move her out of the hurricane's eye into the hurricane itself, and it would batter her, and then wear her away to the zero. Nothing in life had ever hurt her more than sympathy.

"I have to go now," Kit said, turning away. She walked fast, and then ran, in the opposite direction.

*   *   *

OF COURSE I remember you. We were both in a calculus class. We had hamburgers after the class sometimes in the college greasy spoon, and we talked about boys and the future and your dog at home, Brutus, in New Buffalo, Minnesota, where your mother bred cairn terriers. In the backyard there was fencing for a kennel, and that's where Brutus stayed. He sometimes climbed to the top of his little pile of stones to survey what there was to survey of the fields around your house. He barked at hawks and skunks. Thunderstorms scared him, and he was so lazy, he hated to take walks. When he was inside, he'd hide under the bed, where he thought no one could see him, with his telltale leash visible, trailing out on the bedroom floor. You told that story back then. You were pretty in those days. You still are. You wear a pin in the shape of the Greek letter lambda and a diamond wedding ring. In those days, I recited poetry. I can remember you. I just can't do it in front of you. I can't remember you when you're there.

SHE GAZED out the window of the bus. She didn't feel all right but she could feel all right approaching her, somewhere off there in the distance.

She had felt it lifting when she had said his name was Billy. It wasn't Billy. It was Ben. Billy hadn't left her; Ben had. There never had been a Billy, but maybe now there was. She was saying goodbye to him; he wasn't saying goodbye to her. She turned on the overhead light as the bus sped through Des Plaines, and she tried to read some Ovid, but she immediately dozed off.

Roaring through the traffic on the Kennedy Expressway, the bus lurched and rocked, and Kit's head on the headrest turned from side to side, an irregular rhythm, but a rhythm all the same: enjambments, caesuras, stophes.

My darling girl, (he said, thinner
than she'd ever thought he'd be,
           mostly bald, a few sprout curls,
and sad-but-cheerful, certainly,
           Roman and wryly unfeminist, unhumanist,
unliving), child of gall and wormwood (he pointed his
thin malnourished finger at her,
           soil inside the nail),
       what on earth
       brought you to that unlikely place?
An airport! Didn't I tell you,
               clearly,
to shun such spots? A city park on a warm
Sunday afternoon wouldn't be as bad. People fall
into one another's arms out there all the time.
           Hundreds of them! (He seemed exasperated.)
       Thank you (he said)
           for reading me, but for the sake
of your own well-being, don't go there
       again without a ticket. It seems
       you have found me out. (He
shrugged.) Advice? I don't have any
       worth passing on. It's easier
to give advice when you're alive
           than when you're not,
       and besides, I swore it off. Oh I liked
what you did with Caroline, the lambda-girl
       who wears that pin because her husband
       gave it to her on her birthday,
March twenty-first—now that
       I'm dead, I know everything
       but it does me not a particle of good—
           but naturally she thinks it has no
special meaning, and that's the way
           she conducts her life. Him, too. He
bought it at a jewelry store next to a shoe
           shop in the mall at 2 p.m.
       March 13, a Thursday—but I digress—

and the salesgirl,
cute thing, hair done in a short cut
style, flirted with him
showing him no mercy,
touching his coat sleeve,
thin wool, because she was on commission. Her
name was
Eleanor, she had green eyes.
The pin cost him $175, plus tax.
She took him, I mean, took him for a ride,
as you would say,
then went out for coffee. By herself, that is,
thinking of her true
and best beloved, Claire, an obstetrician
with lovely hands. I always did admire
Sapphic love. But I'm
still digressing. (He smirked.)

The distant failed humor of the dead.
Our timing's bad,
the jokes are dusty,
and we can't concentrate
on just
one thing. I'm as interested
in Eleanor as I am
in you. Lambda. Who cares? Lambda: I suppose
I mean, I *know*,
he thought the eleventh letter, that uncompleted triangle,
looked like his wife's legs. Look:
I can't help it,
I'm—what is the word?—salacious, that's
the way I always was,
the bard of breasts and puberty, I was
exiled for it, I turned to powder
six feet under all the topsoil
in Romania. Sweetheart, what on earth
are you *doing* on
this bus? Wake up, kiddo, that guy

Ben is gone, good riddance
is my verdict from two thousand
          years ago, to you.
     Listen: I have a present for you.

He took her hand.
His hand didn't feel like much,
     it felt like water when you're reaching
     down for a stone or shell
under the water, something you don't
     have, but want, and your fingers
          strain toward it.
     Here, he said, this is the one stunt
I can do: look up, sweetie, check out
          this:
(he raised his arm in ceremony)
     See? he said proudly. It's raining.
I made it rain. I can do that.
          The rain is falling, only
               it's not water, it's
this other thing. It's the other thing
          that's raining, soaking you. Goodbye.

WHEN SHE awoke, at the sound of the air brakes, the bus
driver announced that they had arrived at their first stop, the
Palmer House. It wasn't quite her stop, but Kit decided to get
out. The driver stood at the curb as the passengers stepped
down, and the streetlight gave his cap an odd bluish glow. His
teeth were so discolored they looked like pencil erasers. He
asked her if she had any luggage, and Kit said, no, she hadn't
brought any luggage with her.

The El clattered overhead. She was in front of a restaurant
with thick glass windows. On the other side of the glass, a man
with a soiled unpressed tie was talking and eating prime rib. On
the sidewalk, just down the block, under an orange neon light,

an old woman was shouting curses at the moon and Mayor Daley. She wore a paper hat and her glasses had only one lens in them, on the left side, and her curses were so interesting, so incoherently articulate, uttered in that voice, which was like sandpaper worried across a brick, that Kit forgot that she was supposed to be unhappy, she was listening so hard, and watching the way the orange was reflected in that one lens.

Believers

I

My father was a man of singular devotions. For a few years before I was born, he was a priest in the Roman Catholic Church.
As a priest, his countenance—that old word—was eerie. His
light gray eyes gave him, from a certain angle, a quality of rapt
contemplation. At those moments his expression conveyed a
disturbing radiance. He had—I can't avoid saying it this way—
an oddly beautiful face. Many people said so. Rapture was
sometimes visible in his expressive gestures, in the way he
aimed his face at the sky. He had a gift for rapture, strange as
that may sound. As a consequence, women sometimes found
themselves going a bit shivery in his presence. I have spoken to
some of them. Most are grandmothers by now. But they do not
especially mind talking about the past, and a few can be direct.
"It wasn't his fault," one of them once said to me, "but your father made me weak in the knees."

She took a sip of her tea. We sat in her kitchen, at the oil-cloth-covered table. It was a hot day, and tiny beads of sweat had appeared above her upper lip. Hot as it was, she was still wearing a blue scarf, and she dabbed at herself with it. "I never told him, of course," she said, with a pallid smile, "because he was my priest for those three years, and I don't suppose he knew how I felt. Nobody knew, not my husband or my sister. Why should I tell anyone? It wasn't important, you see, that I reacted that way. But I'm older now, and I'm a widow, and you're his son. Women love their priests sometimes. They bring casseroles to the rectory. It's not news. It shouldn't be news to you. Besides, you look like him."

Another one of these ladies said to me, "When he was nearby, my whole body knew it." She didn't smile. She glanced at the ceiling.

"I don't care in the least," she added, "if you know this or not. It doesn't make any difference now. Not the slightest difference."

In addition to his gray eyes, my father had straight sandy hair parted on the left and layered neatly across his head, hair that he did not lose even in early middle age. The photographs of him as a young man suggest a narrow nose and thin lips on a mouth whose corners curved upward, so that he gave the impression of smiling even when he was pensive and did not intend to smile and was not, in fact, smiling. He had a slight limp from a childhood injury. Like many North Germans, afflicted for countless generations by clouds and damp weather, he could be moody, but unlike most of those same Germans, his moods were almost weightless, and the shifts in his emotions were often so quick that watching him was like being stationed in a field over which clouds were rapidly passing, creating patterned successions of shadow and light.

I was the child in that field, over which the clouds passed.

I loved my father, lost calling and all. I might as well say it. I loved him for his instinctual goodness, which was evident to just about everyone who knew him, a peculiar variety of it without righteousness or piety, and for his forbearance, a word rarely used now, because its referent is disappearing. True goodness can be bland. The unworldliness surrounding it often suggests something peculiarly childlike. Most men secretly have a contempt for it. My father was blessed, and cursed, with this quality. He did not hold it aloft as a feature of his character, as some people make a practice of doing, the ones transfixed with hypocrisy and mania. Reader, you may have known, at some time in your life, someone good and quietly honorable like my father. You must try to recognize what I am describing. You must help me breathe the breath of life back into him. I might as well tell you that this is a desperate enterprise.

Finally, I think, his goodness brought him into the arms of my mother. And when that happened, he was vacated of his faith. God, who says of Himself that He is jealous, took His leave of my father. And my father was given this world, the one we live in, for all the good it would do him.

I am, as you understand by now, his son. My name is Johann Wolfgang Pielke. Actually, this being America, everyone calls me Jack. Jack Pielke. My sister is Margareta Pielke. Everyone calls her Maggie. I have inherited my father's gray eyes but very little else from him, despite what the old ladies say, though I have kept faith with one feature of my father's character, and I will explain what that is at the end of my story. I live in western Michigan and work as an electrical engineer, and I am writing this at a table in front of my apartment window, with a view of two largish oak trees outside on the front lawn. (No leaves: it's winter now.) On my wall, to the left of the window, is a picture of the Third Reich's Minister of Propaganda, the failed novelist Joseph Goebbels. In the picture, Goebbels sits in a chair, a

paper in his hand, and he looks toward the camera in the full
nakedness of his rage. I cannot write a word without that man
looking down at me.

This is a story about Goebbels, my father, my mother, and
two Americans, Mary Ellen Jordan, and her husband, Burton
Mitchell Jordan. It is a story about fascism, and believers, a
story of the American Midwest, and of how I came to be con-
ceived and brought into the world by a priest. I suppose that
announcing all this information ahead of time is poor form. I
don't care. My existence is not the point of this story, in any
case.

Here on the desk are two notebooks. One is labeled *"Vögel"*
and the other *"Wildblumen."* Birds and wildflowers. They belonged to my father when he was a boy. The covers consist of a
cheap heavy paper, and my father's name is written carefully
near the bottom. Franz Pielke. It is not in his own handwriting
but his sister's.

The notebooks are written in German because my father
was born into a German-speaking family from Hamburg, from
the same section of that city where Johannes Brahms was
born. My father's parents, Richard and Helge Pielke, moved to
America in 1906, in a great wave of German immigration, and
like many Germans they settled in southern Michigan because
others of their family had settled there and because the modest
farms and flat terrain dotted with its many small lakes looked
like the agricultural landscapes surrounding Hamburg. In
Michigan they borrowed money from other relatives, cousins
who had already crossed, and they managed to get a small loan
from the local bank. With this money, a trivial sum by today's
standards, they bought a manageable farm of approximately
one hundred twenty acres from a man named Samuel Staples

who had grown tired of the relentless demands of farming. Of such men it was often said that they didn't have the spine for serious work. He gathered up his family and took it into Lampert, Michigan, the nearest town, where he opened a dry goods store. The business failed, no one knows why, and Samuel Staples, along with his family, subsequently vanished from the town and from the memories of its inhabitants.

My grandfather, I have been told, planted feed corn and alfalfa for hay, the land in this region being too poor in topsoil and nutrients for much else, and he gradually built up a small herd of dairy cows, along with chickens, pigs, a workhorse named Albrecht, and a mule named Max, some of the usual fixtures of a family farm. At first the Pielkes made almost no profit from their work, but they got by, as farmers did from year to year. About Richard Pielke, my grandfather, no one remembers much except that he was a hard worker and therefore at least an honorable farmer. Like many of his generation, his identity was absorbed into the constant daily labor his life demanded. He worked. He had a quick temper. That's how he was known. Perhaps he took joy in his life, or was aggrieved. No one, except perhaps his wife, noticed or cared about his opinions of daily earthly existence. Among those people, these German-Americans, moods of any sort were common but useless and were generally not remarked upon.

No one remembers much of anything about his wife, Helge, either, except for her accomplishments in raising two children and in helping to run the place. She had one remarkable physical attribute: blond hair the color of gold coins. I mean coins that have been in the pocket for several weeks and have acquired darkness and tarnish. An ancient woman I found in Niles, Michigan, remembered her hair.

"Her hair was so thick, yellow, you couldn't take your eyes off it. And they were Catholics, too, of course," this woman said, from her motorized wheelchair. "The Pielkes were all of them Catholics." She waited. She pointed a withered finger at me. "You, too?"

When he was four or five years old, my father had a habit of wandering off. He wandered down to the barn, where his sister, my aunt, would find him gazing raptly at the livestock. He ambled aimlessly around the house, into the kitchen and through the bedrooms, where he would stare at the curtains blown inward by the summer breezes. He went into the chicken coop and watched the hens. He wandered down to the stream at the back of the fields where, once again, and screaming his name this time, his sister would find him.

"Franzl, you could have drowned," she would shout (in German) as she pulled him back by the arm, yanking him up the grassy rise, through the poplars, back into the fields. "Why can't you stay still? Why can't you stay where I can see you? When my back is turned, you sneak off and then you race away to your hiding places."

"The ducks," he said. "I wanted to see them. Let go of my arm."

"You're not good for anything," she said, giving him another yank. "You're lazy and you think no one notices. I'm ashamed of you."

"Not good for anything," he repeated happily. "*Wertlos.*" Worthless. And then with his arm suddenly free, he would start running across the fields, his legs pumping into the dirt, poom poom poom, as my aunt told me, pushing her index fingers downward alternately, like pistons.

"Later, when he was six or seven, your father could run like an animal. He was a powerful runner, graceful. He looked like a greyhound, like one of those North Germans, one of those Frisians, with their narrow faces. You would never expect it, because he had that dreamy side, just standing around or milking the cows or cleaning their stalls. He'd collect the eggs from the chicken coop and take them up to the house. And then . . . he would clench his fists and start running, and you never saw anything like it. Yes, a greyhound. He was a child athlete, I don't know what to call it, that gift. But he had it. He was always racing."

So that she would know where he was, and what he was doing, my aunt gave her little brother two cheap notebooks that she had saved up for and bought in town, one for *Vögel* and one for *Wildblumen*. She wrote his name, FRANZ PIELKE, on the covers, in large letters. He seems to have not been terribly interested in the *Wildblumen* or animals other than birds or cows. Perhaps no other animals were visible. He sketched only a few wildflowers with his Mongol pencils, starting with *Löwenenzahn*—dandelion—and going on to the *Violett*. Sketching flowers wasn't the sort of thing a boy would do unless bullied into it by his sister anyway. Girls have odd ideas about what their younger brothers will enjoy. He must have been about seven years old at this time, an age when some boys can still be ordered around, but most of them won't be.

He did enjoy drawing birds, though. He climbed up to the loft in the barn and drew the *Schwalben*, the swallows, and his notebook shows them in flight, with tiny dots on the paper for the insects they're chasing. But they look like birds in a nightmare, with curved wings and tiny heads with open beaks. There is nothing cute about them. They are eating machines, feathered bundles of blind appetite. Out in the woods somewhere he must have caught sight of a woodpecker once or twice. Here they are, labeled carefully, the *Kleinspecht,* clinging to the penciled-in suggestion of a tree, with long sharp pointed beaks and irregular white stripes along the back. They aren't beautiful, these woodpeckers; their beaks look like pickaxes.

And here are my father's owls, the *Eulen,* staring straight out of the notebook with eyes so wide open that they make you think of police interrogators probing for a confession. Nothing cute on these pages either, not with these creatures. And not the *Finken,* either, the finches, or the *Habichte,* the hawks, drawn with blank black eyes. How did my father ever manage to get close enough to these animals to get so clear a look? He must have been able to sit quietly for hours in the woods behind the fields or on the ridge close to the stream, waiting and watching, as patient as the birds themselves. Or else he must have found a few of them dead. Like that other observant bird lover, John J. Audubon, he may have propped up dead specimens and then immortalized them posthumously.

My father's birds are generally of two kinds: the razorlike *Raubvögel,* the predators (it sounds more like itself in German), and the other kind, the prey, those that are chased, the *Beute,* whom he has drawn with astonished expressions, doves and pheasants, about to be dropped upon. Some feathered thing— lethally poised, trembling, impatient, deadly—waits for them outside of the picture. The pigeons, with their meek watchfulness, have food in front of them, but they do not eat. They seem to be waiting for a slaughtering and devouring attention to descend on them. They seem to know it is coming.

Whenever he caught my father daydreaming at the window, or staring off toward the woods or the birds in them, my grandfather would roar, "There is no place on this farm for a lazybones!" Down would come the dirt-encrusted callused hand onto the back of my father's head. My grandfather's roaring had no malice in it. His anger was unpremeditated and impersonal. Life was about work, the daily struggle of it. Franz recovered from his father's anger in short order, did his chores, and then ran to a safe spot where he would be absorbed by what he saw.

* * *

As it happens, my grandfather, who did not gaze in rapt contemplation at anything, did not like most trees or undergrowth or shrubs. They offended his sense of arrangement. Trees were the edge of chaos. He considered them un-German, and, as he grew older, in surges of newfound patriotism, un-American. A farmer's business is to clear away nature and create a better and more orderly version of it. The Earth is a kingdom but we must labor to make it so. So he had been told, and so he believed. Scruffy American undergrowth had no place in this order, nor did most trees, except when they provided shade for the farmhouse. Forests were unkempt, a mess.

The farm's outbuildings stood north and west of the house, and beyond the buildings and the fields were several acres of second-growth woods, a mixture of poplars, maples, oaks, and pine. This small forest contained a stream running through it and a small marshy pond on its northeast side that often dried up in late summer. In the spring it was a gathering place for ducks. My grandfather wanted these areas cleared out, and my father wanted them left as they were. My father took his orders and did his chores with a silent patient dutifulness. What he really loved was running and sitting by this pond, watching the birds.

He carried bread crumbs in his pocket for them. In time, the birds gabbled and clucked around his feet, attending him.

In the winter Richard Pielke repaired his tools, fixed up the house, carved toys for his children, and cut down his trees for firewood. The scrub brush that, in his thinking, had no use, he piled in a clearing just beyond where the fields ended, for a bonfire each year on the night of Saint Lucia, December 13th.

The year that Franz was nine years old, Richard Pielke, his father, took him out on Sunday, December 10th, to help him cut down trees and brush and to haul the cuttings in a toboggan to the brush pile and the logs to the back of the house, where the firewood was stacked in symmetrical piles. The shape and standing of a man's woodpile could be seen as a sign of his inner discipline, and Richard Pielke's was so neatly laid that the edges lined up flush, like a wall. The day was thickening with clouds and snow. A light wind blew against the house from the west, and the temperature was 14 degrees Fahrenheit. In the kitchen, my grandmother and my aunt were baking bread.

My grandfather, pulling his toboggan, on which were riding the axe, the hatchet, and the crosscut saw, occasionally looked back to check on his son, who was a few feet behind him. In his dreamy absorbed way, Franz was studying the semi-straight lines in the snow left by the toboggan's wood slats. Occasionally the snow would stop falling, and my father, ambling along, his hands in his pockets, would gaze up toward the sky, checking for birds.

The second time he did so, he stepped onto the toboggan.

"Franz," his father said. "Pay attention to yourself." Franz nodded.

A male cardinal flew from the edge of the forest, up, back, and toward them.

Careless of his direction, Franz stepped again by accident on the toboggan's back edge. His weight pulled taut the rope in my grandfather's hands, jerking him backward suddenly. He lost his balance and almost fell over. The axe rattled and the saw began to slide off. My grandfather became angry. He was the sort of man who had built up his precarious working man's dignity through the years stone by stone, furrow by furrow. Losing his balance in front of his son made him feel ridiculous. He bent down and repositioned the saw. Then, after he had recovered some of his composure, he removed his stocking cap and grunted. Fearing an uprush of his father's anger, Franz at once apologized.

Richard gazed at his son. "You're so serious," he said. "You study everything. Things that shouldn't be studied, these are the things you study. Birds and bugs. Squirrels and worms."

"I'm sorry, Papi."

"No, it's all right," my grandfather said. "It is only that a man cannot be like you. A man must attend to his work, and the work of a man's hands is to the things of the earth. A man looks downward. Do you understand that? A man looks down. He does not gaze off, as you do, upward or around or without purpose in any direction, like one of our cows. Perhaps a woman can do that. A man cannot. Do you understand this, what I am saying?"

"Yes, Papi."

"The saints tell us what a man must do." Richard straightened his back to offer a quotation. "Think of their concentration and devotion. Think of their discipline." He pointed in the direction of his feet. "Do you see this ground? Adam's sin cursed it. 'In toil you shall eat of it all the days of your life; thorns and thistles it shall bring forth to you.' Is this something which you understand? These thorns, these thistles?" He jabbed his finger into the air. "You have seen them here, on our farm? Together we have pulled them up."

"Yes, Papi."

My grandfather sighed. He turned around and gripped the rope again. "What use are the stars or other faraway things, to us here on Earth? No use."

The boy thought: *Navigation. They are good for navigation.* But he did not say anything.

Richard nodded, agreeing with himself, having settled the matter. He said, "Now we must go into the woods."

Having taken the axe and the hatchet off the toboggan, as a kind of penance, and carrying them now, Franz followed his father into the opening of the forest, a space between two old maple trees.

* * *

A bird broke my father's leg that day. Broke it so that from then on he could not run and would have to walk the two miles to school each morning and each afternoon in pain and difficulty.

But I see that, once again, I am anticipating myself. It is a habit of a man who has thought too much about the story he is telling.

They had entered the forest and had proceeded through the graying air and falling snow until they reached a white pine, a tree easy to cut down and good for firewood. My grandfather set to work. After determining the angle in which he wanted the tree to fall, he made a deep gouge in the trunk with the axe. He worked with force, but slowly and carefully, breathing in deeply before swinging the axe, breathing out as its blade fell and the wood chips broke off. When he was finished, he called to Franz, and together they began to saw away at the tree, Franz on one side of the tree, his father on the other.

Franz watched the sawdust spurt out and pile onto the snow. He smelled its clear faraway scent: Greenland! The Black Forest! He felt his back working to pull the saw. Then he felt a familiar sensation, an ache, blooming in his shoulder and arm muscles. He ignored this feeling of tiredness, as his father had taught him to do.

Slowly the piles of sawdust accumulated on the snow at the base of the tree, light brown powder scattered in small pyramids. He knew he wasn't doing as much work as his father, but how could he, being small, a boy?

Crows skittered above them, cawing. His father said, "Yes, good," as the saw went deeper into the trunk. Franz wondered—his arms felt darker as they grew tired, that was odd— if trees ever felt anything as they were axed and sawed. But men didn't ask such questions. They weren't supposed to. He could hear his father's voice inside him. Women could ask pointless questions; that was what they did in life. Men could not. All the same, sure, of course, trees felt it.

Behind him, Franz suspected, no, he knew, there was a wolf watching him as he helped his father to cut down this tree. He didn't dare look. He sensed the wolf on his back. A wolf with bright gray eyes, eyes like his own, and a long muzzle. A male wolf. But a man does not look away from the work he is performing. He gazes down toward the earth, toward the small pyramids of sawdust.

It suddenly occurred to Franz that his father loved his mother but did not like her or women generally. That idea, having no place in his mind to stay, vanished from his thoughts as quickly as it had entered them.

He could have left the tree and gone running through the woods with the wolf, racing him, following him, leading him. No boy in North America could run as fast as Franz Karl Pielke. When he ran, the world blurred out, smeared into vibrating color. His speed was a gift from God. He gave it back to God as an offering every time he ran.

Above the tree, and above the sound of the saw—Franz felt his back turning gray from the work—the boy heard a male cardinal sounding its call. Unusual in winter for a cardinal to chirp and sing. *He sees us,* Franz thought. *He sees us here, just as that wolf does.* A phrase came to him: *I will lift up my eyes to the hills, from whence comes my salvation.*

He looked up. His father said something.

His father said another sentence, equally unintelligible, and the cardinal rose, lifted itself aloft from the tree where it had perched, one spot of red in a landscape of consuming gray, the finest red Franz could remember seeing, and he thought, *God loves me,* and the thought was so layered and thick and unarguable that Franz didn't hear his father crying out to him and reaching toward his left arm, just as the tree fell over and against Franz.

His father, trying to save him from the falling tree, had pulled him into its path, under it.

Above the sound of the tree striking the ground was the sharper, more incisive crack of the boy's leg as it broke.

Cursing himself and his son and fate, Richard Pielke bent down to lift the trunk of the white pine off his son's leg and found that he could not do it. His son was screaming, screaming and screaming and screaming, a child's prolonged agonized wail. What the boy was actually feeling was more shocked surprise than pain, finding himself unable to move underneath a fallen tree, but all that came out of his mouth was noise.

As the cardinal flew away, it saw, far below it, two tiny human figures waving their useless wings.

Above the sound of his own noise, Franz heard his father praying and cursing almost simultaneously, and he heard his father bargaining and muttering and grunting, and then the tree moved off and away from him, and Franz saw his father's face above him, so deeply red that the skin shaded off into purple, the veins bulging. Tears spurted from his father's eyes, tears not of sorrow but of total physical effort at its last limit of intensity. Grimacing, lifting the tree, his father bared his teeth. *He* was like a wolf! Something inside his father's body made a hollow snapping sound, like a fist striking a board.

He lowered his arms under his son and lifted him onto the toboggan.

The axe, the hatchet, and the saw.

Richard Pielke, a practical man and a methodical one, feared losing his tools under the new, the falling, snow. Without them he could not cut wood, and without wood no fires would burn in the stoves. A serious person, even in panic, did not misplace his tools. And this is apparently why, after he had laid his broken son down on the toboggan, he placed the axe near the boy's feet, the hatchet close to his left elbow, and the saw directly over Franz's chest.

With his leg fractured, my father lay under the saw, still smelling of the wood it had cut, and its teeth still warm, as his father pulled him back through the forest the same way they had come. Franz had stopped yelling, though he was in pain and could not move his right leg. Over the sound of the toboggan's shooshing progress over the snow, my father heard my grandfather's boots sinking downward as he took each new step. He also heard his father raging at him.

"How did I get such a son? A dreamer, a good-for-nothing? What did I say to you? I said: *Watch yourself.* That is exactly what I said! Watch the work you are doing. Stop the gazing off in all directions, stop this staring at nothing. But you did not listen. I said it, I told you. I warned you. But you are a fool! I have a son who is a fool! A fool who falls under trees! Whose head is filled with air and birds! A dog would know better than you! A dog would have more sense!"

Franz, stretched out under the crosscut saw, heard his father say these words, and he was glad that the saw was shielding him from his father's angry accusing looks. He turned his face to his right. Bushes glided past. Far in the distance he caught sight of a rabbit, before a stump blocked it. He spotted some dried grayish grass partially crusted with snow. He thought he saw a grackle before a terrible pain reached up through his hip and grabbed him and shook him.

Just then, my grandfather's mood changed.

"May God forgive me," he said. "May God forgive me for what I have done today. I have cursed You, and I have cursed my own son. This is wretchedness."

My father listened to these verbal dramatics in astonishment. He was used to his father's angers but not accustomed to the language of emotional groveling. He didn't like to hear his father speaking this way; it frightened him. Such language made his father helpless and small.

They had left the woods and reached the fields. His father was muttering unintelligibly. Still he pulled the toboggan.

"Whosoever dwelleth under the defense of the Most High will abide under the shadow of the Almighty."

Where did those words come from? Who said them? The boy had heard them somewhere. His father wasn't saying them, but somehow they had appeared in the boy's head.

"Whosoever dwelleth under the defense of the Most High will abide under the shadow of the Almighty." The words took up occupancy in the boy like a tune heard once and repeated endlessly in the memory.

All the way back to the house, and then in the carriage on the way to town, the boy heard those words. He couldn't remember where he had found them. He had heard them somewhere, in church, or he had read them in a book. They could not have come into his mind on their own. No. Impossible. Words could not do that.

He appeared to be growing delirious. He thought God loved him. God's love surrounded him like warm soothing water.

In Lampert, where the town doctor first examined and set Franz's leg before putting it into a splint, having pronounced it a green stick fracture, the boy opened his eyes in a moment between the spasms and brushfires of pain, and he looked up at the bespectacled man gazing back, a whiskey-breathing town practitioner named Henry Foessern working by gaslight, and in a weak voice he said, "Whosoever dwelleth under the defense of the Most High will abide under the shadow of the Almighty."

Henry Foessern stopped what he was doing and gazed for a

moment at the boy. "Is that so?" he said. Then he smiled. The doctor was tolerated and trusted but not well liked in town. He had an unpleasant streak of irony. Drinking fueled this irony so that by nightfall he was usually reading Nietzsche. Inspired by the German philosopher and by alcohol, he would find himself, as midnight approached, revising and amplifying his great lifework, a denunciation of small-town America, which he kept in the drawer in his study and which had now reached two hundred cramped handwritten pages. The book was tentatively titled *Behold, Democracy!* He was a bachelor.

Now, however, he turned to the boy's mother, whose hair, like gold coins, shimmered under the gas lamps, and whose eyes were red with tears. She sat next to her sullen husband.

"This is a very intelligent boy," the doctor said. "I will make a prediction. I imagine he will grow up to be a priest."

2

In the spring of 1937, Father Franz Pielke was hunting for wild asparagus in the woods east of St. Boniface, Michigan, where he celebrated Mass on Sunday and taught biology in the parochial school. He did not consider himself a man much given to life-distorting habits, but he had a secret craving this time of year for fresh-cooked asparagus. It came over him every spring. Furthermore, the search for wild asparagus brought out the boy in him. He felt as if he were on a treasure hunt.

The winter, which had been harsh, and the spring, which had been dry, had reduced the crop. This year asparagus spears were exceptionally hard to find. So far he had picked only a small handful. Though it was still spring, the air in the woods had a dusty golden aura, the dryness of pollen and airborne topsoil.

But nothing good came without some labor. Wild strawberries hid under grass in early June, just the time when the mosquitoes came out. Asparagus thrived in mixed light and shadow, where poison ivy also flourished.

He limped toward a section of the woods where the combination of light and shade seemed to be right. As he walked, he waved his hat at the gnats clustering over his head. He passed a cluster of Solomon's seal, mostly done in by the dry conditions. Their blossoms shivered.

He could smell the asparagus. He had an instinct for it, as some people had an instinct for sniffing out edible mushrooms. Crouching down to avoid hitting his head on a tree branch, he checked the area, but—he groaned aloud—the only asparagus here was past picking; it had already sent out its branches and stems.

He glanced up. Through the trees just ahead of him—he had brought his pocket compass, though he didn't need it now—he saw a clearing, and in the clearing was a man on horseback, waiting, watching for something behind him. His horse was a dappled gray mare, well groomed and beautifully conditioned. As Father Pielke watched, another horse came into view, carrying a woman who wore a hat, riding boots, and jodhpurs. The horse on which she rode was a remarkable brown gelding, also beautifully groomed. Its coat shone in the late spring sunlight. The woman's hair, under her hat, was the color of gold coins.

The man and the woman spoke to each other. The two horses nodded together, evidently stablemates.

Father Pielke, without quite realizing that he was doing so, thrashed his way through the shrubs and undergrowth toward the two figures on horseback. They looked like two people in a book illustration or a painting. It was as if they were posing for someone whose job or pleasure it was to gaze upon them. They were rather grand, at least from a distance; on horseback, they both had excellent posture, like public personalities who know they are being watched. They had no resemblance whatever to any of the inhabitants of St. Boniface, at least those farmers and laborers and merchants known to Father Pielke.

As he finally broke his way out of the wood, Father Pielke stepped over a hip-high sandbar willow he hadn't seen that caught his ankle. He didn't fall. His balance had always been good. But his temporary disorientation and his limp caused him to drop his asparagus spears as he emerged into the sunshine.

The two figures on horseback turned toward the noise he had created. When they saw him, they laughed. It wasn't quite malicious laughter. It was more an I'm-so-sorry-for-you laugh. At that moment Father Pielke knew that they had a fortune somewhere; they had enough money to afford compassion. The woman pointed at the ground.

"You dropped it . . . your asparagus," she said. Her voice was soft and cultivated, faintly Eastern, as if she'd been to college in Massachusetts or somewhere else in New England. Father Pielke nodded and bent down to gather what he'd picked.

The woman's husband said, "Would you like some help?"

"No, thank you. No." He glanced up. "I'd only found a few spears anyway."

"Still." The man shrugged pleasantly. "Fresh asparagus. You must hold on to it. It's not to be wasted." The moment suspended itself between them, and then the man smiled in a friendly way. "I feel that we should introduce ourselves. I'm Burton Jordan," the man said. "And this is my wife, Mary Ellen." The man dismounted, gave the reins of the horse to his wife, and approached Father Pielke, his hand out. "Are you hurt?" he asked. "You're limping."

My father had never met anyone quite like Burton Jordan.

The man's hair was swept back and parted in the middle, Ivy League style, and he was physically imposing, as if he'd played hockey or polo in his youth. His smile was ingratiating and friendly, but his hooded eyelids gave to his face a faintly reptilian quality. He smelled of horse, saddle leather, sweat, and cologne.

"No, I'm all right. How do you do," my father said.

"Fine, thank you." Burton Jordan waited for a moment. "And you are . . . ?"

"Oh, sorry. Franz Pielke."

"Pleased to meet you. You must know something about plants if you can find asparagus in places like this, all this chaotic undergrowth."

"Well," my father smiled, "I do know something about plant life." He felt oddly nervous under the gaze of these two people. "Biology used to be my hobby, and now I teach it."

"Oh, really?" the woman asked. The sun was in my father's eyes, and because of the angle, and her height in the saddle, my father couldn't quite see her. "We've recently moved out here, into the country, and we're just terribly ignorant about all these wild things growing everywhere. We know nothing about it. It's rather scandalous. We really need somebody like you. We live over at Juniper Hill."

"Yes?" my father said. He had never heard of Juniper Hill.

"A few miles over," Burton Jordan said, tilting his head toward the northeast. "We rode this way from there. We've been living there for eighteen months now." He pronounced "been" like "bean." "In the middle of all the unknown and unidentified vegetation. The nameless ferns and anonymous trees. Would you like to see it? After all, you're our neighbor. We could ride you over there, and then, well, I suppose we could drive you back."

"Yes, yes," Mary Ellen Jordan said excitedly. "You must come with us. You must see Juniper Hill. You must tell us what is growing there. You must give names to everything. No arguments, please. Come up here, with me. Bring your asparagus. This horse—his name is Snooze—is stronger and younger than Burton's. It won't be a strain. You're slender."

"Excuse me?" my father asked.

Burton leaned forward toward my father. "My wife wants your company up there on her horse," he said. "Here." He cupped his hands together, and, without thinking, my father put his foot into Burton Jordan's hands and mounted the horse behind Mary Ellen.

"Hold on to the back of the saddle, if you need to," Mary Ellen said. "We'll go slowly. We'll take you to Juniper Hill. I won't do anything dangerous. Not unless you ask me to."

Burton had mounted his horse and was directing it down along a path my father hadn't noticed until now.

"I imagine you could put your arms around my waist if you feel yourself falling off," Mary Ellen said to my father, her face half-turned. "Is that being too forward? Possibly. Only in emergencies, then, Mr. Pielke."

"It's Father Pielke," he said. "I'm a priest."

She gave out a pleased shriek. "But you're not wearing your uniform, your soup-and-fish! How should I have known?"

"Well, we don't, always, you know. Sometimes, we—"

"Burton," Mary Ellen Jordan called out gaily. "This is wonderful. We've captured a priest!"

"Bravo," her husband called back.

Slowly, at the speed of a dream in which leaves are pulled aside from in front of us, they advanced over two cleared meadows and then directed their horses onto a path that led to a corridor between trees so high that they formed an overhead canopy. The afternoon sun broke through the branches and cast its light in unpatterned bursts on Mary Ellen Jordan's hair. Father

Pielke looked down. The woods, he noticed, had gone silent. The squirrels had stopped their customary chattering, the cawing of the crows had died away, and the other birds, usually so noisy with their mating cries, were curiously mute. The windless air surrounded them like a transparent, porous membrane through which they passed. The forest was so still that it might have been encased in amber. The horses walked on, occasionally snorting. The landscape first unrolled itself and then folded itself away. Nothing stirred.

It's because of the drought, Father Pielke thought. *This stillness. That's why it's so unearthly—the woods are dry.*

What time is it? he wondered. *I should be getting back to St. Boniface.* He clutched at his fourteen spears of asparagus. All at once a wind rose out of nowhere and lifted Mary Ellen Jordan's scarf, and the scarf brushed against his face. There was a scent of some flower embedded in the cloth. She was very pretty, he thought distantly, observing the languid movements of her back as she swayed in time to her horse. He could smell her perfume. Odd: to put on perfume to go riding. For what purpose? Well, such things didn't interest him anymore. In the wars of human love he had declared himself a noncombatant. Her hair brushed against his face.

Like every priest he had been through struggles of the flesh, but he had faithfully given over his body and its desires to God, and now he regarded his physical desires the way a museumgoer contemplates a display inside a glass case. Something powerful was there, but it was enclosed and would never get out again into the world, having been carefully labeled and methodically deprived of any further use. Physical longing had always seemed rather uncomplicated and unnuanced and didn't actually interest him very much.

Some priests are interested in sin, transfixed by it. Whereas my father was interested in light, and the designs of God in nature, and the designs of God in man.

I can barely put these words down in this order, but I must. He told me some of this but I'm making up the rest.

"We have captured you, Father Pielke," Mary Ellen Jordan laughed. "And now we are spiriting you away to our castle."

"Yes," he laughed gamely, in return. "I guess I've been kidnapped."

"To the dungeon with you," she said. "From now on, nothing but bread and water." After a pause, she said, "Don't mind me. We get a little bored sometimes out here. We play charades often, and it spills over into daily life. Could you play along, do you think?"

"All right. So what have I done?" he asked, trying to imagine what she meant by *charades*. "To be thrown in your dungeon, I mean."

"Oh, it's just that you're our neighbor. And you have been caught picking wild asparagus." They were now going down a dirt road, which had turned into a sort of driveway, and the road turned slightly to the right. "And we don't know enough people, and the country life sometimes gets us down. And now you must pay. *Voilà.*"

She pointed at the house. Father Pielke's first thought was that he had never seen anything like it, except perhaps in pictures, and his next thought was that it was impossible—no such country houses in this part of America.

Twenty-two upstairs windows faced the driveway—he was counting under his breath—and more than that downstairs, clustered together to the left of the porte-cochère, and the house was so large that from here, some distance away, Father Pielke couldn't see all of the exterior without turning his gaze back and forth. The eye couldn't take it all in in one glance. Despite its size, the house seemed strangely undetailed. It just went on and on and on in a disagreeable way, without what anyone would have called a style, its west-facing white stucco covered here and there by clinging vines and, on the north side of the house, a rose arbor, on which, however, nothing seemed to be growing. An ornamental brick structure the size of a shed on the south lawn had evidently once been used as a pump house; Father Pielke saw through one of its windows a hand pump inside. A vast front lawn gave way to a view of a lake in the distance, a lake he hadn't known about, perhaps privately owned. And the lawn! How was any of this mowed? Who mowed it?

"The caretaker keeps the place up," Mary Ellen Jordan said, apparently reading Father Pielke's thought. "His wife, Felicity, makes the beds. It's beyond us, all that work. And we have ten bedrooms," she continued, "to answer your question about accommodations. Do you think it's excessive? Well, I know it is. But tell me anyway. Be honest."

"You must have many children," Father Pielke said.

"We have one, our son, Edward, but he's at boarding school. So there's plenty of room for guests. Too much room, maybe. Sometimes the hallways echo. It looked grand when we bought it, but it is awfully . . . big." She laughed, a form of dry punctuation: ha ha, in the British manner. "I'm going to take this horse down to the stables. Can you dismount here, do you think?"

"Yes, certainly."

Dr. Foessern had set Franz Pielke's leg so that, although the bone had healed, the nerves had been damaged. Franz lived with intermittent pain just above his knee, and his broken and mended leg—he wasn't sure about the actual clinical reason for this—seemed somehow to be shorter than the other one. His body tilted when he put his weight on his right foot. Now, when he lifted this leg to get off the horse, he had a brief stab of pain in the usual place, which caused him to lose his balance. He felt himself falling toward the earth head first. He reached for the saddle but couldn't get any sort of grip. He landed with his arms out, breaking his descent.

"Oh my God," Mary Ellen said. "I'm so sorry! I should have helped you. Are you all right?" Quickly she got off the horse and eased him to his feet. She dusted off his shirt and picked up his hat. Then she bent over again and collected his asparagus. She had a certain absentminded kindness.

"Fine. I'm just—"

"—Ah, Father Pielke." Burton Jordan, having already stabled his horse, strode up the driveway with his arm out, like an old friend at a reunion, or a host at a party. He shook Father Pielke's hand again jovially. "It's about time we had a priest around here. Shocking, the things that happen at Juniper Hill without a priest to oversee our welfare. No spiritual direction at all. Welcome to Juniper Hill, in any case. You must come inside. Fix the moral climate. View all our waywardness." He was chuckling.

"Burton, dear, Father Pielke fell off Snooze. I wasn't careful helping him down. He might be shaken up. He's just recovering now from his fall."

"As are we all. Ha ha." They both did it, that laugh. "Are you all right? Come inside, Father. You seem unhurt. I see that you are smiling. Please come in. We could use the company. And please, bring your asparagus."

"I told him," Mary Ellen called to her husband as he and my father walked toward the front door, "that we would put him into the dungeon."

"Oh, she tells everyone that," Burton Jordan said. "It's an empty promise. I shouldn't be concerned, if I were you. It's just another one of our games. You'll have to try to get used to us." They came to the front door, with a lion's head knocker. "Do come in."

Father Pielke hesitated for a moment, then stepped inside.

* * *

It was gloomy and elegant. The polished wood gleamed darkly in the front hallway, which led toward a vast sitting room, the size of a lounge on an ocean liner. The rooms were so large that the furniture seemed to have been abandoned, rather than positioned, in the midst of all the empty space. In the living room a sort of bed-hammock hung by chains from the ceiling. The air pulsated with dust motes swirling in the light from the west windows. Pointing here and there as he walked, Burton Jordan explained that the house had been built on the site of a summer hotel that had burned to the ground in the 1880s, when it had been struck by lightning. The land had subsequently been bought by a lumber man named Van Dusen, who built the house, which had then been remodeled by its next owner, the president of the Detroit trolley company, Harold Goodrich. "The Depression came, and Goodrich went bust," Burton Jordan said, leading Father Pielke into the kitchen, where the cook was preparing dinner, broiled pheasant. As Father Pielke watched, the cook pried out several pieces of shot from the bird's breast. Blood leaked off the knife. Without thinking, he put down his asparagus on the kitchen counter. Father Pielke saw a servant's callboard above the doorway. On the board, Burton Jordan explained, each one of the bedrooms had a square, which turned white if a guest pressed a button on a call switch beside the bed. "We bought this place, all of Juniper Hill, for a pittance. You know, the banks foreclosed all these places. The Depression hit pretty hard out here. We had a bit of money from Mary Ellen's father. Grain business, milling and storage, that sort of thing." He paused, as if trying to think of something to say. "Would you like to see the ballroom? Or the billiard room? I expect you don't play billiards. But then I don't know. I don't run across many men in your line of work."

"What do you do?" Father Pielke asked. "If I may ask."

"You may. I'm a lawyer. I work in Detroit. Various kinds of law. Corporate law. Banks. And foreclosures, I'm afraid, are a

large part of my job. The last five years, I must say, the trade in
foreclosures has been quite brisk. It's sad, but . . ."

"That must be disheartening," Father Pielke said.

"My dear fellow, business is business. If I felt sorry for
everyone, I couldn't do my job. Naturally you see the other side
of it. You would have to. I do the money, and you do the feelings and faith. But we're not Catholics here. I can't sham that. I
expect you knew anyway. I fear our opinions are transparent. If
there's a hell, I suppose I'll end up there. Hell. What a curious
idea, and I must ask you about it sometime. It's the revenge of
the weak against the strong." Burton Jordan shifted his position. Close up, he had a massive, intelligent face, roughly handsome, but with an icy brutal expression of quick evaluation
that appeared every few moments just beneath the geniality.

"Nietzsche," Father Pielke said. "You've read Nietzsche."

"Yes. Good for you. Touché. The wonder is that you've read
him. I wouldn't expect a priest to know his writing. They let
you read Nietzsche in the seminary? They certainly don't let
you read Nietzsche now, do they? In church?"

"Well, when I was in school, our family doctor as a gift gave
me some volumes—"

"—Ah ha. The hometown sawbones. Good for him. Good
for you."

"Darling." Mary Ellen had appeared from behind them.
"Are you tormenting our priest? I think that's hardly fair. He's
just got here. Keep still with your opinions until the cocktail
hour. Come with me, Father." She took his arm and led him
away from her husband, who smiled and waved.

Never in my life, Father Pielke thought, have I spent an afternoon like this, with such people, nor will I ever again.

They went to the attic and inspected the game, hanging in
braces. They walked through the upstairs hallways, Mary Ellen

beside him, her hip occasionally knocking against him. She had a determined stride, and she gave the impression of physical strength; she was beautiful, my father thought, beautiful and slightly forlorn in this huge house. He noticed that most of the bedrooms, with their monstrous oak and maple furnishings, had fireplaces and Franklin stoves. "No central heating up here," Mary Ellen said with a laugh. "It's quite barbaric. We must remodel. Do you think, as you must, that this is all a bit pretentious?" She didn't wait for an answer. "Well, I do." Father Pielke found her curiosity about his opinions odd. A housemaid wearing an apron scurried from one room to another down at the end of the hallway. When she saw them, she curtsied before fleeing downstairs. "All the servants are frightened of us," Mary Ellen Jordan said, now walking ahead of Father Pielke at a brisk pace. She shook her head, laughing at herself. "I'm not quite sure what to do about it. It's not as if we can invite them to our parties. They have no conversation. All they can talk about is the weather. We bought this place—did Burton tell you?—fairly recently, and the times being what they are, it was quite a bargain. Burton had always wanted to live on an estate. He'd read Dickens, and all that. Traveled in Europe, viewed the stately homes. I'd read Thackeray, and Trollope. My God, the corruptions of literature. It put all these notions into our heads. Now we're living in one of Burton's novels. Buying this old place may not have been a good idea, but we did it."

She turned around at the bottom of the stairs and glanced in his direction. "What is it? Do I have something in my hair?"

"No, excuse me, I'm sorry," he said. "My mother had hair the same color as yours."

"Ah." She smiled with an expression of grim triumph. "And is she still living, your mother?"

"No, she isn't." She had died of a sudden stroke, but he was not about to reveal a detail of that sort to these people.

"So there you are," Mary Ellen Jordan said, noncommittally.

"That's such a shame, isn't it." She spoke this sentence as if it were not a question. "Well, I shan't get personal with you, dear Father Pielke. It wouldn't do. We mustn't stage the Reformation, or is it the Inquisition, all over again. Don't mind my teasing. Playacting is an old habit around here. We have to fill the hours. Come into the library. I'd serve you a martini if you weren't a man of the cloth. Ah, Burton, here we are, back again from our excursion, our little tour."

Burton Jordan was sitting in a blood-red leather wing chair, reading the London *Illustrated News*. He had not changed clothes. They were two of the silliest people, my father thought, that he had ever met, but he couldn't quite dismiss them, and now, coming into the library, he felt slightly off-balance again.

From floor to ceiling on three substantial walls the bookshelves held volumes bound in leather, mostly books from the previous century—he saw a complete set of Macaulay's essays next to bound volumes of Shakespeare—but with some more recent books, too. One shelf held collections of poetry, T. S. Eliot, Ezra Pound, Stephen Vincent Benet, Robinson Jeffers, and Archibald MacLeish. There was no fiction from the twentieth century in the room, but the poetry went up to the ceiling: Goethe, Heine, and Eichendorff, Edna St. Vincent Millay, Conrad Aiken, W. B. Yeats, and Amy Lowell. There was a complete set of the Harvard Classics, with gold and blue bindings. The next shelves, just above the library stepladder, held the philosophy books: a complete set of Nietzsche, volume after volume of José Ortega y Gasset, Santayana, Marx, Freud, and William James. Next to James's *The Varieties of Religious Experience* was Adolf Hitler's *Mein Kampf*.

"This is quite a library," Father Pielke said.

"Aren't you nice," Mary Ellen said, picking a hair off her blouse. "Well, Burton went to Yale, and law school at Harvard, and it seems to have got him into the habit of reading, and we read to each other, and that's how we ended up out here. Of course a library is so, I don't know, distinguished. Restful. Don't you think?"

"Oh, stop badgering him, darling," Burton Jordan said, from behind the London *Illustrated News*. "He's a priest. You're taking advantage. 'Restful.'" He snorted.

"I'm not taking advantage. My husband, Burton, you know," she said, whispering conspiratorially in my father's direction, "was a friend of Thornton Wilder and he was Bob Coates' roommate, and that literary crowd. You know, sometimes I like it better when Burton is off fishing or hunting. When he reads, I just don't always know where he is. Could you possibly know what I mean?"

"Yes," my father said, although he didn't, exactly. "I'm afraid I have to go. I must get back home."

"We'll get Harold to drive you back in the Chrysler. Oh, my heavens!"

"What?" Burton Jordan looked up.

"Father Pielke hasn't labeled a single plant for us. We're just as in the dark as we ever were. I just *hate* being ignorant. Well, you must come back. Burton, dear, how shall we ever persuade our priest to return?"

"Invite him for dinner. You've got to come back, Father. We need company."

"Dinner? He wouldn't enjoy that, would you, Father? No, I don't think so. Roast beef and mashed potatoes? That's not much incentive." She was leaning back, considering. "Father, would you accept a contribution to your parish, or whatever you call it, if you were to come back?"

Intrigued by its title, *The Revolt of the Masses,* my father had pulled a book off the shelves and was glancing through it. Without quite thinking, he said, "Oh, yes, certainly." A moment later he closed the book and understood what he had just agreed to.

"We'll make it worth your while. Why don't you borrow that book?" Burton Jordan said from his wing chair. "It's not about your Masses, you know. It's about the other masses. The moronic masses. Parasitism. Quite good reading, though you might not like it. Borrow it and bring it back."

"Oh," my father said, "I couldn't do that."

But somehow they persuaded him to take the book. They called Harold, the caretaker and part-time chauffeur, and the gigantic Chrysler was brought up from somewhere, and my father was taken back to St. Boniface in it, carrying *The Revolt of the Masses*. The astonished housekeeper saw him emerge from this sleek black car as she peered out from the rectory window. He had left his fourteen spears of asparagus back in the kitchen of Juniper Hill, where the cook, not having been instructed about what to do with them, and not having the nerve to ask, threw them into the trash.

The Jordans had already invited my father to come out on Saturday afternoon of the following week. He had declined the invitation, and then, thinking of the money they had promised him, had said that perhaps he would be able to come, but he would have to consult his immediate superior, which was not quite true. He didn't think of his lost asparagus, however, until he had arrived back in St. Boniface and was clothing himself in his vestments. He had been looking out of the window and was thinking of a line from Augustine's *Confessions*—something about Augustine and his mother at the window in Ostia—and it was then that he remembered what he had struggled to find, and had lost.

3

I think of this now—my father, the young priest, somehow imagining that he could improve the lot of his poverty-stricken parish by becoming an acquaintance of the richest couple in the county—and I see him, with his thoughtfulness, his eagerness, and his optimism, riding back to Juniper Hill the following week in the black Chrysler touring car that had been sent forth to fetch him, and I want to tell him that he is being toyed with, that the Jordans are playing with him, that he is an amusement for them, these two rich, intelligent, Anglophile Americans, living out in the countryside on their huge nondescript estate modeled on those pictured in English novels.

Across the years, to this desk, to the left of which is the picture of Joseph Goebbels glaring with severe murderousness toward the lens, my father says, in some part of my imagination, what he never did in fact say to me, which is: *Don't worry. I knew what I was doing. I saw through them immediately. I knew who I was. I had my faith. They did not really intimidate me after that first visit, not really. They were silly and shallow, despite their education. You cannot break the integrity of a man who lives in the spirit.*

And I say, *Her hair, the color of gold coins.*

4

My father told Burton Jordan to buy a notebook, and he did, a big leather-bound thing in which the Master of the House drew, in various colors, the plants he had discovered accompanied by his friend the priest and identified with the priest's help. Like a schoolgirl, Burton Jordan inserted flattened flowers between the pages. It is incredible to me that he followed my father's instructions in these matters, but he did.

Burton Jordan's book is here on my desk. Its outward smell is of dust and leather. It takes up most of the space not taken up with the typewriter. When I remove it from where it lies, to drop it back on the pile of other documents, several plants from sixty years ago fall out. Their light scents have aged inside the pages, and they have taken on the acrid sweet-foul odor of compost.

Trillium, cinquefoil, hawkweed, bellwort, foxglove, bluebell.

In his restlessness, Burton Jordan hunted deer in the fall, shot ducks on a game reserve in northern Minnesota owned by a like-minded company of friends with whom he was a partner; restlessness had taken him toward polo, and then away from it, before he had an opportunity to break his neck; to fishing, in lakes and rivers all over Michigan; he shot at grouse and pheasant, cleaned them and hung them in the attic before serving them with excellent wines stored in the cellar from before Prohibition. He explained all this to my father.

In his restlessness Burton Jordan must have read the classics, because I have a copy of *The Meditations of Marcus Aurelius* with his signature in it. I own his copy of *The Revolt of the Masses,* which my father forgot to return. Penciled commentary litters the margins. On page 202, Ortega y Gasset writes, "As regards other kinds of Dictatorship, we have seen only too well how they flatter the mass-man, by trampling on everything that appeared to be above the common level." In the margin next to this sentence, Burton Jordan penciled, "Roosevelt!"

He quarreled with Ortega on page 130: Gunpowder did not doom the supremacy of the nobles and their armor. *"Sed quare?"* Burton Jordan inquired in the margin. "Armor could resist arrows no better than gunshot. Inability to maneuver doomed the man in armor." He corrected Ortega in a small detail about the Swiss army, perhaps a bourgeois army but not because of firearms. "Used pikes, not firearms," he noted. Burton Jordan had, it seems, a thorough education and a good intelligence in search of a set of ideals capable of counteracting the mass man and his laxity and nondiscipline.

On page 201, next to "there will not be found amongst all the representatives of the actual period, a single group whose attitude to life is not limited to believing that it has all the rights and none of the obligations," he wrote, "Conf: 'Mein Kampf.'"

5

"Welcome, welcome, Father. Care to shoot today? Try your aim?"

Fall: a blue-gold autumnal afternoon, and with his customary affable and hearty handshake Burton Jordan met Father Pielke as the priest climbed out of the hearselike Chrysler. Cradled in Burton Jordan's left arm was his shotgun. He was dressed in weekend hunting gear, multipocketed vest heavy with shotgun shells, light olive cotton knickers with calf-high heather gray woolen socks, and Tyrolean hat with goat's-beard brush—the full array for the sporting weekend soldier. It occurred to my father, seeing Burton Jordan in his hunting costume, that he had forgotten to bring back Jordan's copy of *The Revolt of the Masses* again.

"Shoot what?" Father Pielke tried to smile. "Squirrels?"

"Heavens, no. Clay pigeons. Come around in back."

On the terraced backyard, facing the lake, Mary Ellen Jordan stood, garbed in plus fours and severe black leather shoes, aiming her gun out toward the water. An open box of clay pigeons sat near the terrace wall and the rearranged lawn furniture, removed from the front of the yard for the sake of the shooting. She shouted, "Pull!" and a clay pigeon, thrown out by an invisible trap directly below the wall, was launched into the air. She aimed and fired. The blast echoed, my father noticed, for about four seconds. The sound traveled down the hill and rolled back up. If there had been neighbors, they would have heard it, but Juniper Hill as a parcel of land was so immense that there could have been no neighbors, at least none within hearing distance. The airborne disc blew apart so quickly and thoroughly that it seemed to vaporize. After it shattered, Father Pielke couldn't see its pieces falling.

"Nice shot, darling," Burton Jordan said. "Look who's here."

"Ah." She turned to see him, and her blond hair swung around. She smiled in a half-snarling, half-pleased way. She was taking shallow excited breaths. Her face was flushed. Her eyes were as bright and as hard as diamonds. On first sight she seemed to be a few inches off the ground with exhilaration. When she nodded and looked at him, Father Pielke felt it in the pit of his stomach. At some intellectual distance, he recognized her excitement as sexual. She was so pretty, he thought, and there was nothing to be done about it. "Thank God you're here. I've missed you. Our handsome gray-eyed priest. On this divine day. Out of his dungeon for an hour or two. Oh, do give him your shotgun, Burton."

"Ever fired anything, Father?"

"Well, you know I—"

"It's a Browning double-barreled twelve-gauge. Here's the safety. Trigger's down here. Nothing to it, of course. Lead your aim ahead of the wicked pigeon, and the thing will be doomed. Give it a try, and we'll applaud and pat you on the back."

"Yes," Mary Ellen Jordan said. "We'll hoot and holler."

Several guests—there were sometimes guests at Juniper Hill on Saturdays to whom Father Pielke was not introduced—watched from fifty feet behind them. They murmured and chuckled and drank, with a collective sound like the gurgling of happy fish. They were the audience for this show, the show in which the local priest would be invited to practice his marksmanship. Father Pielke now noticed that Burton Jordan had picked up a stein of beer from the lawn. On one side of the stein, Father Pielke could see a college name printed near the top, and then, in the center, a broken Latinate triangle.

VE RI
TAS

On the other side of the stein was one word below a crest.

LUX

"Here," Mary Ellen continued. She put the butt of her husband's Browning against my father's shoulder, aligned his hands, and released the safety. "Close your left eye," she said. "Sight down here. See?"

"Yes," Father Pielke said. "Actually, I've done this before."

"Have you?" Burton Jordan took a quick swig of his beer. He shook his head with ironic sadness. "Probably we shouldn't get you back into the habit of using firearms, though. Not good for a priest's daily work, a twelve-gauge. We'll fill your head with ideas, but, well, no harm done, except for, you know, the inevitable progress of sin. Gives a person a feel for the other side. Ready?" My father nodded. "Pull!" Burton Jordan shouted.

A clay pigeon flew out. Father Pielke followed it and squeezed the trigger. The shotgun roared and kicked his shoulder. He had missed, as he had expected he would. He hadn't fired a shotgun since he was seventeen, when he had killed rats in the barn, following his father's orders. Under his breath, he muttered, out of habit, *"Um Himmels Willen."* For heaven's sake. Laughter and smiles and louder murmuring arose from the happy fish gurgling behind him in the shadows. "Well, we don't expect men of the cloth to be crack shots, do we?" Burton Jordan asked, taking another sip of beer.

"No," Mary Ellen said, "we don't." She waited. "What *do* we expect? We're too unpredictable."

"There's the question," her husband said. "There it is."

"Try again, Father," Mary Ellen suggested. "It's still loaded. Two triggers, you'll notice. There's another one in back."

"Yes." After putting the safety on, and holding the barrel up, Father Pielke made as if to hand the shotgun to Burton Jordan, who did not take it.

"I think you should shoot again," the host said. "Show your mettle and all that. Nothing's ever achieved the first time through."

"But I'm out of practice these days," Father Pielke said. "It's not my line." He wasn't in his vestments, but he suspected that he still looked like a priest to them, no matter how he was dressed.

"Be that as it may. Play up, play up, and play the game," Burton Jordan said, grinning. He strategically used his charm to bully, Father Pielke noticed. He was one of those.

"Didn't you like it?" Mary Ellen asked. "Try again!" More

quietly, she said, "It's odd how you'll come to enjoy doing this. Really."

"All right," Father Pielke said. "Though I don't quite see the point." He limped forward to get a better stance.

"Well," Mary Ellen said, "the point is, you don't want to be just another one of those fussy little church men who can't do anything at all, do you?"

"Now wait a minute," my father said. He checked the safety again and then lowered the gun to waist level. With a flick of his thumb he cracked open the barrel. "I think the day is now over," he said. "You'd better call the car to take me home. I'm done here."

"Oh, now, Father, don't be like that, don't take offense. We were just—"

"—I know what you were doing, Mrs. Jordan. I wouldn't want you to misunderstand. I've appreciated your hospitality in the past, of course. You can make jokes at my expense, if you like; I don't really mind that. I haven't minded. But I won't stay here if you continue to mock my Church. Or my faith. Those are sacred things to me. For them I don't apologize. I'm sorry, but I won't stay here to be the excuse for that kind of mockery. I won't be a show for you." He made an effort to hand the twelve-gauge to Burton Jordan, on whose face an oddly serious look had suddenly appeared.

"I thought you probably had limits," Burton Jordan said, for a second time refusing to take the gun back in hand. "I said so to Mary Ellen. Good. I'm glad that you do. Now see here, Father Pielke, we weren't trying—"

"—The saving of souls," my father said, interrupting him. "Is that fussy?"

"Oh, well . . ." Mary Ellen replied. "Souls! That's rather grand language, isn't it?"

"Yes." He waited. "It's rather grand language."

He bent down and reached into the box of clay pigeons.

They were small discs, about the size of a hand, with lowered edges. He picked one out. "That's what I do. It's my calling. Take this gun, Mr. Jordan." It was the first time he had ever told Burton Jordan to do anything, and the act felt deeply satisfying. Burton Jordan did as he was asked. "Souls are delicate," my father said. "They break. Like this thing."

My father threw the clay pigeon against the low brick wall. It shattered against the brick with a popping sound, and the party guests behind them grew silent for a moment.

"*Exemplum.*" Burton Jordan smiled. "All right, you've made your point. Now shoot again, please." He handed the gun back to my father.

The handing back and forth of guns had a certain ritualistic importance, my father realized.

Father Pielke reset the barrel, switched off the safety, and called, "Pull!" He aimed, fired, and managed to break off the righthand side of the airborne target. When his hearing cleared after the firing, he heard scattered applause. In spite of himself, he felt a quick subtle thrill of pleasure and pride as he handed the Browning to Burton Jordan.

"Hullo." Burton Jordan had glanced to his right. A crow, in a rush of black, apparently frightened by the gunshots, had flown up from the woods to their left and into the space where the clay pigeon had been a moment before. Mary Ellen lifted her gun so quickly that my father didn't even notice her arm movements. The crow flew in a zigzag feverish pattern. Then it was dead and falling, the impact of Mary Ellen's shot throwing the bird outward and dropping it through the air to the bottom of the hill—a long way—in a slow spiral.

"Crows are out of season, dear," Burton Jordan said, chuckling, glancing down the hill to see where the crow had landed. "Good shot, though. Damn thing's as dead as Marley."

"Well, this isn't any crow we'll have to eat."

The color was back in her cheeks. My father saw that she

had a taste not just for gunplay but for blood sport. He had never observed it in a woman before. She was so aroused the tips of her ears were reddening. She looked directly at my father, and he saw her bright teeth, the look of a wolf, animal to animal. Her husband at that moment gave her a prolonged pat on the shoulder, a gesture full of the long intimacy of marriage.

"Congratulations," Father Pielke said.

"Yes," her husband said. "Splendid shooting. Well done."

My father heard a rustling sound, a dry scratching, and turned to his right to see what it was. Just a catalpa tree with long brown seed pods, breeze-blown. Then he felt it coming on him. He thought: uh oh. He'd had these moments before, when time stopped. He gazed at the thick leaves of the catalpa tree. Now, to his right, the Jordans' guests held their drinks motionless in the air, and one woman in a light blue outfit and too much powder and rouge on her face froze in mid-laugh. A kind of fluted shadow-ecstasy traveled up my father's chest and nestled in his heart. Mary Ellen Jordan was still smiling at him, still showing her perfect teeth, but he could look back at her without being recognized, because he had been taken inside this rapture and she . . . well, she resided somewhere else. She was *in* time, going on, completing her smile, ready to do whatever came next. For my father, though, time had halted. But he could still move inside its nonmovement. It was no use explaining these pockets of timelessness to anyone, because no one else he knew had ever experienced them. God did this to him, but for what purpose my father did not yet understand. Inside my father, stillness had taken over the back terrace of Juniper Hill. Nothing stirred.

There they all were, the Jordans and their guests, and the black Labrador, Bertie, standing behind them, his tongue out, and his tail stopped in mid-wag; and the butler with his tray of drinks, his left arm extended like a department store mannequin, grasping a drained highball glass, vestigial ice cubes still at the bottom; and over there, the catalpa tree, immobilized. Everything and everyone transfixed. No breath of air trembled a single leaf. A bird, a sparrow, rigid, was hanging in the air to his left, as if pasted there to the sky. Was this some kind of blessedness—hadn't St. Theresa of Avila reported on such moments?—or was it the beginning manifestation of epilepsy? On the lake, the waves curled and then confounded any sequence of anything by not moving anywhere, in any direction. Where was he, my father, in all this?

Inside his body my father's spirit turned toward the sun, but the sun's rays were blocked by the house; they did not want him. He heard two bell tones, one high, the other in the middle range, the range of the human voice. In front of him, and invisible, but like a sheet of wound fabric, eternity unrolled haphazardly. Inside his body his spirit bowed its head. *Lord,* he asked, *what is Your will? What do You ask of me?*

Squeezed from the things in front of him and behind him came this:

There is no death.
That which is, shall never die.
There is a plan. And you must suffer for it.

"Father Pielke!" Mary Ellen Jordan touched his shoulder. "Father Pielke! Yoo hoo. Gracious. You get such looks on your face, I can't bear it sometimes!"

"Sorry." He rubbed his forehead.

"Such a faraway look. Is our catalpa so magnificent?"

"It's a beautiful tree," he said.

"Yes," Burton Jordan agreed. "Quite beautiful. Large white blossoms in late spring." He waited. "Bit of a mess with the bean pods, though, this time of year."

"He goes into spells, our priest," Mary Ellen said to no one in particular, shaking her head, fiercely preening. "He's here, and then, well, he isn't here, for seconds at a time. Whatever are you thinking, Father? I worry about you. Mustn't go through life in a daze!"

"He's probably thinking of his Sunday sermon. Am I right, Father Pielke?"

"In a way," my father said.

"You look like a man in love," Mary Ellen Jordan said, gazing at him with ironic gloom. "In love with a tree. Rather a safe love, I should say. Well, I shouldn't say such things at all. It's quite tactless, I admit it. In any case, welcome back to the world." She whispered something to her husband, and her husband nodded.

"My wife," Burton Jordan confided, in a low tone, "rather likes it when you get into those states. She's quite keen on believers. And partisans of every stripe. They bring her to a low boil. But enough of this. Back to our shooting. Remind me to show you something later, Father."

My father watched as the man and the woman of the house practiced their aim for the next half hour, firing shot through one clay pigeon after another. Mary Ellen's percentage of hits was higher than her husband's, Father Pielke noticed. She was a woman of practiced but whimsical sensuality. How odd she would be, if she ever discovered she had a soul. She'd probably try to sell it, first thing.

By late afternoon, he had been escorted back into the library. The books gave off their customary aloofness and comfortable tedium. The air smelled of dusty leather and gin. Somewhere else in the mansion, just barely audible, guests were clinking the ice in their highballs and laughing. Father Pielke had been given a glass of brackish-tasting iced tea. A soggy mint leaf floated on the surface. He was sitting on the sofa waiting for Burton

Jordan to come down from upstairs and reading a book of essays about English agrarian revolts in the early sixteenth century when he heard his host's footsteps.

"Ah. Here we are." Jordan came into the library, waving a check. For the first time, Father Pielke noticed that over the entrance to the library, above the lintel, was a recessed shelf on which rested a plaster reproduction, about twelve inches high, of a Cathedral of Notre Dame gargoyle, painted brown, horned, head in hands, tongue out, miming contempt. "Something for your time, Father. Made out to your parish. I'm sure they can use it. If there's anything irregular here, let me know."

My father glanced at the check. The gargoyle glared down at him. The check was for the sum of three hundred fifty dollars. He felt a split-second of pleasure, but only that: pleasing as the gift was, he had been expecting more. Burton Jordan's generosity was a bit drab.

"Thank you." He waited. "It'll be put to good use. We need—"

"—Don't mention it." Burton Jordan waved his hand and smiled. When he smiled, his canine teeth, which were sharply pointed, gave him the appearance of an elegant silver screen vampire. "You've been kind to come out, kind to help us here. Your usual tasks must take up most of your schedule, after all."

"Yes. But I like to get away to your house, to Juniper Hill, if I can." He swallowed, making an effort to stay on the side of truth. In this place, he wasn't always sure where truth lay, or whether he should care. "It's so beautiful here. It's quite a change for me."

"Good of you to say so." Burton Jordan sat down in the wing chair. "I suppose it's not your usual fare. What do you usually do on Saturdays, Father Pielke?"

"Why don't you call me Franz?"

"All right. Franz. What do Saturdays hold for you?"

"It depends. I'm the assistant priest in the parish. I visit the sick and . . . well, the dying. I perform weddings and baptisms. Funerals, on occasion. My parishioners come to talk. Our parish is like so many others. I assist Father Martin in hearing confessions, and I—"

"—Yes, yes." Burton Jordan nodded his head quickly and impatiently. He was not very good at listening; he didn't do it willingly. "Tell me, does it bore you, ever?"

"Bore me? No, not very often. That's an odd question."

"Well." Burton Jordan lifted his head, as if he were thinking. "The truth is, I don't quite understand you, Father. I have never really known any Catholics before, much less priests. My family members were never acquainted with any of them. My father was a doctor who practiced in Minneapolis, and he considered Catholics to be rather, shall we say, ground floor. We were all lapsed Protestants, you know, my parents and great grandparents, and Unitarians, when we were religious at all. My father used to read Ralph Waldo Emerson to us in a loud voice. I don't have any feeling for what you call your faith. It's a mystery to me."

"It's a holy mystery," Father Pielke said.

"No, no, that's not what I mean at all." Burton Jordan fixed my father with a steady look. He leaned back, handsome and shrewd, and the leather creaked. In his way, he seemed fatigued. "I mean that I don't understand why anyone would really *want* to believe what you believe. I don't get it. Look around this room, Father Pielke. This library is full, it's choked, with history, with stories. Some of these stories are about your Church, during the Middle Ages, and some of them are about other matters, and all of them give us accounts of what humans have done and what they like to do."

"Yes?"

"Well." Burton Jordan stood up. He towered, a bit, over Father Pielke. He did it for effect. "People do what they like to do, don't you think? I think so. And what they like to do, Franz, if you're asking me, is as follows." He leaned forward, as if he were addressing the boardroom. "Men like to hunt and to kill. Their aim is to dominate. They take considerable pleasure in it. They like power. They all try to get power over one another. They enjoy the shedding of blood. Bloodshed never bores anyone, does it, have you noticed? Young men gang together by blood instinct, and they hold territory by blood instinct, and they rampage. They have leaders and foot soldiers and initiations. These hierarchies are written into our brain cells. Men like to take women." He stopped, sat down again in the leather chair, and crossed his legs. "Give them half a chance, they'll just take as many women as they can, unless some ponderous morality stops them. A few men are born to lead, but most have a slave mentality. Some men conquer, and some men work in the post office. That's how it is. Most want a strong leader, a warrior, to lead them. They have no clue otherwise. They must be convinced that their subservience is to a common good."

He took a breath and smiled. He was pleased with what he was saying.

"Patriotism is an effective sham to get the lower orders in line. Read Machiavelli. And the women, their role in all this? Well, women like to be overwhelmed, don't they? They seem to. The ones with intellect don't use it, that's my impression. Never have. They just scurry around. Men—men of courage—live on power and lust and warfare, Father. Perhaps it's a shame, but that's how it is. There are those who build and create, and then there are the parasites. I'm sorry. I'm making speeches. All the rest of this"—he waved his arm toward the terrace, visible through the back windows—"is theater. I'm a student of history. History tells me is that it's always been this way. Power is the force that drives life forward. The battlefield clarifies everything. The battlefield is the laboratory of human character. Life isn't about anything else. Aggression isn't original sin. It's where life starts from, what it's about. It certainly isn't about love."

He was speeding up. The smile had almost disappeared from Burton Jordan's face. The buttons of his blazer glowed and sparkled. His smile twinkled with practiced insincerity.

"If you ask me, and I know you haven't, Jesus lied." Burton Jordan raised his eyebrows in mock astonishment at his own statement. "His lies were so attractive that people believed him. You see these silly baffled women in church. They pray that the lies of Jesus are true. You see them clucking on the sidelines of the arena. Women and children live in illusion. Men shouldn't. They can't. That's why I don't understand you. I like you. Why don't you admit that men enjoy warfare? That may be bitter news, but it must be acknowledged. And what your Church does is to pretend that what I've said isn't the case. But it is. Every man with guts, and some experience of the world, and a decent respect for truth, will say so. Only the sheltered and the self-deceived think otherwise. You take Hitler, for example. This fellow Hitler is a rabble-rouser and a boor, but at least he says what he means." He held out a silver bowl. "Care for some cashews?"

"No, thank you." Father Pielke waited a moment. "People accuse *me* of sermonizing. You seem to have a taste for it, too."

"Well, I'm a lawyer. It's a habit. No doubt I've offended you."

"You haven't," Father Pielke said. "I . . . I know those arguments." He was trying to think of Burton Jordan as an exhibit of something, but he couldn't think of what. He found it difficult to accept, week after week, kindness and generosity from a man he thought was entertaining and dislikable. All these social ideas—who cared about them, anyway?

"And you disagree?"

"No, I don't disagree." From the side table, he picked up a

small paper knife, used for slicing through uncut book pages, and balanced its tip on his finger. "Not exactly."

"Well, then?"

"Burton, I'm just a country priest. I can't do apologetics. But why debate this?" Father Pielke asked. "You've read all these books. Okay. But they're just observations, and you're pretending that they're facts. But they aren't. They're opinions. If they were facts, you wouldn't have to try to convince a harmless guy like me." He was beginning to sound like a Jesuit. They both were. He stopped himself, then continued. "You're a gentleman of education and leisure with a hankering for the battlefield. Well, fine. All I know is that ours is a fallen world, with all its cruelty, but I'm not convinced that we're destined to behave like the brutes you claim we are. It's not inevitable. It isn't. I *know* it isn't."

"How do you know? Whose opinion should I have?

"Well, God's, of course. And it's not an opinion."

"Oh. I see. God's. There you are. Please, Father Pielke, don't be sanctimonious with me. Your virtues are cloistered and celibate. But I can tell that your intelligence is not. Well, let's not argue anymore. I like you too much. Oh, by the way. I said I had something to show you."

"Yes. You did." Father Pielke held on to the letter opener. He was no longer aware that it was in his hand. By now, Burton Jordan had pulled down, from a high shelf, a branch with small bright yellow flowers and was holding it out for examination.

"Do you recognize this?"

My father glanced at it quickly. "Certainly," he said. "It's witch hazel."

Burton Jordan put it between the leaves of his plant book and began to label it.

"If you don't mind my asking," Father Pielke said, "how do you reconcile all your social theories with this interest in identifying plants?"

Burton Jordan closed his book, straightened up and smiled. "A gentleman," he said, as if he were reciting a phrase from a conduct manual, "knows the names of all the vegetation on his land. Franz, are you going to assault me?" He pointed at the knife in my father's hand.

"Oh, sorry." My father put it back on the table.

"Bit of the beast in you." Burton Jordan chuckled again.

6

They took him to the basement. There he saw the room filled with wet cell batteries for the electric lighting. (Rural electrification came to Juniper Hill the following year.) He saw the storage room with its shelves of canned stewed tomatoes. Applesauce in Mason jars. Tomato juice in Mason jars. The tomato juice was sometimes improperly prepared. Air got into it. It would ferment. Then it would explode, blistering the walls of the room with reddish ooze. Someone in a servant's uniform was always cleaning up the mess down there, with tomato-stained mops and pails. They took him back to the billiard room with its cozy inlaid woodwork. It seemed as if they were always giving him some tour or other of the house and the grounds. It occurred to Father Pielke, as he was guided, once again, through the tiresome chandeliered dining room toward the ballroom, that the whole point of Juniper Hill was to excite admiration and envy. The visitor was roughly forced, bullied, into feeling enchantment. Without enchantment there was no point to any of it. Without enchantment it was just pumpkin time. My father's visible boredom with the sheen and glitter sent both the Jordans into frenzies of charm, charm without letup, charm cloaked in anecdote, a relentless unsatisfied sadistic sociability. They even offered to have his portrait painted.

Why was he there? What had he done? He had mastered one version of nature, with his detailed knowledge of living created things, their names and attributes, and the Jordans wanted that for themselves, the Father Pielke version, so they could entertain their friends with it. They wanted everything money could buy. Now they had a pet priest in a silver kennel. Who else had that? They had large appetites, and they could buy in quantity. They didn't want to believe his version of anything; they just wanted to own it.

But when they focused their attention on him, he couldn't turn away. He felt the onset of a large event among the three of them, huge and lifesaving, and its excitement for him was not lessened by his not knowing what it would be.

He had studied and learned to love the details of forests and fields through which he had limped, bordering the houses of his parishioners. He still owned the notebooks from his childhood to prove it. He had disciplined himself to love those who came to Mass at St. Jerome's, had heard their confessions, understood their strengths and frailties. The old ladies have told me that he was a good priest, absentminded, maybe, and prone to daydreaming, but a wonderful listener all the same. Not a brilliant priest, but patient and kind. In a farm community no one wants a brilliant priest around anyway. They want a child of farmers in priest's robes. In their houses he would chat, discuss the crops and the weather, pass the time, listen, and give counsel. He would be stern or gentle, depending on what the situation and the love of God called for.

He was a simple man, and his faith was straightforward. And of course he was handsome. There was that, too.

He had much in the world to love. He was celibate physically but his soul was prodigal in its passion and loving kindness for the world he inhabited, plain as it was. But the Jordans had introduced a taste for a grand prize in him; they had planted an ambition in him. That's my guess.

The Jordans saw their chance. And they pounced.

By August they told him they were planning on going to Germany the following summer, the summer of 1938. They were interested in the great social experiment, they said. They wanted to take him along. He spoke perfect German, after all. He was a requirement. He was an absolute necessity.

You must come with us, they both said. Please. Dear Father Pielke, we need you. You must see it all for yourself. We will reward you handsomely. Come to Germany, they said to my father. History is being made there. It's the wave of the future. You must accompany us on our travels. You must agree. Mary Ellen Jordan's eyes glittered with a sort of feral charm, fixing him with harsh aggressive insistence. Inform your bishop, or whoever is next in the pecking order, that we will give a generous gift to your church, a memorable gift, if only you come with us. A gift of considerable size! And a gift to the archdiocese, if that's necessary. We will talk to the bishop himself, if need be. We won't call it a bribe. We'll find another name for it. Money will not be an issue. Money is never an issue. Why should it be? And of course all your expenses will be paid.

Really, they said, with their suave manners. Really, do you have a choice?

He inhaled their perfumes. He would win them over. He would return to his parish with thousands of dollars as a reward for his services.

I see them smiling, and their white furniture pleasantly arrayed out there on the immense preposterous elm-shaded lawn, the happy couple beaming at my father, amused at the great joke, amused at themselves, at what they have concocted, their plan to spirit their handsome priest, their interpreter, off with them into the Black Forest, just like the Erlking carrying away his stolen goods.

Unlike my father, I am not a Catholic. Nor am I particularly scrupulous about my language or my feelings. This is my version, my imaginings, of what happened, no one else's. Therefore, I can say what I want to say. And what I say from my distance of fifty years forward into the future is, God damn both of them.

7

"I met your father soon after we moved to St. Boniface. I was seventeen, and my father—your grandfather—was a pharmacist. But you know that, of course."

I nod. I ask my mother to continue. The cut flowers I have brought in, mostly snapdragons, for their brilliant yellow and red colors, stand in a vase on her coffee table close to the ashtray. She curls her mouth up skeptically.

"I really don't see the point in this, Jack. The past is . . . well, sometimes the past is best left in the past, don't you think? Sometimes you just stir things up by bringing it all back."

"Your father was a pharmacist," I say, prompting her. "Grandfather Ed. Speak into the microphone, okay? It's over here."

"All right." She exhales impatiently, a sound I know very well. She touches her hair with her hand, a nervous gesture. "Yes. A pharmacist. A druggist. He was the druggist in St. Boniface. I helped him in there, after school. I cleaned up at the end of the day and helped with the accounts, and sometimes I worked behind the soda fountain. The previous druggist had, I don't know, retired or something. Or the doctors dispensed their own medicines. People moved out of that town when they could. Wasn't a very pleasant place. Bland and dusty and flat. Are you sure you want to know about all this?"

I assure her that I do. I tell her, again, how valuable her memories are.

"You're mistaken," she says, and there is a long silence. I smile at her, to urge her on, but she won't smile back. Just when I start to wonder what I will have to do to get her to start talking again, she takes a hankie out of her pocket, blows her nose, glares and smiles at me simultaneously, then continues. "Drugstores have to be very clean. They're not like hardware stores. Customers don't like the least little speck of dirt in a drugstore. Makes them think the pills are dusty. Can't have that. So, anyway, I swept and mopped and dusted and straightened. I worked late sometimes. Your father, he was Father Pielke then, came in sometimes to chat with us. I noticed him. He was one of the two priests at St. Jerome's. Maybe I even talked to him. I don't remember."

My mother is lying to me—I'm sure of it—so I get aggressive. "Did you find him attractive?"

"What kind of question is that? Really, Jack. For heaven's sake."

"I don't know." I shrug. "An ordinary question."

"It's not an ordinary question when you're talking about a priest, Jack, or your own father. Use some judgment. What are you suggesting?"

"Come on, Ma. This is only a little family history. All I asked was if you found him attractive."

"Well, of course I did, dear. Now turn that thing off." She points at my cassette tape recorder. "Turn it off."

"All right." I pick the recorder up and fiddle with the volume control. The recorder keeps on running. "Okay, it's off," I tell my mother.

"Why are you asking me all this? You know this whole story. You've heard this story before many times. You're making me feel like a monkey on a leash." She waits for a moment. "No, that isn't the right expression, is it?"

"Sorry, Mom. I don't mean to. I just want it down on tape. Also, I just need to understand," I say.

"All right, Jack. Understand this. I was a young woman. People said I was very pretty. I could pick and choose. I was well-spoken. I wasn't cheap or anything like that. After I married your father, we had to leave town because of what people said about us, but it was complicated. Everything about love is complicated, especially the way it comes and goes. And it goes, more often than not. Your father had his female admirers. He was very good looking. I was attracted to him, but not for that. Still, I didn't try anything." She means: not at first.

"What attracted you about him?"

"You really want to know, don't you?"

"Yes, I do. Come on, Ma, it's not such a strange question."

"It's none of your business, and you wouldn't understand anyway."

"Try me."

My mother sits up. Now, in her late sixties, her brown hair is turning gray, but there are odd traces of elegance in her. She has striking blue eyes, and she has kept trim by daily walks, and she likes to wear rather formal skirts and blouses. I admire her, though I think she is a bit disappointed in me, in the way my life has turned out. I glance toward an Italian cedarwood chest on the other side of the living room.

There is a long silence. Then she says, "Men don't understand things like this. You won't understand. I don't even know why I bother to tell you. But it was his limp." She waits. "He came into the store once, a smile on his face, and those rimless glasses he wore, and his hair combed back and his gray eyes that the women admired, but it was really the limp." She looks directly at me. "You probably can't understand this. Nobody nowadays would. But he was so sweet and vulnerable, I couldn't take my eyes off him. And then I got sick."

"The pneumonia."

"Yes. Why do I bother telling you anything? You know it already. You could talk into your own microphone. You don't need me. Well, anyway, I walked home from the store one night in the rain, and I had forgotten my hat. This was autumn, one of those chilly soaking rains, and I got a cold and then the cold turned into pneumonia, and I was laid up for quite a while, and your father paid us a call, a visit, I guess, to cheer me up. My mother had been worried about me, high fever and so on, and she asked him to drop by. He was the priest for the youth in the parish, you know. He came into the room where I was, his hands clasped in front of him, but he was relaxed and he told me a joke, and we talked for a while and then we said a couple of prayers together. He didn't know what I was praying for, of course. I was trembling the whole time."

"The fever?" I am being deliberately obtuse. I want to get a rise out of my mother.

"Jack, honey, please. You're an adult." My mother is exasperated with me again. I don't always enjoy provoking her, but our battles are sometimes the most intimate moments we share. I want to pat her hand, but it's not the right moment for that. "I shouldn't have to explain this to you. I had a music box near my bed. It was carved like a little Swiss chalet. And your father wound it up. He played it for me. He listened to it before he left. It went like this."

To my horror, and amazement, my old mother starts to hum the tune that her music box used to play. There is something terrible about this, and I can hardly bear to listen to her, but I do.

"And then, every time I wound up that music box, I swooned a little, thinking about him. But it was just puppy love.

An infatuation. Lots of girls had feelings like that for Franz. It was a safe love, because he was a good priest and above suspicion. You could tell that about him."

"How could you tell?"

"How could you tell?" she repeats. She fixes me with what people call a baleful look. "You don't know anything. It's pretty late in the day for me having to explain this to you. There's a concentration men have when they're paying attention to you romantically. Like they're about to leap over a chasm and they're calculating how far they'll have to jump. Sort of a single-minded look. He didn't have that. No. He'd look right through you. He was seeing God through you. In you. He didn't stop with the person, he went all the way on to God. A real priest doesn't have trouble with women because that's the way he sees people. And your father didn't have trouble, either, until after he got back from Germany."

"The trip he took with the Jordans."

"Those awful people." My mother, here on the seventh floor of the retirement home, looks out at Lake Michigan and the Outer Drive and the Chicago skyline. She didn't have to move here; it was her choice. It's a sunny day, summer, and the yachts are taking their pleasure on the waves. My mother is content to watch them. She won't say anything more unless I ask her another question.

"What happened when he got back?"

"That's enough for today. Honey, I'm tuckered out."

"Just two more questions, Ma."

"I don't think so. I'm tired. I want to take a nap before dinner."

"In a minute. What was Dad like after he got back from Germany?"

"He hadn't been corrupted, if that's what you're asking."

"No, I didn't say that."

"People want to make everything simple," my mother says.

"They want to make everything into black and white. *Schwarzweiss,* as the Germans say." Suddenly, and with great vehemence, my mother says, "Where would you be if he hadn't given way?"

I shrug.

"Or your sister, either! Nowhere! So don't you be so judgmental with me!"

"I haven't said anything, Ma. I didn't make a single judgment."

"I can tell from your face," she says. "You keep needling me and needling me. What do you want me to say?"

"Just the truth."

"Oh, and that's so simple? You think everything's so simple, with your electrical diagrams, with your machines! Well, it isn't. You've guessed all this. You know all this. You just want to hear me say it, don't you?"

I simply gaze at her. I love her but I have to get something out of her, for my own good.

"I was beautiful and I loved him!" she says. "What do you want me to confess to? All right, I'll say it! I seduced him! There. I said it. He came back from Germany, and he wasn't the same. He wasn't the same, and I could tell that right away, and I was so in love with him that nothing would stop me. But he let it happen! He didn't before, and then he did."

"How did it happen?" I ask. "Exactly?"

"Oh no," she says. "You've been prying enough. You want me to feel guilty? Don't you think I've thought about what I've done all my life? Don't you think he thought about it, too? I was in agony for him. Love is an agony sometimes, honey. That's how it is. You want to know how I got him to . . . no. That's private. That's what a man and woman do together. It's private and it's over and it's years and years ago. Leave me alone now."

"Ma," I say. I lean over to hug her.

"Leave me alone." She is weeping. I am filled with shame. She is right, of course: I know most of this story already. Up here, on the seventh floor of this building, I have made my mother weep. "I seduced him, and I'm not sorry. I seduced a priest. It wasn't a mistake. I will never say that it was a mistake. I don't care what you think. I would do it all over again." She points a finger at me. "We loved each other all our lives, your father and me. We had two children. We had a wonderful life together. And who do you love, Jack? Exactly?" She flings my word—"exactly"—back at me. On rare occasions, my mother has a mean streak.

I pick up my tape recorder and shut it off. I kiss her on the cheek. "I'll see you tomorrow, Ma."

She is still pointing. "Who do you love, Mr. High and Mighty? Who's there to kiss you when you come home?" She is so composed, most of the time, it's difficult to watch her when she's like this.

"Tomorrow, Ma." I am out in the hallway by now. I am closing the door.

But I can still hear her voice. "Don't you go judging me, honey. You, of all people!"

8

It was arranged, the trip, intermediaries were empowered to transfer cash to the archdiocese, bishops and archbishops and cardinals were no doubt enlisted, and somehow they were persuaded to release my father from his pastoral duties to accompany the Jordans. I haven't gone prowling through the records of the archdiocese to find out what was promised in whispers to whom, and I won't, because even if they decided to let me

look in those records, if they had a lick of shrewdness, and I
hope they did, the Church functionaries would have had the
sense to destroy each and every document related to Father
Pielke's trip to Germany in June and July of 1938, a subject of
no great pride to anyone now: Well, yes, um, that was permitted, was that permitted? Yes, it seems that something of the
sort did happen, but it is a footnote to a footnote, see how the
paper itself recording these arrangements is yellowing? No, is
gone, is absent, is shredded? What an unjolly subject, what a
nonhappy time, and what did you say your purpose was in
bringing up these matters now, Mr. Pielke, to no one's apparent
credit? Oh, too bad. There's been a slight housecleaning, all rel-
evant documents are in fact missing, actually nothing is known
about any of those events, it is possible, is it not, that these
events, these "events" you claim have happened, did not happen at all, we beg your pardon, Mr. Pielke. Goodbye, good day,
God be with you, as the door closes and the tongue of the lock
slips into the slot of the door.

Actually, I'm sure they would have been perfectly coopera-
tive and civil. I'm making this up. I just don't have the heart to
go over there to check those details out.

Sometimes I think I'm not the right person to tell this story.
Late at night I have these bouts of shivering. I try to write a
scene and I go into another mentality, and the scene I write is
not the one I intended to write. The themes and characters veer
off and they don't come back to me. There's nothing I can do
about it. My mother doesn't want me to write this and my sister
Maggie doesn't want me to write this, and Goebbels is staring
down at me from his picture on the wall.

I don't think that I can be trusted.

9

On the Broadway Limited to New York City, Father Pielke, sitting in his coach seat, watched the Ohio landscape rush past. He had a headache. The headache felt like fine china dishes being dropped, one by one, to a hardwood floor. Alongside the track, the telephone poles set up a rhythm of numbed spasms. In their Pullman car compartment, the Jordans, those rascals, had been playing honeymoon bridge all morning, and a festive lemony odor of martinis drenched the air when Father Pielke checked in on them. They seemed puzzled, though pleased, to see him, as if it were an absurd and wonderful coincidence that he should be on the same train that they themselves had chosen. Mary Ellen seemed to have developed a temporary form of asthma; she would turn away from Father Pielke and look down toward the floor, a handkerchief in her hand.

Every few minutes, back in his coach seat, Father Pielke would close his eyes and offer a prayer for his own safety, for his soul and the souls of the living and the dead. At times his prayers were shorn of content. He would just gather up all his emotions and pass them along to God in a great heap, like a basket of laundry.

He would take out his passport and stare at his photo, then return the passport to his pocket. When he realized that he had started a new nervous habit, he instructed himself to stop doing it. The next time he reached for his passport, he immobilized his hand in midair and then brought it back to his lap.

Seated across the aisle from him was a man traveling with his son, a boy who appeared to be about seven years old. Wearing eyeglasses, the boy sat in the window seat transfixed with the sights passing by and often announced excitedly to his father the appearance of a cow, or a silo, or a brightly painted barn. He was one of those children for whom nothing in the world had yet become routine. Father Pielke liked him immediately.

The boy's father said he worked in radio. He introduced himself, in an oddly resonating voice, as Horace Hornsby, and his fingers clamped down on Father Pielke's hand like a spring-loaded bear trap. "And that's Albert," Horace Hornsby said, pointing to his son, who waved with friendly politeness at Father Pielke before turning back to the sights of Ohio. "We're both Lutherans," Horace Hornsby said. "I hope you don't mind."

Father Pielke smiled. "That's quite all right."

Returning the smile, Horace Hornsby's face had a strange indeterminacy. My father couldn't tell how old Hornsby was because the boyish vacant eyes didn't fit with the huge voice coming out of the man's chest cavity. There was an effect of glottal amplification somewhat belied by the modest friendliness of the man. He was carrying a Sinclair Lewis novel and a copy of *Time* magazine.

"Where're you going?" he asked Father Pielke.

"Germany. I'm taking the S.S. *Washington*, sailing from New York. Three days from now."

"Germany!" Horace Hornsby rolled up his copy of *Time*. "Frightening and impressive. Well, there's not much to be done about that place right now. The fascists have all that energy, and who knows where they get it from. It makes you think that the democracies can't compete, with all their quarrels and inefficiency. They say that Germany is the wave of the future. It might be. Albert, are you hungry?"

The boy shook his head without turning away from the window. Father Pielke rotated to see what the child was seeing. They were outside Sandusky, and they were an hour late. Spindly maples passed close to the tracks.

"Chaos," Horace Hornsby said ruefully, and Father Pielke thought for a moment that Hornsby meant Ohio. "All those fellas do is debate and debate and debate, and meanwhile they line their pockets. What bothers me is, the democracies set people to quarreling without any purpose. And Roosevelt's like a storekeeper who opens the store and lets anyone take what he likes off the shelves. Oh, I shouldn't talk politics. It's a bad habit in my family. Talking. I'm in radio, after all. We're going to New York for a couple of things. I'm doing an audition. That's what I have, my voice."

"It's a powerful voice."

"That's right," Horace Hornsby nodded. "It's my meal ticket." He held out his arm. "'Carter's Little Liver Pills! Buy them today at your local drugstore.'"

"Yes, indeed, that's quite a voice. Where're you from?" my father asked.

"Worthington, Minnesota," Hornsby said loudly, but the amplification had no effect on the words. The words stayed the same.

"And what did your folks do?"

"They were farmers," Horace Hornsby said. His voice had skidded downward and quieted to conversation level. He rubbed his throat with a passing nervous gesture.

"Mine, too."

"Yes?" Horace Hornsby looked down at his son and absent-mindedly patted his head. "So you left the farm, same as I did? You didn't like the work, either?"

"No," my father said. "I liked the work. My vocation lay elsewhere, though."

"Yes, true. I can see that." Hornsby tapped his book. "It was just too dull for me, that work, and too hard. So, you're going to Germany!" My father nodded. "Did you know the Nazis make radios so cheaply that everybody can buy one? They want everybody to listen to the radio. They want everybody tuned in.

That way, everybody hears the same thing. You have to admire that."

"Why?"

"Why? Because when everybody hears the same thing, everybody responds in the same way. That's power and solidarity. You don't have all this fool and mess, all this inefficiency we've have here all the time." He opened his mouth and laughed, showing his small white teeth, though Father Pielke could detect nothing funny in what he was saying.

"What's the other thing you're going for?"

"What?"

"You said you were going to New York for two reasons."

"Oh, I guess I did."

"I don't mean to pry."

"That's all right," Horace Hornsby said. "To tell you the truth, I'd rather talk politics. You know, people, they say things about war, how it might be coming. But I think Roosevelt's not that stupid. And besides, war over what? You know, Father, I'm a reader. I keep myself informed. I think a person should. And this week General Marshall said—and I read it right here in *Time* magazine—that domestic insurrection poses more of a threat to our country than Europe does. Domestic insurrection, that's number one as a threat. Number two is South America, all those good neighbors we've got down there who hate us and are flinging their pitchforks at us." Horace Hornsby took a breath, as if all this insight had tired him out. "And then, General Marshall says, Europe, war in Europe for any reason. But nobody wants to get into a ruckus with the Nazis. What good would that do?"

The dishes in my father's head kept falling to the hardwood floor.

"And who says it can't happen here?" Hornsby's voice was rising again. He was the kind of man, my father guessed, who increased the volume of his voice when he wasn't quite sure of the truth of his statements. "Sure it could, and maybe it ought to. War," he went on, doggedly, "would be the last resort." He peered down at the book in my father's hands. "What's that you're reading, Father?"

"Oh, nothing that would interest you, I expect. St. Thomas Aquinas."

"Ah huh." Hornsby nodded. "Is it about miracles?"

"A bit. Not this section. Not really. Not very much."

"Because, well, that's the other reason my boy and I are going to New York."

"I don't understand," Father Pielke said.

"My boy isn't well. He looks well, and he's strong, but we need to see a specialist."

"What's the trouble?"

Hornsby leaned over and whispered two words in Father Pielke's ear. Father Pielke did not understand them—they were sounds, not words. But he felt he could not ask Hornsby to repeat them. He shook his head, then thought better of the gesture, and nodded.

"I love my son," Horace Hornsby said. "He's the world to my wife and me."

"Yes."

"I just don't know what we'd do if anything happened to Albert."

"I'm sure things will work out."

"I'm not sure they will. Father, you're a Catholic. And I'm a Lutheran. Our faiths divide us. But they shouldn't divide us over a child. This is selfish, I know, what I'm about to say. But I'm going to ask a favor of you." Horace Hornsby put his hand into his slightly greasy hair. "I don't ask you to pray for me. You don't have to do that. But maybe, in your next prayers, you'll do me the favor of remembering my son. And maybe you'll ask

God to stop this terrible thing that's killing my boy." He said these last words almost inaudibly. "Would you do that for me?" He waited. "We need all the help we can find."

"Yes," Father Pielke said. "Yes, I will."

"Thank you." Horace Hornsby seemed to relax inside his suit. He took Father Pielke's hand, then turned toward his son, and rubbed the boy's left shoulder. His son smiled at his father, and Horace Hornsby bent down and adjusted the knot on the little boy's necktie.

10

On the *Washington*, traveling third class—the Jordans were in first, where Father Pielke never saw them—he stayed for the first day in his room, only leaving it for meals. He had his reading and his rosary, and the flood plain of his thoughts. The room was so far down in the hull that it had no porthole, just a circular ventilation outlet, discharging air that smelled like newspapers soaked in warm grease. Father Pielke found that the rocking of the ship made it difficult for him to concentrate. A faint wisp of nausea had made itself felt here and there in his body, the realization that he had been a fool to agree to this trip. He had allowed himself to become the butt of a stupidly elaborate and quite expensive practical joke. He had let his desires get the best of him.

By the third day of the crossing, however, he had found his way to the ship's library. The librarian was a young woman, a brunette, who recommended to him several histories of ancient Rome and the Caesars. He said that, though he was a priest, he wasn't going to Rome, and she replied that it didn't matter: The Caesars were so interesting that they would just take you away from your troubles, Catholic, Protestant, or Jew. Not that a priest had to be taken away from his troubles, of course. She wore a quite a lot of makeup, but the carelessness of its application made her seem innocent rather than worldly. Probably she was in search of a husband, and Father Pielke thought to himself that, with her charm and bossy friendliness, she would soon find one.

Carrying his volume of *The Twelve Caesars,* Father Pielke went limping out onto the ship's deck. He held onto the book with his left hand and the railing with his right. The day was clear and warm, and the sea breezes, with their distant airy saltiness, suddenly opened his spirit. The ocean's blue clarity and uninterrupted calm was contagious; he began to feel calm and clear himself. He was the child of farmers, after all, and the Atlantic Ocean was something new in his experience, for which he could feel thankful.

For once he didn't care what the Jordans had in mind.

He stood at the railing, breathed in the sea air, gazed at the horizon, and felt his life enlarging through this series of accidents. What a relief it was to get free of pointless fretfulness! To want little and to fear nothing, to feel a salt breeze on your face and to be grateful for it. In the distance a few strings of cirrus clouds floated around the aimless unambitious sky.

He walked down to the ship's chapel and recited the Veni Sancte Spiritus to himself. At the back of the chapel, in the last pew, rocking in time to the swell of the waves, Father Pielke prayed for his sister, for his parents, and for those souls in need of comfort and those in distress. When he came back out onto the deck, it was dark, and the wind had risen a little. He felt unburdened and, somewhat to his surprise, powerful. He had no idea for what purpose this power was intended. He faced the bow of the ship; Europe was up there, ahead somewhere, and he was aiming all of his innocence at it.

II

In Hamburg for the third night he waited in his room in the Hotel Diana until two hours past sunset. For the last two nights he had gone out walking and had found an old man in a park who sat on a bench and quietly recited poetry. Father Pielke had enjoyed listening to the poetry—it was a relief of some kind—and planned to hear it again. Just now, however, someone outside was shouting for help. He went to the window, drew aside the curtain, and peered out into the street. Summer nights put no one to bed in Hamburg, and men and women were still up and walking along the Seewartenstrasse. But no one seemed to have heard what he had heard. They walked on their errands with determined and imperturbable steps.

Down below, at the corner, was a woman in a blue squarish hat accompanied by a tall man in a sea captain's uniform with a high stiff collar. Neither of them stopped or waited. They just continued on. Two SS officers walked past, laughing. No one was strolling. He hadn't seen anyone strolling so far in Germany. All of these citizens advanced powerfully toward their destinations, looking like doctors on the way to emergency surgery.

"*Hilfe!*" Help. There it was again, fainter this time. The night walkers continued on their errands. But one woman, perhaps a tourist, stopped. She lifted her head in the European manner, as if she had heard a tune. When she did, she saw Father Pielke standing at the window. They exchanged a glance in the dark. Then the woman shook her head, one tiny flick. She rushed forward, crossed the street, and was gone.

Father Pielke wanted to leave the hotel. Ever since the *Wash-*

ington had steamed up the Elbe and docked in Hamburg, he had felt tired. Yesterday, he had, in a manner of speaking, escorted the Jordans around Hamburg. During the past twenty-four hours he had shown them Alster Lake, interpreted for them in restaurants and beer halls, and consulted the maps for them when, on a whim, Burton Jordan had decided that he wanted to drive to what turned out to be a nondescript park outside of the city and view the wildlife, the birds particularly. So they had set out in the Jordan's hired car, a shiny black Mercedes, to the Grossensee, where for a rushed half hour they had observed the German ducks, the mallards, the *Löffelente,* which had looked exactly like the ones in the States, feather for feather.

The Jordans seemed to be in a rush at all times of day. They had to see everything, but once they cast their eyes on a monument, or a park, they had to see something else. It was as if they were buying up sights for a traveling collection, a museum on wheels.

At the window, Father Pielke began to pray for the person who had cried for help. The prayer died out a moment after it began. Prayer was useless in Germany. He had noticed this the minute he had stepped off the boat. Prayers fell as dead as stones here as soon as they were uttered, were inwardly unanswered, and the fact was so obvious to him that he had been spiritually perplexed since he had arrived. In this place, speaking to God was like trying to carry on a conversation with a fully dressed corpse.

Something else seemed to have taken over, in that realm. It was alarming.

He stood up, feeling resolute, and headed downstairs.

He limped through the hotel lobby, where the walls had been decorated with wallpaper showing Burmese pagodas, and he made his way out into the street. The air smelled curiously of burnt sugar pastries. He didn't know which way to walk but decided to head north on the Zeughaustrasse toward the Brahms Memorial, a few blocks up.

At night the city, badly lit, had a somber stony alertness, and not just in the Reeperbahn red light district, but everywhere. An insomniac consciousness seemed to animate the place.

After passing the Brahms Memorial, he turned off onto Kaiser-Wilhelm Strasse and lowered his head when he heard thunder, followed by a dutiful minute or so of rain. When he raised his head he saw several uniformed soldiers heading toward him on the sidewalk. He wanted to cross the street immediately to make way for them but decided against it. But he had hesitated, and they had noticed.

One officer was tall—a shadowy display of buckles, black unscuffed leather boots, and medals over a stale meaty background odor either on his breath or in the street—and he had a horselaugh that seemed to come out of some deeply infected and pocketed cavern in his body. His lips were so thin that his mouth looked like a lesion in his face. Father Pielke heard the cry for help once more. It echoed over the stones of the street, traveling down the Kaiser-Wilhelm Strasse toward the Rathaus, starting a journey toward the Hauptbahnhof, toward the North Sea. And now, all his senses alert, he heard, from an upstairs window, a woman, a mother perhaps, softly singing, *"Es war einmal ein treuer Hussar."*

Three of the men glanced over at Father Pielke, and then another one of the soldiers, a boyishly handsome youth, walked crisply toward a doorway, where he vomited. The other soldiers studied him, their arms folded, and a few of them laughed, though it sounded like dogs barking. When he was finished, the young man took a handkerchief out of his pocket, dabbed at his mouth as he smiled grimly, and returned to the group. All this happened quickly. But the street had meanwhile taken on an odd silence. The woman singing *"Es war einmal ein treuer Hussar"* had stopped. Everything had stopped, and for a moment Father Pielke wondered if one of his paralyzing time tricks was about to occur. Father Pielke gave the soldiers a quick nod. The men turned away from him, whatever interest they had had in him having died, and as they turned, Father Pielke noticed that they had managed to coordinate their movements so that their arms and legs were in an odd synchronicity, like gears meshing in a large machine.

Father Pielke did not think of himself as a brave man but found himself unfrightened now, somehow exempt from the fear he thought he would ordinarily have had, and he started walking again. He found himself on the edge of the park—he still didn't know its name—with a flower garden ringing its east edge, the flowers themselves indistinguishable from one another in the dark, and benches here and there near the plantings. On the north end of the park was a train or bus station. He sat down on a bench near the old man who had been there last night, and the night before.

The man wore a woolen suit with rather old-fashioned tailoring, and it did not look like comfortable summer wear. It had the rough, approximating lengths of shoulders, trousers, and sleeves characteristic of rural Sunday clothing; most of the men in Father Pielke's parish wore baggy clothes like that. The old man clutched at a walking stick with some sort of dog's head—it looked like a Weimaraner—carved on the handle. In his other hand he held a cigarette.

The man glanced over at Father Pielke and nodded. It appeared to be his habit to twist his head back, examine the stars, then lean forward to examine the grass, before reciting.

"Es fällt ein Stern herunter," the old man said, as if now inspired, *"Aus seiner funkelnden Höh!"* He was saying the words slowly, with evident seriousness. *"Das ist der Stern der Liebe,"* he went on, solemnly speaking to the flowers, *"Den ich dort fallen seh . . ."*

I see a star that plummets
From all its sparkling height.
Love is the star that's falling
Plunging out of sight.

In front of him, on the opposite side of the park, was a beer hall, and from its open door came the Horst Wessel Lied, sung loudly and drunkenly. From another window Father Pielke thought he heard a Brahms intermezzo.

This night air is full of voices, he thought.

The old man finished his recitation, but the Horst Wessel Lied continued. There were many verses—something about it seemed unstoppable—and they were all repeated, as if the tale could not be told often enough, or at sufficient length, to satisfy those who sang it. Father Pielke heard a dog barking and, coming out of the dark as faintly as the starlight, another cry for help.

He didn't care if he slept in this country or didn't sleep. If sleep never overtook him, he would manage to conduct his waking nights one way or another.

At that moment he heard, from behind him, the metallic crunch and shrieking-chrome ripsaw sounds of a collision. These noises were followed by the tinkling of broken glass falling to the pavement, the hiss of steam rising from a smashed radiator, and the whirring of a hubcap rolling circularly, like a child's top, some distance away on the street. Father Pielke stood up—the old man beside him had not gotten to his feet, he had not in fact moved at all and seemed to be ready to recite another poem—and Father Pielke saw, now that he could get a view, an automobile that had jumped the pavement and collided with a light pole. The driver's side door was open, and the driver lay halfway outside the car, his head on the pave-

ment, traceries of blood dribbling downward. As Father Pielke
moved closer, he could see the blood forming into a pool the
size of a half dollar.

People were now shouting from the upper windows. A small
man with sleeves rolled up, showing hairy arms, pushed past
Father Pielke toward the accident victim. He lowered the man's
legs out of the car onto the pavement, then put his fingers on
the man's pulse.

Meanwhile, Father Pielke found himself in a small crowd of
quiet curious onlookers, moving forward together. In America, he thought, these people would be shouting suggestions,
or calling out questions. They would all be collaborating.
These citizens—a married couple dressed in similar woolens,
a young student carrying opera glasses—studied the man on
the ground as if they would be questioned, later, on his de-
meanor. They were all so studious here. He heard them muttering, now and then, but the sight of the victim's blood had
caused Father Pielke to lose his German. Someone said, *"der
Notarzt kommt,"* and Father Pielke thought: *Why would they call
a notary?*

He edged forward. *"Herzschlag,"* someone said. Heart attack.

And now he felt himself being taken in hand. "Come forward, please." The same small man with hairy arms was leading
him toward the body on the ground. With his other hand he
was waving and pointing. In a low voice, almost at a whisper, he
said, "Father, this man is dying." He released Father Pielke's
arm and took off the sweater he himself was wearing and
placed it over the body lying there. The pool of blood had ex-
panded; now it was as wide as a tea cup. "Dying quickly, I think.
Though I am not myself a doctor, I believe so." He grabbed
Father Pielke's elbow. "Please do something." He touched Father Pielke on the arm. "Consider this poor man."

"What shall I do?"

"As you would when someone is dying . . ."

"You mean the last rites." Father Pielke was struggling with his German. "The man cannot confess, I have no oil . . ."

"Nevertheless, he is dying. We cannot have technicalities now. Can you not pray?"

A sense of burgeoning calamity bloomed somewhere along his spinal cord. Father Pielke kneeled. He exhaled and took the man's right hand in his left hand. Making the sign of the cross over his forehead, Father Pielke said, *"Ego te absolvo, si capax es."* He waited, then began praying again, speaking quietly for God, for himself, for this nameless wreck of a human body.

As he was nearing the end of his first prayer, the man's eyes opened. His eyes were blue, and when the pupils exposed themselves, they were hugely dilated. His bald head shook, and drops of blood flew off onto Father Pielke's sleeve. "Where are my glasses?" he said. He squinted. "Who is this priest?"

"I am Father Pielke."

"Get him away from me." The man put his hands down, and with astonishing speed and strength, lifted himself up, making an almost inaudible groan as he did. He glanced down at his feet. Someone had taken off his shoes, or they had flown off at the moment of collision. "Get this priest away from me!" he shouted. Now he turned his back to Father Pielke and began, very unevenly, to walk away. He looked like someone up on stilts, staggering sideways once for every two steps forward. Like a silent screen comedian, he dusted off his lapels.

"Wait," Father Pielke said. "Someone stop him." For a moment it seemed that the crowd was mesmerized by the man's recovery, stricken into passivity with admiration for it, and then two men emerged, took hold of him, and managed to get him to sit down on the sidewalk. A moment later, a doctor appeared from a sirening medical ambulance that had just arrived, squatted down near the man without shoes, and began taking him in hand. The doctor stopped his work long enough to proclaim to the onlookers, "This man is all right. Everyone can go home now."

"*Ah, der Notarzt,*" the short man said, as if the whole event had now concluded satisfactorily. He glanced up at Father Pielke and smiled wanly. "I was mistaken," he said. "He was not dying after all, as you see." He pointed a stubby finger at the priest. "Or else he was dying, and you brought him back to life. Who can say. A miracle, perhaps. You don't speak German like a German. Where are you from, sir?"

"America," Father Pielke said.

"America? No doubt the prayers are young in America," the man said, somewhat obscurely. "Perhaps they still work there. Here in Germany the prayers are old and used up. Perhaps God . . ." He didn't finish his thought. Instead, he reached into his pocket and pulled out a coin. But now it was my father's turn to feel insulted, and he backed away quickly and limped off down a badly lit narrow street. "Stop!" he heard someone say. "Stop!"

Turning a corner, he found himself near a pub with a steamy front window bordered on two sides with a sort of ornamental ironwork in a pattern of curlicues. To the side, another window was open part way. He glanced in through the window and saw, at a table with several other people engaged in active conversation, a woman whose back was to him, but whose hair was the color of gold coins. Facing her, speaking rather loudly and animatedly to a chubby man with bright red cheeks who sat on her left, was her husband, Burton Jordan. He was speaking German, speaking it rather well, though with an American accent. The chubby man was nodding and puffing away on a pipe.

Everyone was nodding. Father Pielke stared in through the window.

He made his way inside. Mary Ellen saw him first. "Ah, Father Pielke!" she said, rising up immediately. "What are you doing here?" She asked the question in German.

"I was out walking," he said. "I witnessed an accident."

Burton Jordan glanced up, a smile frozen on his face. He had been drinking beer and his expression displayed a certain degree of strained affability.

"Come outside," Mary Ellen said. "Burton," she said, "you stay right here. Herr Schillinger, don't you move, either. We don't want to lose you."

She took his arm and together they walked out, the patrons of the Kneipe watching them as they went.

12

"An accident," Mary Ellen said in German. "Was it serious?"

"I thought so," Father Pielke said. "I began last rites. And then he returned to consciousness." He breathed out twice, to compose himself. "Mrs. Jordan," he said. "You were in there, speaking German. I heard you. And here we are speaking it now." His words sounded idiotic to him. "Could you explain? I don't understand any of this. What are you doing? What is this theatrical about this time?"

"Ah, yes. You have found us out," Mary Ellen said, switching back into English.

"What? What have I found out?" he asked.

She tugged at his arm. "Our little masquerade," she said. "Our play." She moved ahead of him by several steps.

"You speak German," he said, embarrassed at his own obviousness.

"Oh, yes, I speak German. So does Burton, of course."

He stopped. "In that case, Mrs. Jordan," he said, "why am I here?"

"Because we invited you," she said, "and you accepted."

"That's not what I mean." He noticed himself growing agitated, or perhaps angry—he wasn't sure which it was. "Why did you ask me to accompany you on this trip? What purpose does it serve?"

They had reached another street corner. Father Pielke was quite lost, but he could see a canal nearby, the water flowing placidly underneath the bridge, reflecting the vacant stars.

"What purpose?" she repeated. "What purpose?" She laughed. "No purpose at all! A traveling companion, that's what we wanted, that's what we asked for. A naturalist, too, to identify the shrubs and the wildlife. And of course we're going to help your parish, financially. Wasn't that the plan?"

"Oh, I don't believe you when you say that," he told her. "I haven't believed it for some time now. But I don't know what to believe instead."

She shrugged. Under the streetlight, he saw her smile. "Walk me over there." She pointed at the small bridge over the canal. She took his arm again. Then she said, "You're probably right not to believe me. It's not wise. I'm a prevaricator. I can't help it. I was always one of those awful *imaginative* little girls, one of those little showoffs."

When they reached the canal, she walked out to the center of the bridge and stopped. "Tell me, Father Pielke," she said, "why *do* you think we invited you along on this trip?"

"I can't say."

"Oh yes, I think you can. I think you can say, if you give it a moment's thought."

"Why don't you just tell me instead?" he asked.

She was gazing down at the water. She shook her head in a

demure, ladylike way. "No, I don't think so," she said. "I don't think I'll tell. I'd rather not do that. Please, try to say. Save me from being explicit. Do you have no idea?"

"No," he said. "None at all." It wasn't true. He did have an idea, and it was growing, and it had an astonishing specificity, and he saw suddenly how late it was for him to have this idea.

"None at all!" she laughed. It was not a pleasant laugh, being closer to a groan. "None at all." She shook her head. "All right, then," she said, "you want your answer? Then look at me."

In the dark Mary Ellen Jordan turned her head. She was wearing a hat, with a veil turned back up near her forehead. The look she gave him altered slowly, as if thoughts were being rearranged or destroyed below the immediate surface of consciousness. And then what she wanted to show him rose up to her eyes, brightening them, and her expression took on its feeling and fastened it there. Her face actually began to redden in a blush. The intensity of it struck him so hard that he felt it in his stomach. No woman, no one at all, had ever looked at him that way, with such an arrogant aggressive longing, and she held it, and he wondered why he had never caught her before this moment gazing at him with this nakedness of feeling. She had been careful, she had been watchful: That was why. No, he hadn't been paying attention, he had been oblivious, gazing at his birds and his plants.

"Oh, no," he said.

"Now you know," she said, turning away. "The little cat is out of its little bag."

"But that's impossible," he protested. "What are you thinking of? What does your husband think?"

"Do you know what I tell him? He sits down during the cocktail hour, and I say to him, 'Oh, the priest? Father Pielke? I like to have him around.' And he says, in that way of his, 'Well, so do I.' We wanted your company. That's all. Just your company. We had no deeper darker plans. Don't worry, I won't corrupt you. We needed an excuse." Father Pielke wondered what she meant by that, but she rushed on before he could ask. "It's safe, after all. You're quite safe, to start with. There won't be any *seductions,* after all. There won't be any *talk.* You're above suspicion, aren't you? Above above above suspicion." She was starting to sound giddy.

"This is ridiculous," he said. "It's childish and ridiculous, and if you think that I—"

"—I don't think anything," she said, with sudden bitterness. "I don't expect anything. I haven't said anything, have I? No, I don't think so. I have said nothing to you. You're simply talking about what you think you have seen. The three of us—you and my husband and I—are on this little tour of Germany. Not a long tour, either. A browse, here and there. And it would be the least you could do, Father Pielke, not to make blunt what has been unvoiced. I myself can't be blunt. I'm a woman. I am Burton's wife. Subtlety is the only refuge I have. Do me the favor of leaving me my refuge. Oh, you know, we—Burton and I— we were day after day out there on Juniper Hill having our fun, our rustic pleasures, having our theatricals, and somehow, I don't know, somehow this other thing happened, this emotion, this emotion involving our visitor arrived, and it was ridiculous, wasn't it? It *was* ridiculous. But one plays, you know. That's very important to Burton and very important to me. And after all, here you are, in Europe, for free. Are you complaining, Father? Is that it? A complaint?"

"I don't—"

"Do you know how the German women say goodbye, Father?"

"No, I don't. Well, they say *Auf Wiedersehn,* of course, and they—"

"No. This is what they do." She reached down for his right hand, took it in her left hand, and pressed it to her chest, so that his arm was crossed over her breasts. She breathed deeply twice, and he felt her breasts rise and fall. He had never felt a woman's breast as an adult. He could tell his life was shattering. She was throwing rocks through the glass of his soul. "It is the German way," she said. "Now, I think it would be a good idea if you escorted me back to the Kneipe."

A banner with a swastika on it hung across the front of a stone arched building to their right as they walked back. The city was a forest of symbols, swastikas and the lightning bolts of the SS, hammers and castles and skulls. The symbols, Father Pielke thought, were alive, they were standing up and walking, scurrying about, goose-stepping triumphantly, abducting and kidnapping the humans. From a great distance Father Pielke heard a faint human outcry in which groaning and imploring were mixed.

"Did you hear that?" he asked Mary Ellen Jordan.

"Hear what? No, I heard nothing."

"The night is full of sounds," he said. "I heard a . . . it was a shout or a call. A woman, I think," he added. He was very tired. The words were tired little animals making their way uphill.

"Lovers." She glanced at him. "Husbands and wives. Women and girls, boys and men. Hamburg, Father Pielke, is a city renowned for every form of vice. Such an interesting place, don't you think? It makes one feel so alive. Permission is granted here. There's so much—"

"—Don't tell me," he said. "I don't wish to hear what you think there is so much of. You had no business inviting me to accompany you. If I could leave now, I would."

"Oh, don't be like that. You're being disagreeable," she said. She touched her hand to her hair. "And worse, I think you're being dishonest."

"It's interesting," he said, "that my mother had hair the same color of yours."

"Yes," she said, "you told me once. I caught you looking at my hair. A woman's hair—did you know this?—is her glory, Father. It is her radiance. And your mother's hair resembled mine? Well, there you are."

"I was devoted to her," he said. "She encouraged me in the priesthood. My father never did. He was . . . more practical." It shocked him suddenly that he was already confiding in her.

"A singular devotion." She pressed her lips to his cheek and went back into the pub. Burton Jordan gave her a small guarded wave as she returned.

After several moments, during which he felt his vocation slipping, just slightly, away from him, like a glove coming off a hand, Father Pielke began to make his way back to the hotel.

In bed, lying awake, he continued to hear cries for help, without origin and without location.

13

In Munich the Jordans' plans were confounded. The Hotel Aragonia had never heard of them and could find no record of their reservation. After making several calls, the Jordans and Father Pielke found themselves at the Grand Hotel Mussmann, which was not grand at all, but instead occupied the end of a block uncomfortably near the warehouse distinct, close to some factories and abandoned yards scattered with debris and trash.

"This is very un-German," Mary Ellen Jordan said from her hotel window. "We can't stay here." On the wall next to her was a calendar hanging from a nail with a photograph of the Rhine and a quotation from Clemens Brentano. Father Pielke sat in a chair near the door reading the *Frankfurter Allgemeine*. When he looked up, he tried not to see Mary Ellen Jordan but the calendar instead. The Germans had calendars everywhere, usually with photographs and quotations, he had noticed. They had an unnerving obsession with time in this country. The Germans were like housekeepers that way. It seemed as if you might be arrested for not knowing what day it was. There were calendars in the restaurants, in the train stations, in the apothecary and the stationery store. They were displayed aggressively. Wherever there weren't calendars, there were clocks, chiming and ticking and bonging and clanging. The soldiers' boots on the pavement sounded like clockwork to him. The goose steps were like pendulums.

"All we have to do is sleep here," Burton Jordan said. "We don't have to stay here. Our whole purpose . . ."

Father Pielke looked up. He was more than slightly curious about what Burton Jordan would say. The man had an easy, relaxed hypocrisy. Remarkable curiosities of speech and manner flowed from it.

". . . Our whole purpose," he repeated himself, as if giving thought to what he was saying, so that he could score a profundity, "is to enjoy ourselves. Isn't it? And to learn something about what is going on here. Historically. And to see the sights. Need I remind you that—"

"—I have an idea," Mary Ellen broke in. "Let's leave this hotel this very instant. What does one do in Munich? Where does one go?"

"The English Garden," Father Pielke said, from behind his newspaper.

"Yes, yes, the English Garden." Mary Ellen's voice was a bit too bright. Its timbre was becoming fragile. "I can't stand this wallpaper. Look at these awful designs. They make me feel quite mad. Let's go this very minute. Burton, do I look all right?"

"Ravishing, my dear," he said, reaching for his handkerchief. He didn't do anything with the handkerchief. He put it away. "Darling, never lovelier."

At the English Garden, near the Chinesischer Turm, Father Pielke watched several children playing a game of tag, using the trees as hiding places. One of the boys had a limp. My father watched him closely. The boy's ears were large and protuberant and gave his face a sort of elephantine appearance. When he shouted, the boy produced a guttural German village dialect. The Jordans had gone off for a minute, claiming that they were hungry and had seen apple tarts for sale. Good riddance. The limping boy began to shout playfully and raised his arms as if they were controlled by invisible wires. Father Pielke was having some difficulty understanding what the boy was saying until he realized that the game, which he had thought was a game of tag, was actually a variation of Get-the-Jew. Whoever was the Jew had to evade the pummelings of the others by hiding, or by turning another player into the Jew. But no amount of observation could make clear to Father Pielke how this transformation occurred.

It seemed that a boy had to hold down another boy and rub him, or scrape him, somewhere on the face, and then on the wrist, in order to turn him into a Jew. If the procedures weren't followed exactly, the intended victim would leap to his feet and say, "I'm not the Jew!" and rush off in a different direction.

Father Pielke, in an effort to find relief, gazed upward toward the trees. They had their usual blank vegetative indifference. No refuge, nor relief there. The children took their game off toward another section of the park, and Father Pielke was left alone near a bench, watching a chickadee, a *Tannenmeise*.

A couple walked past, engaged in discussion.

". . . but Germany must nevertheless—"

"—no, no, a waste of our time! They do not think, they have views."

"Ach, Poland! A land unworthy of its people . . ."

The couple disappeared behind a curve in the path. The Germans all seemed to be discussing Germany these days, as if they were all engaged in a great laboratory experiment. He would have found it a relief if the Germans now and then talked about the weather or the sorrows and rewards of love. He didn't expect discussions of God, but all the talk about politics oppressed him.

The Jordans had returned, and Father Pielke felt himself being piloted toward the Ludwigstrasse with nudges and taps and squeezes, while their affable conversation, as harmless as the squeaking of mice, played about his head. Yes, we found something to eat, it was delicious, such wonderful pastries, you should have accompanied us, and we fell into a wonderful conversation with a young man, a Dr. Schantz, so young to be a doctor, he told us how death is sometimes beautiful, he said—unusual for a doctor to say it!—that death is the mother of beauty. That's quite an idea, isn't it, coming from a doctor?

Ahead of them, in the Odeonplatz, they saw some sort of commotion.

A young woman whose head had been shaved was being pushed off a streetcar, and as she descended she was surrounded by well-dressed men who were prodding and tapping and pushing her. They were now joined by some women, who were shouting and jeering. It registered on Father Pielke that, to the side, a solemn-looking man, possibly a Gestapo agent, was watching this scene with silky silent pleasure. Father Pielke couldn't understand why the woman with the shaved head was the object of so much attention until he had walked close enough to the crowd to see the placard across the woman's breast. Her face was flushed but absented, as if, somehow, she had been absorbed into a deep recess of herself.

Across her breast the placard read:

I HAVE OFFERED MYSELF
TO A JEW.

Father Pielke found himself several steps in front of the Jordans. He turned around. Burton Jordan's face had its customary imperturbable calm. Mary Ellen, by contrast, was leaning forward, like a spectator at a sporting event. She clutched at her purse with both hands. Then she raised herself on tiptoe to see better. The tips of her ears were reddening.

Father Pielke glanced back at Burton Jordan. Burton Jordan was enjoying his wife's pleasure as a witness. And then Burton Jordan did something that my father never forgot, something that stayed with my father for the rest of his life.

Burton Jordan winked.

Without thinking about it, Father Pielke rushed forward into the crowd in the Odeonplatz. He had little experience in fistfights. But his spirit was large and exalted with fury. He first took on a large lumpy man with scorched-looking hair who was shaking the placard-carrying woman. He forced himself between the man and the woman and took aim at the man's face, and before he himself was struck he felt his fist separating the cartilage of the man's nose from its anchoring. Another man wearing a hat hit Father Pielke in the jaw, and in the moment of shock that followed, he felt himself being kicked in his bad leg. The dove fluttered in Father Pielke's heart, and he turned and landed one good punch, one solid blow against the man in the hat, before he was knocked over. Blood flowed out onto the street from his nose and his mouth, and, feeling the presence of Christ for the first time since he had entered Germany, he raised himself up, his fists out, before he was struck again, several times, and was brought down semiconscious to the gray stone pavement.

14

They were on the train to Berlin. The private compartment was roomy, but it had been made smaller by Burton and Mary Ellen Jordan's displeasure with Father Pielke and his behavior. There was a sour and almost acrid quality to their anger with him that was disturbing the air. Father Pielke, with his comic black eye, was no longer a good idea. He had turned into a bad idea, even a dangerous idea, from the Jordan point of view. Father Pielke didn't care. He was pleased with himself, pleased with the trouble he had gotten himself into and managed to get the Jordans into—the parade of police and Nazi officials, who had to have explanations, who had to be wheedled, smartly placated with explanations of American innocence versus Germanic knowingness and omniscience, one small official with a small dangerous power having also to be bribed—this almost athletic pleasure living next to the fear he had begun to feel, thick steady fear, a monotonous blanketing, a solid weight of oppression, as if graves were being dug in every backyard in this country, in every village, a hobby this was, graves dug with delicious excitement, graves growing larger and larger as people called from the windows for help. . . . He grimaced out of his new fear and pleasure.

"Oh, look," Mary Ellen said, pointing at the rushing landscape. "What a pretty little house."

"A house?" Burton Jordan glanced at it. "Oh, yes. There it is."

"I didn't see it," Father Pielke said.

"Didn't miss much," Mary Ellen said grimly. "Anyhow it's gone."

"Tell me," Burton Jordan said, turning with theatrical compassion toward Father Pielke, "how's that eye of yours?"

"Better, thanks."

"It looks pretty terrible. You're quite the little scrapper. You got us into quite a scrape, back there."

"Yes, I'm afraid I did."

"Well," said Burton Jordan, "one more city to go. Berlin. Tell me, Father Pielke, do you plan to stage another anti-Nazi rally for our benefit? Another display of pugilism? On the streets of Berlin? I feel we should be warned."

"No," my father said. "I have no plans to do that."

"Good," Burton Jordan chuckled, "because if you do, I'll leave you where you fall. Dammit all, I won't risk my safety if you become headstrong again. These Germans mean business."

"Tell me," Mary Ellen said, swiveling away from the rushing landscape to fix her gaze on Father Pielke with a sort of smoky attention, "what is it about you and the Jews?"

"It could have been anybody," Father Pielke said.

"Ah, but it wasn't," she said. "It was about the Jews. About that placard. That woman wasn't even a Semite, she just gave herself to one. What difference does it make to you, a Catholic? And a priest?"

"Yes," Burton Jordan said. "What is it about the Jews? Your church doesn't like the Jews better than anyone else does. Less, actually, now that I think about it."

"It was wrong," he said. "What they were doing to that woman was cruel and wrong."

Burton Jordan leaned forward. "Was there ever a Jew whom you loved?"

My father lied: He nodded. In fact the only Jewish person he had ever known was the proprietor of the farm implement store in St. Boniface, a nice enough man—but, no, he didn't *love* him, not in the way Burton Jordan meant. Father Pielke could have said, *It wasn't the Jews, it was your wink,* but he kept his silence for a moment, having, he thought, had the privilege to witness an evil in a relatively pure form: an attack on an innocent, and the wink that went with it, not only the infliction of suffering but its conversion into spectacle, an entertainment for others, a sideshow. That was what had enraged him and enlarged his heart's knowledge of his own proper place in the world. At last he gathered himself and said, "You two have made me desperate." He waited. "I could almost do anything now."

Neither of the Jordans bothered to follow this absurd comment, coming from this ridiculous fellow, their traveling companion, dressed like a priest.

15

"Of course," my mother says, "nobody would remember any of this if she hadn't gotten up on Goebbels' car."

"Where was that?" I ask.

"Berlin," my mother says. "They went to Berlin after Munich and then they flew back to Hamburg and took another boat home."

"She jumped up?" I ask.

"The running board," my mother says. "Cars always used to have running boards in those days. They always said she was pushed, though."

"Pushed onto the running board?"

"They were in a crowd. Your father was somewhere behind her. It was one of those big Berlin streets, and, you know, motorcades went down them, all the big Nazi officials, maybe this was a smaller street, I don't know. Me, I've never been to

Berlin. All I know is that she ended up on the running board of Goebbels' car, and because it was summertime, he was riding in a convertible, and he had a conversation with her. They spoke, those two."

"What did they say?"

"I wasn't there," my mother says to me. "That conversation is lost to the ages."

16

The failed novelist, Joseph Paul Goebbels, former Catholic altar boy, his right clubfooted leg braced by steel, lamed for life, author of a novel *Michael Voorman: A Man's Fate in Leaves from a Diary,* and a play, *The Wanderer, a Drama in Eleven Scenes,* editor of *Der Angriff,* Reichsminister of propaganda, professional shouter and liar, Hitler observer, prop and support, filmstar-struck womanizer, expert—method finder—in mendacity, father of Helga, Hilde, Helmut, Holde, Hedda, and Heide, all subsequently killed with glass cyanide capsules in the Führer bunker, labeler of Jews as "parasitic beings" and "demons of decay," a man of delicate sensibilities who was nauseated by filmed scenes of torture, shorter by several inches than the other members of the Nazi inner circle, spectral dwarf of history, had his conversation with Mary Ellen Jordan, American, in July of 1938 as his motorcade headed toward the Leopold Palace on Wilhelmplatz.

One must imagine Mary Ellen Jordan standing with her husband, Burton Jordan, at curbside in Berlin, on Kurfürsten-damm, often chosen by Hitler for motorcades, with a crowd of tourists—for there are still tourists in Germany in 1938—and Germans behind her, and one must imagine Father Pielke standing in this crowd, observing it, and Mary Ellen Jordan herself, of whom little is visible except for her hair, the color of gold, mostly concealed now by a hat she is wearing, a compact circular blue hat held in place by hatpins, and one must imagine the collective insuck of breath and the excited murmuring in the crowd as the motorcade is spotted and its approach is announced and acclaimed by the mostly well-dressed men and women and even children screaming quietly with excitement, standing there to observe the spectral dwarf as he passes in his open convertible, a Mercedes, silently powered by a pantherlike V-8 engine, the driver instructed to go at a moderate speed, not rushing, because power is not rushed, power takes its time, power displays itself to the worshipful crowd, hysterically reverent, standing in the shade of these Berlin trees, lindens, for example, for which the city is famous.

One must imagine my father being jostled back and forth as he watches Mary Ellen Jordan standing on tiptoe to get a better look at Siegfried, which is how she thinks of Goebbels' Mercedes, although Siegfried should be white, not black, as this car is, and one must imagine the crowd noise and clustering of consonance and syllabic plosives and grunts and continued chirping cries of wonder and excitement, which even my father, the priest, knows to be sexual, as this car, carrying this clubfooted man, approaches: the women in the crowd sounding more like birds with every passing second, the men more like large fierce grunting circus animals prodded by sticks, and now, at last, *there he is,* the spectral dwarf, who must look up to the taller uniformed members of the inner circle, smiling, if that is the word, toward the adorers and observers lining the street, no, smirking is perhaps a better word, the Reichsminister does not smile, he smirks and grins and glowers, he does nothing for himself anymore, whatever he does he does for National Socialism and for Hitler, but in any case his car, Siegfried, approaches, and the crowd moves forward as if collectively taking a crowd breath that warps in the direction of the Reichsminister, and in this crowd movement that yearns toward the street, toward the Mercedes, toward Goebbels himself, Mary Ellen Jordan, a frustrated woman, in her way, the tips of her ears reddening as they sometimes do, Mary Ellen Jordan, American, leaps or is pushed onto the running board of the car, whose fine metal door sill she grips, so as not to lose her balance and fall off, with the result that, several feet back, my father sees Mary Ellen Jordan, dressed rather elegantly for the occasion, standing on the running board, disappearing down the street in the motorcade that does not stop for her, does not stop for anything, so that now she vanishes in the distance and is gone.

But one must imagine in addition the initial look of alarm on the face of the Reichsminister, a man noted at no point in his earthly existence for physical courage, upon seeing this face-powdered woman springing up toward him and now holding on for dear life, and the looks of alarm and rage on the faces of the bodyguards reaching for their pistols, until the Reichminister sees the woman flushed and excited, even smiling, having now at last found the measure of her passion, and he says, having seen her wedding ring bulging under her glove, *"Guten Tag, gnädige Frau,"* and Mary Ellen Jordan also says good afternoon, and from her accent Goebbels can tell at once that she is not German, something about the pronunciation of the vowels is foreign, but, beyond that, something in her face makes him think that she is no danger to him, so he makes a single gesture toward the bodyguards, a quick sweeping of the hand from left to right, and they put their pistols away.

It is then that they have their conversation. A Midwesterner, after all, is typically polite. A Midwesterner will try to make a social effort.

They talk about Germany, and its future. They talk about the great plans.

In front of the Leopold Palace the Mercedes stops. Goebbels says, *"Heil Hitler"* and Mary Ellen Jordan says, *"Grüss Gott."* One must imagine her getting down from the running board in her hat and gloves and her blouse of the palest purple, and one must imagine her breathless and quivering.

17

Sick with love, her nightly thoughts perfumed by the image of Father Franz Pielke, who had come to her bedside when she was sick with pneumonia to talk to her and to console her, Ingrid Shepherd was working in the drugstore, sweeping the tile floor behind the soda fountain and gazing somewhat dazedly in her boredom and adolescent melancholy at the colored syrups in the apothecary jars perched on top of the cupboards. This was late August 1938, and it was a Tuesday when she looked up from her work and saw the object of her thoughts, Father Pielke himself, walk into the drugstore, and she saw that he was changed.

He was still dressed as a priest, but he didn't look like a priest anymore. The yearning was gone from his face, that and the boyishness, the assistant-to-the-angels look he had before he went to Europe. He saw her, and his eyes settled on her, and he said, "Hi, Ingrid," and there was something painfully opaque in the look he gave her. But she knew that look. It was a look boys gave you when they had started thinking about you and were wondering what their next move would be.

"Hi, Father," she said. "You're back." Her heart was thumping so hard that she couldn't think of anything else to say.

"Yes," he said. "I wonder if you could pour me a cup of coffee."

She straightened up to show off her figure, and she reached up and with the back of her hand swept back the hair that had fallen onto her forehead, a womanly gesture, and she saw Father Pielke watching her, so she began to watch him back.

"And how was your trip to Europe?" she asked, setting down the coffee in front of him, and smiling, she hoped, not too broadly. "How come you've come down here?" She realized her questions weren't connecting with each other.

"Oh," he said, unpracticed in guile, "I came in to see how you were feeling. I remember your pneumonia."

They started to talk. The conversation was pleasantly shallow. Ingrid could see, as through a pinhole, a glimpse of her life flowing outward toward the future in the company of this man. She began to plan a scandal to facilitate her possible, no, probable, no, inevitable, life with him. At least, that's what she tells me now. She now claims that she knew what would happen.

This is what she said to him: "You know that place, those woods, behind the city park, sort of near the river? I've been walking there, and I've seen these berries, I don't know what they are exactly, I mean I don't know their names, I guess they could be poisonous, so I haven't been eating them, but I almost have. And . . . I remembered how you knew so much about the woods. I know you know so much about plant life, and I was wondering, because you're an expert, and I know you love to teach everybody the names of these plants, if you would some day tell me what they are."

He was gazing at her, and he said he would tell her. My mother knew, at that moment, that everything in life, down to the details, had been decided millions of years ago, before we got here. It was all fated. We're working from scripts written at the beginning of time, only most of us don't know it. She felt the inevitability of her life with Father Pielke as a stroke of the greatest luck.

18

A son should not imagine his parents' courtship, but at some point, before or after my parents' wedding, my father, who had fallen out of love with God and found himself drawn instead, and with surprising violence, toward the helpless, that is to say, toward the human, saw Ingrid Shepherd in her nakedness. Let's say that they were in the woods to which Ingrid had invited him, and he had identified for her the berries that she had not recognized: they were blackberries, and after learning this fact, she persuaded him to walk toward another part of the woods, a section of hills and thick undergrowth and shade. Say that it was a warm day in late autumn. Say that the air had a tang of burnt leaves on it.

We cannot imagine the soul without its clothing of flesh. We have no image for the soul except for the body that incarnates it, and we really cannot imagine rapture without the physical source from which it springs. My father had a gift for rapture, and when he looked upon this woman—gazing, as he must have, with a desire and a possible shame that was new to him—he saw her hands, and feet, and breasts, and neck, and then he saw her body as one life. He saw the beauty of this woman's body—the beauty of this woman—as a sufficiency. He had now seen a woman beaten. He had heard cries for help. Other scenes had pressed themselves upon him. This woman, now, was all he needed for an image of the soul. He was lost in her. That feeling overpowered all the previous ones.

I like to think of them in the woods, my father lying on his back—making love to my mother, who was hellbent on scandal—but gazing up past my mother toward a cardinal in the branches above him, flitting from tree to tree. I like to think of him seeing some feathery thing overhead as they bring themselves together.

And at that moment, with that, he gave up his former vocation and took on a new one, which was to love Ingrid Shepherd for as long as he lived.

It is, after all, an old story. A person, drawn toward abstractions, toward what used to be called "higher things," is brought down—we never say "is brought up"—to the physical world.

He left the priesthood. My mother is a strong woman, unapologetic about the life forces that govern her. He never again felt God moving in him. Germany had started a process in him that led him to my mother. And he never looked back. Mary gave way to Venus, an older goddess.

He moved to another town with his wife. In the schools, he taught the names of plants and animals, and when compelled to do so, he taught German. He raised a family, which included me.

19

All this happened a long time ago. Most of the witnesses are gone or, if they are still alive are deeply irritable, as my mother is, with the crankiness of aging people who do not want to give up their treasures to someone who is not likely to appreciate them. Today I have brought flowers to brighten up her room and a new biography of Susan B. Anthony.

"You should tell your own story," my mother says. "That's an interesting one. You're pretty interesting, if you ask me. You're a regular Pandora's box yourself."

"Someday," I tell her. "I'll do that someday."

"Sure you will. Hand me that water, will you?"

I pass her her glass of water. There seems to be some lemon rind floating in it.

"You know who you should talk to?" she asks me. I shake my head. "Burton Jordan, that old gasbag. He's still alive. Lives in a suburb of Seattle somewhere."

"What?" I say. "That's impossible. He'd be about ninety-seven years old."

She shrugs. "I'm only telling you what I know. And what I heard was, the guy's got pots of money, and he's still got most of his faculties intact. He talks and talks. You'd like that. Isn't that the phrase? 'Faculties intact.'" She snorts. "You could turn on that tape recorder of yours and let it run and run. Just hours and hours of old guy blah blah blah. Yes, he's still alive. You should go see him."

"How do you know he's alive?" I ask her.

She looks right at me. "He sends us Christmas cards."

"Burton Jordan? Christmas cards? With notes?"

"Sure. Sometimes with notes, sometimes without. *Love, Burton Jordan.* Isn't that something? God, you're a snoop."

20

A few small matters in this story have been resistant to imaginative reconstruction. Such as: How does a person recover from a bout of fascism? Particularly if that person is an American. How does he go on being charming? Charm sometimes has a habit of taking its leave of you.

Burton Jordan is listed in the greater Seattle telephone directory, and when I call his number, I reach the housekeeper, who tells me that Mr. Jordan would certainly enjoy a visit from me and would certainly be pleased to talk about the past. Except for the housekeeper, she tells me, he lives alone. He is clear in his mind, she says, about most things. She gives me directions on how to get to his house from the airport.

I make the flight reservations. One week later, I am in Seattle. On the way out from the airport to his suburb, where I have been directed to find Burton Jordan's house, I find that I am somewhat unsteady and disoriented. Perhaps I need lunch. Possibly I could use a drink. Somewhere close by the Sea-Tac Mall, I stop at a large, off-the-freeway bar and restaurant called Mr. Harold Hamburger, and after waiting in the foyer for ten minutes and standing amid the glittering young professional-managerial class of suburban Seattle, I am seated and served by a young woman whose breast-tag identifies her as Wendee. I order the Harold Hamburger and the Harold Salad but after judiciously considering the Harold Hamburgbeer I order a double Scotch, with water on the side.

The effect of the lunch is like a soft bludgeoning, and by the time I arrive at Burton Jordan's house at 3465 Periwinkle Way, I am not quite as alert as I would care to be. I have seen nothing but shopping malls, strips, freeways, power lines, and housing developments. Twice I have pulled off the road to let a siren-roaring fire truck pass. I am keyed up, jumpy. The flower gardens and the lawns in this neighborhood are overcultivated and overfertilized, and they sport a kind of hysterical saturated coloration, which in my current mood I label as Suburban Lawn Fascism. Stop that, I say to myself, it's only a neighborhood, and I get out of my car, carrying my tape recorder.

The house is a modest bungalow. I see no evidence of pots of money. The housekeeper, a woman in her early fifties with salt-and-pepper hair and a firm manner, meets me at the door and leads me into the living room, which smells vaguely of fireplace ash. Everything here is pleasantly nondescript: family photographs propped up here and there on the side tables, semi-abstract art on the walls, wall-to-wall carpeting, ornamental hurricane lamps, some antique furniture. The housekeeper says her name is Frieda, invites me to sit down, and says that Mr. Jordan will be with me shortly. She smiles, but it is a peevish smile, and I realize that my breath probably smells of Scotch. I pop a breath mint into my mouth and check my watch. I set up the tape recorder on the table. It's fifteen minutes before one o'clock.

In one corner of the living room is a card table and a chair. A game of solitaire has been abandoned on the table. Whoever played this game was close to winning it.

I look out the north window at a bird feeder. A junco, I think it's called, is feeding there.

In the other corner of the table is yesterday's Seattle newspaper, folded over to the crossword puzzle. The crossword has been filled in with an old man's shaky handwriting. Nevertheless, it has been finished. I skim the puzzle. Seventeen across, four letters: "coughing opera heroine": MIMI.

"Hello, hello."

Into the room from the hallway, supported on his left by a mahogany cane, and with his right arm extended as if for balance, comes Burton Jordan. He is the most distinguished looking elderly man I have ever seen. He is ninety-seven years old and still handsome. It takes me a moment before I realize that his hand is extended for my benefit and that I am meant to shake it, and so I do. He gives me a good strong grip. I nod and smile and tell him who I am. "Oh, yes," he says, "I know who you are. Please sit down."

I let myself down into the sofa on one side, and Burton Jordan sits down on the other. "Whee," he says, as if sitting down is an adventure for an old man, which perhaps it is. "Care for a drink, Mr. Pielke?" he asks.

"Not just yet."

"I have a martini before lunch, myself. Don't think it'll

shorten my life, do you? Frieda," he calls, "is my martini ready?"

"Yes, Mr. Jordan." She brings in a small glass of clear liquid with an olive in it and puts it on the table next to the sofa.

Burton Jordan takes a sip. "Heigh, heigh," he says. He closes his eyes for a moment, allowing me to take a long look at him. His hair—his hairline has never receded—is gray but full and is swept back from his distinguished forehead, and he has a large head and features, a host-of-the-party appearance, except for the cold and distant eyes, a face that makes me think of the English actor Rex Harrison playing one of George Bernard Shaw's elderly characters, like Captain Shotover, a man of power and opinion, a brilliant saturnine despot who commemorates indecencies. He is wearing a green plaid sport coat, a plaid tie stained with food spillage, and a pair of yellow trousers, and on him this outrageous color combination appears to be perfect and accurate and just, the daredevil dress code of multimillionaires at the country club who are carefully managing the exploitation of the world's resources: go-to-hell hues on beautifully tailored clothes.

Suddenly I notice that he is taking a long look back at me.

"Had a haircut lately?"

"Uh," I say, "I had one last week."

"You were cheated," he informs me with a small smile. "And are you trying to grow a beard?"

"I've had this beard for ten years," I tell him.

"It doesn't do you justice, in that case," he says. "You should shave it off." He has the habit, I notice, of command. "It's scraggly. Well, what do I care. I'm as old as Methuselah. Keep your beard if you want to. It's nothing to me if you want to look like that. You have the appearance of someone on the Bowery, and I must say I'm disappointed, but, well, who cares?" He takes another sip of his martini.

"I'm sorry you feel that way, Mr. Jordan."

"Let's not argue," he says. "Let's just say that your haircut and that beard wouldn't meet a payroll. Well, be that as it may . . ." He coughs. Then he recovers himself. "'Twasn't the cough that carried him off,'" he quotes from somewhere, "'but the coffin they carried him off in.'" He chuckles and takes another sip of his martini. Then he seems to gather himself together. "Now. To what do I owe this visit? You aren't going to ask me for money, are you?"

"No," I say quickly. "I wanted to ask you about your trip to Germany with your wife and my father in 1938." I tell him that I am collecting information about my father's life.

"Because I have a lot of money," he says, apparently not having heard me, "several million dollars in fact, and I can't give it away to anyone who asks."

"Mr. Jordan, I'm not here to ask you for any money. I'm not here for that. I just want to ask you about your trip to Germany in 1938."

"Oh, yes," he says. "That trip. Who did you say your father was?"

"Father Franz Pielke," I say, using his old title.

"Oh, yes," Burton Jordan says. "Father Pielke was a priest."

I explain that he left the priesthood and became a teacher and fathered me.

"Yes, of course. Sometimes I remember, and at times I can't. Why did he shed his priestly vestments?"

"He fell in love. He fell in love with my mother. He wanted to have children. I'm curious about it."

"I have several million dollars," he says. "I can't give money to you merely because you ask for money, Father."

"No, no, I'm not Father Pielke," I say. "I'm his son."

"Oh, yes," he says, "That's right. Forgive me. I'm as old as Methuselah. I forget things. Are you certain that you wouldn't like a drink?"

"No, thank you. I just wanted to ask you a couple of questions about your trip to Germany. Why did you take my father along? You spoke German, didn't you?"

"He taught me about the plants and animals," Burton Jordan says. "I was sure he knew about the German plants and animals. Couldn't have been that different, one country to another."

"Then why did you tell him that you didn't speak German?"

"We had to trick him. In the spirit of benevolence, of course. We gave his parish several thousand dollars. He wouldn't have come otherwise." The junco outside the window is pecking away at the seeds. In the kitchen the housekeeper rattles the plates as she prepares sandwiches. This place smells of ash, and I find I am having some trouble breathing.

"Mary Ellen loved him a little, you know," he says, looking at me. "I can't give you any more money." He waits, raises his head with dignity, and says, "I have several million dollars. I can't give it all away to anyone who comes to ask for it."

"No," I say. "Of course not."

"She loved him, but it was harmless," he says, finishing his luncheon martini. "I would have done anything for Mary Ellen, anything. I loved her terribly. She wasn't about to do anything *wrong,* you know. She wasn't a woman for scandal. You should get your hair cut. We both wanted to go to Germany. It was entertaining. A place of interest. But that's so long ago. I don't remember any of it."

It feels to me as if time is running out. "Were you interested in Hitler?" I ask.

"I worked for the War Production Board. Here in this country. During the war."

"That would have been later. But in 1938, were you interested in National Socialism?"

"Hitler?" He waits, then remembers. "He was a four-flusher."

"A four-flusher?"

"It was all a bluff," Burton Jordan says. "That's what we discovered. And they tricked us. They planted all that Nazi propaganda in the car we hired."

"What was a bluff?"

"What?"

"You said it was all a bluff."

"I don't remember. And I'm not in the confessional, Father." His face has changed, softened. "I have my notebook around here, with my drawings of the plants. I drew them just as they appeared to me. I outlined the leaves. I outlined the seeds. The spring blossoms, they're in there, pressed between the pages. I did it for her. She wanted to know the names of things. Father Pielke taught me; he named the plants and animals."

"Did your wife jump up on Goebbels' car, or was she pushed?"

"That's so long ago, Father."

"I'm his son. I know, Burton. It was a long time ago. Do you remember?"

"I'm trying to do my best. What does the poet say? 'I grow old, I grow old . . .' But I don't grow old. I *am* old. You were asking about Goebbels' car. She said *'Grüss Gott'* when she left him." His eyes are closed. Suddenly his eyes are open again, and he seems quite alert, awakened from his nap. "She was pushed. That's what I always say."

"She didn't jump?"

"Well, maybe she did," Burton Jordan says. "She was quite spirited. After all, Mary Ellen was a Jew."

In my mind, a tree falls over, pinning me underneath it.

"Of course, she wasn't a kike like some of them," he continues, in his imperturbable manner. "She never shouted like some of those sheenies you run into now and then. Her mother was Jewish, didn't you know that? And the rabbi cursed her mother for marrying my father-in-law. Cursed them both.

Some sort of Jew curse, to the effect that all their children should die before they did. And do you know, Father, all their children did die before they did? So the curse worked. It's funny about curses, how effective they are. Ah, but Mary Ellen. She had beautiful hair, you know, and she never carried on. She had wonderful manners. Did you ever join one of those anti-Jew militias, Father?"

"No," I say.

"That's good. Well, why would you. They're made up of rather common people with commonplace ideas. Vulgar. Running around in fatigues. Quite silly. You never get a country organized *that* way. You never liked me," Burton Jordan says. He isn't looking in my direction, but toward the wall. His eyes, behind his glasses, are vitreous and rheumy. He looks like a lizard, white with age and mouth half open, sunning himself on a rock. "For a while, I thought we were friends. We took those walks through the forests and you showed me the ferns and the underbrush and the trees. Mushrooms, too. You could identify all those, and you pointed out the ones that were edible, and we brought them back for Mary Ellen, do you remember, and they were cooked up, sautéed in butter, as I recall. Still, you never liked me. Oh, well. Be that as it may, I am ninety-seven years old. Are you coming to my birthday party next year?"

"Yes," I say. I have been resisting the impulse to strike him. What good would it do? He is too far gone for that.

"I'm so old, I remember Harding. I was at Yale when he was elected. I was studying and somebody, this fellow we called Spook, rushed into our room and said, 'Guess what? They've just elected Warren Gamaliel Harding!' The front porch President. He died of a busted gut." Burton Jordan eyes me suspiciously. "You should get a haircut," he says.

"Yes," I say. "I suppose I will get a haircut."

"Good," he nods. He closes his eyes. "I'm tired, dear boy," he says.

"Mary Ellen," I say, hopelessly tangled up in all this. I look around the room for something on which my eye can rest, and I see a silver cigarette box, the old-fashioned kind with a hinged lid.

"I would have done anything for her," he tells me. "Absolutely anything. It was her idea."

"What was? What was her idea?"

"It was all her idea. That trip. Everything. I got all my ideas from her. She was a believer, you know. She was a heroic woman and she took great leaps into what she believed in. That takes courage. How I loved her. You simply had no idea. If she had an opinion, it became my mine. I never had an idea in my life that wasn't hers. She died a few years ago. I think she was disappointed that we didn't see Father Pielke after we got back from Germany. I don't think she liked it very much when you got into that fight, when you got that black eye. She had a bad heart. But she lived a long time. You have no conception how much I loved her." He leans forward to confide in me. "I'm never going to die," he says. "I have great-grandchildren now. I've outlived everyone. I'll outlive you." He gives me a curious laugh.

"I don't think so," I say.

"Time to go," Burton Jordan tells me. His eyes are closed. "Time to go."

"I was . . ." But I can't say that I was glad to meet him, either. I can't say that I was happy to make his acquaintance. I am stumped. The customary pleasantries fall away from me.

"Come to my birthday party," he says.

"All right."

"I'll be ninety-eight years old. I'm pretty well fixed. But I can't take it with me. Let me know if you ever need any money."

"Yes," I say.

"Sure you don't want a drink?"

"No, I don't think so."

"I wondered, because you smell of Scotch."

"Well, I had a drink on the way out here."

"You shouldn't drink, Father."

"No, I don't suppose so." I stand up. I turn off the tape recorder. "Goodbye, Burton."

"Goodbye, Father." I am halfway to the door when he says, "Bring some mushrooms, next time you come. Oh. And God bless you."

I turn around. "Thank you," I say, before I rush outside. I lean against the rental car and for a moment, standing in the driveway, I breathe the air that everyone else breathes, and I am back, I have returned, to 1995, in a suburb of Seattle, where the lawns are manicured and fertilized and the gardens are enriched with nutrients so that they grow with deep ultrasaturated colors. Inside the house on Periwinkle Way, the elegant old fascist in retirement is taking a brief nap or has been awakened and is eating his sandwiches.

I do not know how I find my way back to the airport. I am not sure how I find my way back to the gate, among the other travelers, and then make my way to my seat by the window. But I do.

21

I take down the picture of Goebbels from the wall above my desk. It is the famous photograph by Alfred Eisenstadt in which the minister of propaganda, seated in a chair, looks at the camera with an expression of the purest expressive malevolence. I do not need this picture anymore. I am close to the end of my story.

You have never met anyone quite like me. Passing me in the street, you might think: There goes a quiet-seeming, unremarkable gray-eyed fellow, a threat to no one, not particularly striking in any of the usual ways but not distinguished by ugliness or disfigurements. Not exactly handsome—no, you would not say that. You would not say that I had any shining physical features to melt anyone's heart. I have not resented the somewhat anonymous qualities of my appearance.

No, it's not that. But if you were to come inside my apartment, you would notice a slightly bare quality to the interior, the absence of what used to be called "the woman's touch." Because I live alone here, and because I have married but never started a family, my rooms lack some of the typical signs of familial affection. There are no crayoned pictures attached by magnets to the refrigerator, nor are there photographs of children's faces in my bedroom or in my study. The furniture here is comfortable, in fact everything about the place is tasteful and mildly welcoming, but nothing about it gives me away.

For the most part, I am a happy man, contented with my work, with what I am able to do within the range of my capabilities. I have hobbies. I play banjo in a local bluegrass band, and I meet every week in a square dance group. I sing in a local choral society. Music has left its traces in me.

I repeat: I am a happy man. You would be pleased to make my acquaintance.

So were my two wives. I did my best to love both of them— they were both fine and attractive—but my feelings went blank at certain stages with them, and they knew it, and they could not endure it. They were jealous. I had the preoccupied air of a man who is carrying on a romance elsewhere. But I was doing no such thing. I loved both of them and then found myself incapable of expressing that love. As I grew to be an adult, I developed a hunger for perfection, the worst appetite, and the most damaging a husband may possess. Living in the same rooms with them, I absented myself from my wives, a terrible process I was incapable of terminating. When they asked me, *Why are you doing this, where are you going when you drift away like that?* I said, I'm here, but they knew I wasn't. Any woman would leave a husband like me. And they did.

I have kept faith with my father's celibacy.

I have kept faith with my father.

He was a kind and loving parent to my sister and me. He built a dollhouse for her, taught me the names of the plants and animals, even taught me the intricacies of playing shortstop. But he was a dangerous father because you could not see his faults; it was hard to get some distance on him. He had a strange kindness, so large that you could not find your way around it.

He seemed content with his life. When I asked him why he stopped going to church, why he never went to Mass—my mother still did—he said, "It doesn't work anymore, Jack. He doesn't answer." He mimed dialing a telephone, holding it up, and then putting it down again. "No point in doing it if He doesn't answer."

It's funny to say so, but I think he had a talent for parenthood, but a genius for rapture, and he lost the only place he had to put that rapture, the only faith that deserved it.

22

My father lives several floors down from my mother's apartment. I like to visit him on the weekends in the early morning, when the sun shines through his east window, illuminating the floor, the cut flowers that are brought in and placed in a vase on the table opposite his bed.

First I go up to get my mother, where she lives in her apartment on the seventh floor. I bring her her mail, her new copies of *The Nation* and the *Utne Reader.* I give her a kiss and she takes my arm, and I escort her onto the elevator, and we go downstairs. She steps into my father's room and then comes out in a few minutes. She tells me that she'll see me later; she's going to take a cab downtown for some shopping. Then I go in.

My father suffered a stroke several years ago, a stroke followed by several others, and for two years now he has been able to say nothing. One must converse with him through the eyes. He must be helped to perform most of his daily actions. But I love him——he is the only person on this earth whom I have loved with this intensity, even in his silence, even in his helplessness—and I am willing to be disabled by my love for him, no matter what it requires of me. Why should I apologize now for loving my father so enduringly?

I stand in the doorway. I say, "Daddy, it's me."

My father turns his face toward me. His face is fixed in an expression of rapture. He turns this expression toward me.

I approach him where he sits. I sit down next to him. My father does not say anything to me now. He does not speak anymore, and I am not sure what he hears. Sometimes I read a word or two in his face, a word that escapes but is not spoken.

I lean toward him. I kiss him on the cheek. My lips touch the bristly gray hairs where the nurses have shaved him carelessly.

I tell him about my week. In his head the earth moves slowly toward the sun, then slowly away. Every so often, a bird alights on the sill outside his window, and his eyes turn toward it.

For two years he has had his sights set on something, but he cannot tell me what it is. Sometimes I help him up to his feet, and we limp together down the hall, back and forth on what you might call a walk. I hold him up. We pass the silent others. I adjust myself to his limp. I limp with him, stride for stride. Though those are not quite the words for what we do.

Sometimes I hum songs to him. *The rising of the sun,* I sing, *the running of the deer.*

The earth moves through the darkness of empty space as we do this.

The morning passes. I lean forward, my ear toward his lips, in case he has anything to say. On rare occasions he seems almost able to pronounce a syllable, and once, when I was very tired, I thought I heard him say a word, no louder than a whisper. The word was *"Hilfe."* But I do not think I actually heard him say that word. I think I may have just imagined it.

My father sits in utter silence, and it is there that I go to see him.

At the end of my visit, I say, "Goodbye, Daddy," and I kiss him again, before I go.

My father has my heart in chains.

I never know what time it is when I leave him. He follows me out of the room with his eyes. I think he loves me, as he did when we were younger, when I was a child in his house.

I have two gifts: one for happiness, and one for sorrow. Both these gifts belong to my father and will be returned to him.

One night my father rose from bed and wrapped himself in his bed sheets and stood facing the wall until they found him.

Once I am outside the building where my father lives on the second floor, the floor where constant nursing care is required and received, five floors down from my mother, who lives on the seventh, I always stand and confront the sky and the sun, if it has not been hidden behind the clouds.

And then I proceed down the sidewalk, where you would not particularly notice me. Slowly, step by step, I head down the block until you cannot see me anymore. I vanish into the crowd.

23

In my mother's room there is an album of photographs. One of the photographs shows my father as a child, after his accident. He is seated next to his sister and his mother. They are together, outside, facing directly into the winter sun. The air, with the light angled close to the winter solstice, must have been very cold. You can see their breath. My aunt's right hand blurs from shivering. I do not know who took this picture. Perhaps an itinerant photographer traveling across rural America.

The breath hangs in the air, the vapor of exhalation. The spirit.

And behind my father's breath, you notice his eyes. They look back at you, as if he had seen something fall on him, and it aged him instantly.

You see those eyes, and you think, my God, he was only a child.

ABOUT THE AUTHOR

Charles Baxter is the author of three previous collections of stories and two novels. He lives in Ann Arbor and teaches at the University of Michigan.